I0662631

Bianchi

By

Natasha Hughes Smith

The Reflections Series

Cover Design by Faith Riggs

This is a work of fiction. Names, characters, businesses, places, events and incidents are either the products of the author's imagination or used in a fictitious manner. Any resemblance to actual persons, living or dead, or actual events is purely coincidental.

Prologue

Please be advised that the characters in this novel deal with real-life issues; issues that may have a triggering effect on some readers. Additionally, the story takes place in the 1970s resulting in the use of some terms and language that were loosely and frequently used during those times; however, those terms and slang may or may not be appropriate or acceptable in the current era.

Chapter 1

The city was no longer the height of prosperity as it was in his youth; the vibrant city was gone. It could no longer boast of its grandness and wealth. What replaced it was grittier, meaner and a growing vastness of blight. The 1967 Detroit Riot was one of the deadliest and most destructive riots in American history leaving forty-three dead, 1189 injured, 7,200 arrested and more than 400 buildings destroyed. The riot of '67, left an ugly shadow over the city causing wealthy white families to increase their flight from the city.

As the next decade rolled in, there was more of the same leaving in its wake poorer people gaining access to grand homes without the funds for proper upkeep or wealthy families renting them out, but no longer concerned about maintaining their grand appearances.

The same could be said about Ricky Bianchi's industry of business. The mob world was changing and increasing its involvement in areas that most mob families had tried to avoid. Ricky was determined that he would avoid it at all cost; whereas others were blind to the threat. It was often a topic of discussion as the families met to discuss business and the issues they were facing. Surprisingly, it was slowly becoming an issue within his own family; he and his father were debating the topic more than what Ricky thought was necessary or should be done.

Ricky's family mirrored what was happening in Detroit. Like most, his father, Carlo, uprooted the family from their mansion in the stately historic Woodbridge neighborhood to Grosse Pointe Shores. Unlike some who didn't care for what dollar amount they sold their abandoned homes, Carlo demanded top dollar as he wanted to ensure that a *worthy* person occupied the home. Carlo maintained a passionate love for their old community and continued his involvement in their community groups and projects.

Ricky sat contemplatively in his office at the family's funeral home; it was one of their legitimate businesses that help funnel and cover up their less than respectful and unlawful business practices. It was becoming challenging to run a profitable business the old way with the decrease in jobs and the fleeting prosperity. He seriously considered the number of ways he could secure his own prosperity during these lean economic times.

Everything around him was changing and it was disheartening to Ricky; he had seen his best friend, Bernard Barrington, become a ruthless man in business and even in his relationships when provoked. Ricky missed his friend of old and enjoyed the rare moments that spirit shined through. However, he was more concerned with this new type of mobster that didn't have any respect for the old ways, women and family. Ricky felt that they were more of a threat than the developing recession he saw on the horizon. His peers were blind to it and unprepared for it, just as they were to this new mob.

Ricky's frustration grew every time he read the newspaper and watched the news. He had reached out to the families again to schedule a meeting to discuss his rising concerns. He was growing tired of trying to get them to see the threat; it was like his entire world was blind to the writing on the wall. It was a heavy burden for him to see it clearly and everyone else around was in denial or willingly being blind. He knew he needed to organize another meeting with the families. He summoned a courier to deliver notices to the Dons.

"Yes, Mr. Bianchi.", responded the courier as he entered the office cautiously.

"Deliver these invites to all of the Dons immediately.", instructed Ricky as he handed the letters to his employee.

The courier noticed the stern expression on his boss's face; so, he knew that the request required urgency.

"Yes, sir! Right away.", informed the courier hoping that Ricky would notice his dependability and promote him soon.

"That will be all.", dismissed Ricky as he picked up a cigar and lit it hoping that taking deep puffs would calm his nerves.

Ricky was feeling restless despite all of the work he had to complete. He needed and wanted to feel some reassurance that things would be better. It was at times like these, that he wished he had settled down like his friends. The warmth of a devoted and supportive wife would do his mind and body good at the moment. If he were honest with himself and his friends, he would admit that he had become bored with his standard type of woman. They were loose, often selfish and money-hungry; definitely not the type of woman a man makes a wife and for sure not one with which he would have children.

Ricky eyed his reflection in the decorative glass paperweight and noticed a grey hair. His youth and wild party days were indeed behind him; he was becoming his father before his very eyes. Shit thought Ricky as he pulled the solitary hair and then reached for the phone to call his best friend.

"Hello, Ester, my dear. How's the best secretary in town?", teased Ricky as his secretary walked in annoyed by the remarks.

Ricky looked apologetically as she tossed the paperwork on his desk. Ricky found it humorous that she got jealous when he complimented any other female help. She joked that he was her 'work husband'.

"Hello, Mr. Bianchi. I'm well and yourself?", asked Ester straining to be polite instead of annoyed at the forever handsome playboy. She hated to admit that she loved his jokes and his teasing.

"My dear Ester, I'm doing so much better now that I hear your soothing voice.", Ricky said the words oozing his sex appeal. Ester cleared her throat as she fought a tingling sensation.

"I'll transfer you to Mr. Barrington right away.", informed Ester as she quickly prepared to transfer the call. Darn that Ricky, she thought, he always made her wish for younger and more carefree days. "Mr. Barrington, Mr. Bianchi is on the line.", Ester said in an annoyed tone she reserved for Ricky alone. Bernard smiled knowing full well that she secretly enjoyed Ricky's flirtation.

"You can transfer the call. Thank you.", informed Bernard eager to speak to his old friend; speaking to him reminded him of the good times. "Hello, old chum! How are you?", greeted Bernard.

"Don't start that shit; I've been calling myself old enough as it is.", Ricky corrected his friend.

"Sensitive. You need to accept the fact that you are an old man, just like the rest of us. Get a wife, have kids and let the grey grow in. I know you're dyeing it.", joked Bernard, yet being serious about his friend needing to settle down.

"Fuck you! I do not dye my hair. The only truthful thing you've said is that I need to settle down.", confessed Ricky surprised to hear the words from his mouth just as Bernard was or even more so.

"Hold the fucking phone. Did I hear you say that I was right ... that you need to settle down?", inquired an entertained Bernard, who sat beaming from ear to ear with a smile that would make the strongest of women give in.

"Seriously, yes. These are some challenging times ... stressful times and it would feel good to come home to a woman ready to take all of my stress away. You know what I mean?", asked Ricky then immediately regretted the question since Bernard was no longer married to his first wife and the love of his life for the last four years.

"Yeah, I used to have that.", remarked Bernard hating to remember his beautiful wife and the life that was now gone. "Well,

I just have to make do with what I've got.", said Bernard with regret in his voice.

Ricky hated that he reminded Bernard of his loss; it was a loss that still plagued him despite remarrying. His current wife, Vanessa, was no Josephine for sure, thought Ricky. Ricky quickly changed the subject to a lighter note. He was invited to a party that was being hosted by one of the Italian councilmen who was up for re-election; it was an unofficial fundraiser of sorts; perhaps he would invite Bernard.

"Councilman Rossi of Woodbridge is throwing an unofficial campaign fundraiser for his Italian community supporters. Would you like to come?", asked Ricky assuming that his friend wouldn't attend and if he did, he would attend alone. Bernard wasn't eager to show off his new bride as he had with his first.

"Normally, I would say no; but since you are interested in finding a wife all of a sudden, I need to be there to protect you from yourself. You'll pick the sleaziest one there!", joked Bernard as he only slightly exaggerated his friend's taste in ladies.

"There might be some truth to that statement …", laughed Ricky remembering his wild exploits and the hundreds of times he tried to pass off some of them to Bernard. "Man, I *am* getting older now. All of you, pussies, I call friends are married and have a bunch of kids. I can't be the only one having fun.", joked Ricky.

"So, when is this fundraiser?", inquired Bernard as he sat with his legs crossed in his brand-new office space in suburban, Birmingham, Michigan.

"It's in a couple of days. It'll be at the Rooster Tail at 8 pm.", informed Ricky glad that his friend had agreed to join him. He didn't feel his most confident around the uppity elites unless Bernard was there as a buffer.

"Great, I'll plan to see you there. Should I financially support this crook?", asked Bernard calculating if he might need another councilman in his pocket.

"He seems to be one of the good ones. He truly looks out for his community. That's not just the Italians ... Blacks, Greeks, whoever lives in his *community*. Like anyone else he does like to get his hands greased from time to time.", Ricky expressed his sincere appreciation of the councilman, but Bernard was less trusting as he had become extremely cynical of men.

"Well, that's refreshing to hear. Most of us good men have been corrupted over the years; I know I sure have.", confessed Bernard. "Count me in for support. I'll see you then, Friday night."

"Sounds good. Ciao.", Ricky hung up the phone as his thoughts immediately went back to the problems at hand.

As of late, amusement was ever fleeting and in short supply. Perhaps that was why drug usage and dependence were on the rise, thought Ricky. It was time for Ricky to make his short drive home; however, that evening the drive seemed strangely long. He resolved in his mind that he would have to be an agent of defiance to not only his father but the business itself.

The night had come and gone, but Ricky woke without having had much sleep. What he did have was a resolute mind to stand up to his father's ever-powerful presence. Although, his father, Carlo, had retired; he still maintained a chokehold from his retirement recliner. Ricky felt it was more of a *cock* hold; it was an offense to his manhood and it was time to put an end to it. They had an unusual relationship; it was one of love and hate. Carlo loved him as a son but hated him in business simply because Ricky was a reminder that he was fading and only a shadow of the man he used to be. Subsequently, Carlo often pushed back by advocating for things that Ricky was adamantly against.

Carlo scheduled a meeting to discuss the *new* direction of the family business, but it was nothing but more of the same talk he had been saying for almost a decade now. Carlo's plan went against everything the Bianchi family had stood for; this was nothing more than a sad attempt at a desperate man to keep power, thought Ricky. Ricky too was a little antsy, but he was not going to allow the times or circumstances to change his character. He needed to hold onto what little of it he had left.

Ricky stretched as he slowly got out of bed; he felt stiff and weighted down with the burden of his decision. He slowly walked to the large bedroom window that provided him a view of Lake St. Clair from his immense two-story Italian Renaissance Revival home. The beauty of the limestone home flowed to its backyard where limestone continued as pavers surrounding the pool and sitting area. It was also used to build a short fence to encase the sitting area so that it was separate from the pool. The yard continued to extend past that area to the majestic waters of Lake St. Clair and his boating dock. He would often ride his boat down to the Detroit River where his funeral home was located.

The three Bianchi generations before him had created a fairytale life of wealth, reach and prestige, but would it all fade leaving his unborn children with nothing? Or would the line end with him right along with the wealth? It was a question his nagging father faced him with on a constant basis. He didn't want to be the shame of his family's demise. He wouldn't, couldn't allow it. He was born into wealth, he couldn't imagine a life without it; he had to keep it, but at what cost?

Ricky completed his morning routine and then joined his father in the study where they both poured a cup of coffee and ate bagels. Both eyed each other over their cups as they sipped; neither ready to begin the difficult discussion that would ensue. Surprisingly to Carlo, Ricky took the lead.

"I know you want to take up some new family business ventures, but I'm not in agreement. I have some legitimate business affairs that I have been discussing with Bernard in which our family would do far better to invest.", Ricky said forcefully as he stared intensely at his father. Carlo was neither impressed nor intimidated.

"Really now. The times have changed; I don't like it any more than you do. However, if we are going to maintain our power and wealth, we have to change with the times as well.", informed Carlo as he paused from sipping his morning coffee.

"I hear you and I do understand your view, but I think we can get by a little longer with the gambling and number running being our main focus. I already agreed with you a few years ago to add money laundering to the mix and more drugs.", informed Ricky reminding his father that he had conceded on some things already.

"Indeed, you did; that was the only smart thing you've done recently!", Carlo indicated as his annoyance with his only son began to boil. He raised his hand to silence the rebuttal that was on the tip of Ricky's lips. "Don't you know there are proposals right now to make numbers legal and the state will run it!", Carlo said in an elevated tone.

"Yes, but who knows if that will even pass or how profitable it will be for them; however, I'm working with Bernard on some business proposals concerning that.", commented Ricky as he even doubted his own words about the profits.

"Oh, it's passing and that will hit our profits hard. We have to expand our dealings in drugs. Now, we dabble, but we need to be chief. Hell, add sex trafficking if we have to. Whatever it takes!", demanded Carlo as he spat coffee and bagels from his lips unintentionally with the passion of his resolve.

"For Christ's sake, I refused to add sex trafficking to our business.", Ricky said in shocked indignation at his father's words as he slammed the China cup on the end table. He couldn't believe the despicable things his father was saying.

"Wait a fucking minute, you listen to me! You are not going to tear down what my grandfather built in this city!", shouted Carlo as if Ricky didn't know their history.

"You listen, mother ...", Ricky smiled inwardly as he realized that he had called the bastard a motherfucker so much in his head it was finally ready to come out. "Father, I'm in charge of this family now and I am not doing that!", Ricky shouted at his father.

They had a well-established love-hate relationship that was on the verge of becoming just plain hateful if Carlo continued to interfere. Ricky's mother, Bianca, neared the study and was concerned by the arguing. She hated that their only son did not have a better work relationship with her husband, but her face would be a constant shade of blue if she intervened every time. But she was willing to take her chances today; her husband was getting too old to keep this up. As far as she was concerned, he was on borrowed time.

"Stop it you two! Ricky knows what he is doing, Carlo. You just need to trust him.", Bianca chastised her stubborn husband.

She entered the study with her hands on her hips, but Carlo was cocked, loaded and ready for her with a response.

"Get outta here!", ordered Carlo.

He didn't need her sweet-talking him out of doing what *he* knew was right. He was like butter in her hands, but today concerning this dire matter, he couldn't let her reasoning persuade him.

"I'm done here. I already have some things in motion and they do not include your plans for the family business.", insisted Ricky.

He hated to be disrespectful, but he knew that his grandfather and his great-grandfather before him would roll over in their graves if they could hear what Carlo was proposing. Ricky just wouldn't allow it. He felt that the name Bianchi was one of respect, not just because of the power they willed, but their honor. Ricky felt there was nothing honorable about the direction of this new generation of mobsters.

Bianca circled back to the study after Ricky left. She was not going to be dismissed by her husband; not this time when his and Ricky's relationship could be hanging on by a thread. She boldly approached her husband and removed the cup from his hands to be sure she had his attention.

"You've got to let go and trust Ricky to run the business. You trusted him in years past to be your muscle.", advised Bianca to her stubborn husband.

"That was different.", Carlo defended his position.

"How so? He has a sharp mind and he thinks outside the box no matter what he does. If you keep interfering with his leadership, you'll ruin your relationship forever.", Bianca shared her wisdom.

"What will I have left, if I let go?", questioned Carlo feeling defeated.

"You will have me. Isn't that enough?", offered Bianca.

Carlo felt ashamed of his actions and treatment of his son; the last thing he wanted to do was hurt and disappoint his wife.

"Yes sweetheart, you are enough. I'll fall back and trust him to keep our business afloat.", proclaimed Carlo as he reached for Bianca's hand to kiss it.

Ricky had planned to go into the office after his meeting with his father, but after that exhaustive conversation, he didn't have the energy or desire to work. After hearing his father's bull,

13

the only thing that would help him was a good romp. The one chick he could depend on for that was Giovanna; he could always depend on her for a good fuck, thought Ricky.

Before heading out, Ricky doubled back to his bedroom suite to spray on some cologne; then he would travel across Jefferson Boulevard to Giovanna's condominium just a few miles west of him. Ricky scurried past the family's head butler, Nicolas Alverez, as he proceeded to the garage to hop in his brand-new 1970 Lincoln Continental Mark III. It was black as night with white interior trim and leather seats; it had the latest features including a car phone.

Ricky prided himself on being a modern man; he like having the latest gadgets and wearing trendy clothes. He was the model of style, flare and sex appeal. There weren't many men that could match him in the area. He was tall, slender and handsome; he stood 6'4" with lean muscle. He was as confident as he was handsome. He had dark olive Italian skin with curly black hair; hair covered most of his body. His arms, legs and chest were covered with soft curly black hairs that smelled of his favorite cologne. He owed much of his features and skin tone to the family's secret African American heritage.

His looks and body belied his age; most middle-aged men had let themselves go and were looking more like their fathers than men of youth. He and his close friends were in the minority; they teased each other about becoming old, but their very presence commanded the attention of the ladies and the envy of their peers. Unlike most of his peers, he didn't look like a desperate old man with a younger woman. Ricky's lover, Giovanna, was almost ten years Ricky's junior, but he was easily able to match her stamina with his own passion and litheness.

As he drove to her home, he thought of how times like this made him appreciative of her being nearby and that he could trust her discretion to never venture near his home. He had made her well aware of her station and that it would never change. Fortunately, she was satisfied with that and the perks that the arrangement offered. She just hoped that if he ever married, he would maintain their arrangement.

It was a beautiful spring day with the sun bouncing off the beautiful apartment and condo buildings lining Jefferson Boulevard. Ricky felt as refined and powerful as his freshly washed and polished Lincoln. He was glad that the beauty of Jefferson Boulevard hadn't faded as some of the other areas had. He looked forward to his time with Giovanna; she was a stunning piece of art created by God himself. She was tall, voluptuous with skin soft as silk; her voice purred with sex appeal and he loved her long jet-black hair.

Ricky wasn't into blondes like most guys were. He appreciated the depth of desire contained in the blackest of hair; the blacker the better as far as he was concerned; he felt it represented power and commanded attention. Giovanna had that presence about herself as a result he was always tempted to bring her to events, but he didn't want to send mixed signals. He wasn't one to play mind games; he wouldn't hurt a woman that way, not even a lover.

The closer he got to her condo, the stronger the pull to her body became. He was wound up tightly after a harsh week of dealing with his father and the constant threat of change. He needed to clear his head of all thoughts of business and the best person to accomplish it was waiting with the sexiest of lingerie just miles away. He was sure that if he could clear his mind of worry, he could free it up to devise a plan.

Finally, thought Ricky, as he pulled up to the valet at the beautiful Water Board Building. It was one of the many gems of the city; it was built in 1929 and designed by Louis Kamper. Ricky owned the 3-story penthouse where Giovanna lived; he had bought it for her to live there a decade ago after only knowing her a few months. She was the type of woman who managed to get what she wanted financially from men and Ricky was her number one and only benefactor since they met.

The valet recognized Ricky and rushed over to his car to open his door. Ricky pulled out a twenty-dollar bill and handed it to the attendant.

"Take good care of my girl.", instructed Ricky as he left his current, most precious love in the hands of the valet.

"Of course, sir as always!", reassured the valet as he smiled at the generous gangster.

He didn't know for sure of Ricky's profession, but he was willing to bet that twenty on it. Ricky entered the building and took the private elevator to the penthouse suite. He smiled as he thought of how impressed Giovanna and her friends must be by the place. No wonder she gave him a good romp whenever she saw him. Hell, he thought with a smirk as he eyed his reflection in the mirrored elevator, I'd fuck myself too if I were her. He checked his tie as he eyed his appearance. He wore one of his favorite navy-blue pin-striped suits with a white silk shirt and a silk navy-blue ascot tie. His look was not complete without the matching silk pocket handkerchief and gold cufflinks. He winked at his reflection before exiting the elevator on the 20th floor of the massive twenty-three-story masterpiece.

Ricky used his key to enter the penthouse that was one-third of the upper 3 levels, positioned on the backside of the building so that the resident had access to views of the Detroit Riverfront. If he enjoyed condo living, he would have moved here himself, but he much preferred a home. He felt a home was better suited for raising a family; a family for which his mother was beyond anxious. Despite all of that, he thought the penthouse had a nice vibe to it.

Giovanna had remodeled the place a few times since he moved her in; the latest décor was Venetian mixed with trendy post-modern furniture with terrazzo flooring throughout. The foyer was lined with tan terrazzo with a beautiful crystal chandelier and a Persian rug of hues of blue and taupe creating an intricate circular pattern with a marble-topped round foyer table with a brass base. Giovanna set in the dining room; it was another well-decorated room. She furnished it with cream Venetian style formal dining room furniture with a fresh flower centerpiece that she had delivered daily.

He could see that she spent his money well to create an inviting and stylish home for herself. At least, she wasn't wasting it on drugs and booze as some previous lovers had done. That was one of many attributes he appreciated about her, but the number one attribute was *that* body. He noticed her sitting in the dining room drinking coffee and eating croissants. She had on a red baby doll lingerie with her red high heel mule slipper with red fox trim. She was a stunning woman, she wore a messy pin-up that was done without care, but made her look irresistible to Ricky as he eyed her legs that were endless.

"Hello, Vanna.", he said as he ran his hand up from her ankle to her thigh then up to her breast where his hand lingered as he squeezed and pulled her nipple making sure that he kissed her passionately.

The passion and frustration within him exploded as he slipped her breast out of the lingerie and began to passionately suckle and kiss it. Giovanna's gasp of pleasure fueled him even more, prompting him to lift her and carry her to her bedroom.

"Ricky!", laughed Giovanna, "I haven't finished eating my breakfast. Put me down." She by no means wanted him to stop and he knew it.

"I've got something better for you to sip and suck on.", laughed Ricky as he carried her onto the private interior elevator up to the second floor where the bedroom was located; they both anticipated the devilishly kinky time that would follow.

Ricky was the aggressor as he laid her on the bed, but she flipped the script as she rolled him over pinning him between her thighs. She like to play the role of the shy lover as their foreplay began, but she quickly reverted to her natural personality as the vixen. Giovanna was not one to shy away from sexual pleasures nor would she stop before she was fulfilled.

Her power play thrilled Ricky and he succumbed to her display of power while laying anxiously awaiting her next moves. She quickly stripped him of his suit jacket and took her time unbuttoning each button slowly as she allowed her strap to fall from her shoulder revealing both breasts to Ricky. She tossed her hair as she helped him remove his shirt then she leaned over him so that her hair would tease his skin sending his nerve endings into a frenzy.

He tried to regain control of her as he reached for her with his right arm, but she pressed it down with her left foot. She quickly unzipped his pants and pulled his manhood out with ease since Ricky hated underwear. She expertly maneuvered his erect penis to her mouth as she licked the shaft then deep-throated the huge shaft hoping to swallow its contents with one quaff later. Ricky's hips thrust upward as he smashed her head down to ensure the full of him stayed in her mouth. As she gagged, she forced his hands back as she repositioned her body so that she could slide her hips on top of his long and thick erect penis.

She rode him like he was a wild beast that wanted to toss her off its back as she grinded deeper and deeper until they both quivered, shook and moaned in pleasure. What a fuck thought Ricky as he rolled her off him so that he could head to the bathroom to freshen up. He entered the adjoining master bath that provided a stunning view of the Detroit River and Canada.

"What a way to start my day off girl! Fuck!", shouted Ricky as he washed up and then noticed that Giovanna was approaching.

She leaned on his back and planted several kisses as her nails combed through his chest hairs.

"Was it good enough to take me to Dittrich Furs? I have my eye on a nice mink.", questioned Giovanna as she took his manhood in her hands once more. Ricky moaned as her hand pulled and stroked his penis.

"You give me another round like that last one and I'll buy whatever you want from Dittrich. No price limits whatsoever!", informed Ricky as he removed her hand so that he could turn to face her.

He swooped her slender frame up as he buried his head in her voluptuousness as he carried her to the sunken tub beneath the window. He pushed her back so that she dangled in his arms by her hips as he licked, sucked and delighted in her.

Giovanna's hands helped balance her in the tub as Ricky skillfully used his tongue to toy with her clitoris. However, with each tantalizing lick, her arms became weak from desire and delectation. What an easy way to get what she wanted, thought Giovanna; she felt sorry for women who didn't know how or refused to use their sex appeal to get what they wanted.

"We need to restock the pork chops, Billy. And this time, make sure you put the freshest toward the front. I don't want us selling old meat unknowingly!", shouted Vittoria at the newly hired staff.

She was so frustrated with every single new hire as of late. What happened to the good neighborhood kid that was looking for honest work after high school graduation? It seemed that everyone had college aspirations leaving good small businesses scrambling for good help. Despite her frustrations, she enjoyed managing the meat market when her father was away. He didn't think it was such a good idea, but she was after all his only child. There was no one to take over the business but her.

"Billy, watch it!", shouted Lorenzo, Vittoria's father who entered the store unexpectedly. "You don't have the loot to cover the cost of any broken jars!"

Lorenzo prided himself in having a large variety of spices and sauces for cooking.

"Sorry boss!", Billy spoke nervously as he quickly straightened the jar on the shelf with one hand while barely balancing the box in the other.

He was a little too clumsy for a job with breakables, but he was desperate for work. It was either work or be put out of the house by his father.

This is why I needed a son, God, thought Lorenzo as he eyed the store. Despite Vittoria being a dame, she did a good job perhaps even better than him, thought Lorenzo, but he could never tell her that. Vittoria noticed the glimpse of pride in her father's eyes as he surveyed the store. She knew he was proud of her work and loved her dearly, but he wasn't an affectionate man nor good at expressing feelings other than anger. So, when he fussed Vittoria found it humorous because she knew that he meant the opposite when it came to anything he said to her about the store.

"All of this stocking should be done long before you turn that close sign to open! Customers shouldn't have to deal with you in the way while they shop the aisles.", Lorenzo shouted in his deep baritone voice that rumbled throughout the store as he walked to the counter.

Vittoria followed behind him so that she could receive any further instructions without him yelling across the store.

"Yes, father. We will do better tomorrow.", said Vittoria with a smile as she thought they must have done a great job if that was the only complaint.

"You are not coming to work tomorrow.", informed Lorenzo as he brushed her aside so that he could place the daily till in the cash register.

Vittoria glared at her father knowing that he must have something up his sleeve that she wouldn't like.

"Why not?", she asked bracing herself to be annoyed.

"I want you to attend Councilman Rossi's fundraiser in my place. You can represent our side of the Rossi clan. Besides, it will be good exposure so that you can find a husband.", announced Lorenzo as he placed the bills in the drawer without ever looking at his daughter's irritated expression.

"No thank you. I have some accounting to do tomorrow. I've already planned my day.", insisted Vittoria.

"And my plan trumps yours. So, Vit, I want you to go shopping today and go to the salon tomorrow afternoon. You are an old maid and becoming the butt of jokes throughout the neighborhood and family. I don't even want to repeat the distasteful things they say about you. No Rossi should ever be considered a joke!", Lorenzo shouted the last sentence as his anger started to boil as he recalled some of the hateful words said about his precious baby girl.

Vittoria tried to reason with him, but he would have no more discussion on the matter.

"Pappa, please...", began Vittoria, but was silenced.

"End of discussion. Go to the local boutique the moment they open today and put the dress on my tab.", Lorenzo ordered as he walked away toward his office.

Lorenzo hid his tears as he walked away. He had such a beautiful daughter, yet the world couldn't see past her tight bun which hid long luxurious black hair that reached her buttocks. She always wore trousers, an oversized t-shirt and men's work boots. She insisted on wearing them reminding her father that the boots protected her feet while carrying heavy boxes.

She didn't dress like most women of her generation; she didn't wear the tight mini-skirts, high-heels and tight blouses revealing cleavage. There was nothing, sensual, elegant or even feminine about Vittoria's appearance, but underneath, there was a stunning diamond in the rough that Lorenzo hoped that one day a good man would notice.

As for Vittoria, she had given up hope that she would ever marry. She knew that she was different than her peers; she always had been, so she shouldn't be surprised that her path had taken her in a different direction. She was thirty-two, not married and only had gone steady with one boy when she was twenty. If she was honest with herself, she didn't even know how to act around a man; at least not how to be flirtatious or sensual. She could laugh and joke with them, be one of the boys and that was all. Her mother blamed it on all the hours she spent with her father. She was far closer to him than her mother and perhaps her mother was right, she thought.

She would take the place of the son that her father never had, the one that would someday take over the business; there's where her comfort lay, taking care of the accounting books, stocking shelves and assisting customers. That was her joy, her comfort and a way to forget her shortcomings as far as the world and her mother were concerned, she had. She knew that her father was heartbroken as he entered his office; it broke her heart to disappoint him, but she couldn't control how men saw her. She rushed over to his closed office door to reassure him.

"Pappa, I promise I'll go to the fundraiser for you. I'll try my best to look pretty. I want you to be proud of me.", Vittoria cried out the words to her father.

He felt ashamed that she would ever doubt his appreciation and pride for her. He quickly left his old oversized chair to open the door.

"My precious baby girl,", he said as he held her shoulders and stared deeply into the rich caramel brown eyes of his six-foot-tall daughter then pulled her into his embrace, "I am the proudest pappa there ever could be. One day, a great man will find you and give you the honor that you deserve!", cried Lorenzo as he held her close so she wouldn't see the tears that she heard in his voice.

Vittoria held him close as she smelled the familiar scent of her father that always provided comfort whenever she was frightened and she was still that same frightened little girl in so many ways. Of all the things she could face, marrying a man and being intimate scared her to death, but she would do it for her father's sake if nothing else.

Ricky felt alive and powerful as he drove to his office. After his romp with Giovanna, he had a resolute mind and determination to forge ahead with his plans without allowing the former Don Carlo to interfere. In fact, the old Don would soon realize it was time for a new king to emerge from his coattails. Ricky had decided that he would call his pal, Bernard to discuss a possible new business venture. Instead of waiting to enter the office, he made the call from his brand-new car phone; he was the envy of his peers, one after another bought one to keep up with him.

"Hampton, Inc. Mr. Barrington's office, how may I assist you?", answered Ester with a light and airy greeting.

"Hello, Ester baby. How are you this beautiful afternoon?", flirted Ricky as he always loved to do. Ester's voice instantly turned stern.

"Busy. Just one moment for Mr. Barrington.", informed Ester as she prepared to put him on hold. "Mr. Barrington, your playboy friend, Mr. Bianchi, is holding. Shall I transfer the call?", inquired Ester hoping he would say no so that she could deliver the message.

"Wonderful. I could use a break. Yes, transfer the call please.", instructed Bernard eager to hear what witty discussion Ricky had in store.

"Yes sir.", responded Ester who had been tempted to ask if he was sure, but she realized that would be her acting devilish.

"Ricky! What's new my friend?", asked Bernard anticipating an exciting story.

"I'm feeling like a brand-new man after a good romp with Giovanna. You are about due for a good fuck, aren't you?", laughed Ricky.

"Ha, ha, ha. The last time I did that I ruined my marriage to my precious first wife. Now, I just say fuck it. Who needs sex anyway? It's overrated if it's not with someone you love.", informed Bernard who was about to delve into a serious mood, but decided he wouldn't allow that. "So, who are you bringing to the fundraiser tomorrow?", said Bernard changing the topic.

"To be honest, I had contemplated asking Giovanna.", Ricky notified Bernard.

"Giovanna! Man, don't you know that you don't take a whore to a ball. You don't see me bringing my wife, do you? Just come stag like me.", warned Bernard to Ricky's laughter.

"Ouch! That's cold Barrington.", joked Ricky.

"What can I say, you're starting to rub off on me.", laughed Bernard as he thought of a way to turn his insult into a positive. "If you go stag, you'll be free to site-see and maybe meet a nice lady there. You don't want the streets to start talking about you …", laughed Bernard.

"The streets can kiss my ass. I do what I want to do. When I'm ready, I'll get married. Damn, you all are so anxious for me to be miserable like you. When I do tie the knot, something tells me she'll be different than any woman I've ever dated.", insisted Ricky who was becoming more and more ready to settle down.

He realized that the effects of a good time quickly wear off and he was left with no one in whom he could confide. He was starting to yearn for that type of relationship he saw with his parents, Bernard's parents and even what Bernard had with his first wife. He was quickly building a reputation to eventually be called an old playboy and for Ricky that was embarrassing, but he'd never let Bernard or anyone know that.

He parked his car outside the rear entrance to the funeral home; it was the official entrance for any mob dealings or secret meetings. One of his people rushed out to see if he needed assistance with anything. He dismissed the underling so that he could wrap up his conversation with Bernard. He remembered why he had actually called him and decided to mention it before getting off the phone.

"Hey, I just arrived at my office. I originally called to discuss the contract for the gaming machines. What's the update?", asked Ricky.

"Looks like we are lined up to get the contract here in Michigan as soon as the legislation is passed. We also have secured five other states as well.", advised Bernard of the good news.

"Excellent! Well, I'll see you tomorrow then. Ciao.", Ricky expressed his excitement for the news.

"Ciao!", said Bernard in response.

Ricky was thrilled with more great news of the family's legitimate businesses expanding. He, unlike his father, realized the more they expanded they could survive this strange wave of change that was happening in the mob world. There was no way Ricky would allow their legacy of wealth to fade with the times.

Chapter 2

Antonella swiftly walked into Vittoria's bedroom and threw back the curtains to let in the glorious bright morning sunlight. It was indeed a glorious day, thought Antonella. She was thrilled that Lorenzo had convinced their daughter to attend the fundraiser. She prayed that today God would grant them a miracle and allow a rich gentleman to introduce himself to their only child before her eggs dried up.

"Good morning, Vit! Wake up, darling. I need you to try on that dress you brought home. I want to make sure it's not too frumpy.", exclaimed Antonella as she was determined that the dress showed off her daughter's curves.

Time was over for modesty, thought Antonella, Vittoria needed a man to be drawn in by her body. Vittoria rolled onto her stomach and covered her head with the quilt; she had tossed all night over her promise. She hated she had promised her father that she would go; even as she was trying on dresses at the boutique yesterday, there was dread in her eyes. So much so, that the owner picked out a stunning dress for her because each one that Vittoria touched was not fitting her age or figure. Vittoria tried on the final dress, the one the owner insisted she bought and what she saw in the mirror frightened her almost to tears. Her figure was curvaceous, enticing and unbelievable; she didn't recognize the woman in the mirror. That woman reflected back at her could command any man to do whatever she wanted, but Vittoria also knew that a woman like that was always a moment away from danger. She felt that women like that were not safe around men.

"Enough foolishness. Out of bed, you go!", demanded her mother as she pulled the quilt and sheets back reminding herself of years past when Vittoria was a little girl. In so many ways, she still was, thought Antonella.

"Ok, Ma.", whined a reluctant Vittoria.

She walked toward the hall bathroom like a child who had been scolded with slouched shoulders.

"You really outdid yourself picking out this dress Vittoria!", shouted Antonella so that Vittoria could hear her while in the bathroom.

She admired the dress in her arms as she envisioned her daughter being the belle of the ball just like Cinderella. The dress the boutique owner demanded Vittoria buy was a stunning sheath dress in rich burgundy with sequence embroidery of shades of pink and white adorning the top of the strapless bodice. It would flow the full length of her six-foot frame and accentuate her round hips, buttocks and voluptuous bosom. Antonella was close to tears as she continued to imagine her daughter entering the party and the eye of every man being drawn to her. She knew it would be a special night indeed, she thought.

"God, please let my baby girl find love tonight.", whispered Antonella as she hung the dress on the back of the closet door so she could make the cross of Christ on her chest. She turned her attention to Vittoria. "Don't lollygag either. I have your breakfast ready and right after that, I'm taking you to the beautician to style your hair.", ordered Antonella.

She was not going to let her daughter get in her own way, not today, she thought.

The day had an odd feel to it and it felt even odder with the thought of visiting Giovanna, he felt more interested in the festivities of the evening. Ricky decided to only work a half-day and skip going to see Giovanna. When he called to inform her, she was quite annoyed by the news. However, he cushioned the blow of disappointment by promising to send someone that morning to drop off his credit card so she could buy the fur she wanted.

He planned to get a fresh haircut and wear his new tuxedo. He had never been eager to attend a fundraiser before especially without a date, but there was something different about the day. As he drove to the office, he caught himself thinking about how he would put together his ensemble. His new tuxedo was a three-piece mod velvet navy-blue suit with a broad lapel. He would pair it with his white Italian silk shirt and a navy-blue and gold paisley bowtie. To make his look complete, he would wear the genuine gold cufflinks his maternal grandfather, Luca Jilani, gave him for his eighteenth birthday. Like his best friend, he too was the apple of his grandparents' eyes. So, he had eight eyes scrutinizing how long it was taking him to settle down, that of his parents and his grandparents in heaven.

Vittoria looked at herself nervously in the mirror as Kim, the beautician, added the finishing touches to her hairstyle. Vittoria had a luxurious head of jet-black hair; it was thick and long-reaching her buttocks. It presented a tremendous task for Kim to curl and style, but she enjoyed the challenge. She chose a very popular look of the day worn by Charo; it was a partial front ponytail pulled to the top with her soft baby hairs brushed in place to frame her face. She meticulously curled large sections of hair so that the curls could cascade down Vittoria's back and shoulders.

Vittoria brought an heirloom that her mother insisted that she wear to the event; she had argued with her mother that it would serve better to wear it at her wedding. She had unconsciously smirked while making the statement and her mother caught it and replied that she had an even more impressive one for her to wear at that time. So, in other words, Antonella was not going to let Vittoria talk her way out of wearing it. Vittoria handed the hair comb to Kim with a frustrated sigh.

"Oh, goodness! Vittoria, this is stunning. Mrs. Rossi intends for you to snag a husband tonight!", exclaimed Kim as Vittoria laid the beautiful hair comb in her palm.

It was intricate with faux pearls and rhinestones. She placed it securely at the base of the ponytail; it looked more like a tiara than a comb. She gasped at Vittoria's regal appearance after placing the treasured piece; she was completely at a loss for words. She had yet to even apply any make-up; Vittoria was a rare natural beauty, thought Kim.

"What's wrong?", questioned Vittoria as she tried to turn her chair around to face the mirror, but Kim's firm grip on the chair stopped any effort of doing that.

"Just hold still, let me apply your make-up, then you can look all you want.", insisted Kim firmly as she reached for the loose powder to apply a light dusting of color as a base for blush and eye shadow.

Vittoria had the most beautiful olive skin; there wasn't a blemish to be seen so, Kim didn't want to apply too much powder. She wanted to maintain Vittoria's natural beauty; she only wanted the makeup to be a modest enhancement. Kim applied black mascara, then traced Vittoria's complete eye with eyeliner to the corner of her eyes. She then layered shimmer bronze eye shadow atop the thin line traced on her eyelid. Kim used the cat-eye makeup style to highlight Vittoria's expressive caramel brown eyes. She was becoming so excited about her workmanship that she wished she could attend just to see everyone's reaction to the stunning belle of the ball.

"All set!", Kim informed her reluctant client as she nudged her from her seat. "Off you go! Don't look now. I want you to experience the full effect once you've put on your gown.", smiled Kim as she ecstatically said the words.

Vittoria was obedient as she grabbed her sweater to leave. Most girls would have been excited to receive such special treatment brought on by the day, such as a new dress, makeup and a trip to a beautician. But it only brought on feelings of anxiety for her. As Vittoria exited the shop like a disappointed school girl,

Lorenzo was in awe and close to tears as the stunning timeless beauty emerged from its doors.

"Oh my God!", whispered Lorenzo as he quickly exited his car to assist his daughter.

She needed to get used to being waited on hand and foot; she was bound to meet a worthy admirer tonight, he thought as he opened the car door.

"Be careful my darling. Don't sit on your curls.", he warned; mesmerized by his daughter.

She truly was a one in a million, a diamond in the rough wasting away at his meat market. No more, he thought; he would call his cousin to ask that he make sure Vittoria mingles and doesn't runoff.

Vittoria sat quietly and pensively as her father drove them home. She noticed that he was constantly wiping tears from his eyes. She just knew that she must look like a desperate fool and he was sad that he would be disappointed yet again. She was thankful that there was only a side-view mirror on the driver's side; she could not stand the thought of seeing her overly done appearance.

As they pulled up outside the house, Vittoria saw her mother waiting anxiously at the open door. It was as if her mother sensed that she would be arriving home any minute. Antonella opened the door and wave frantically at her daughter.

"Come on! We have to get you dressed. We can't have the councilman arriving late at his own event.", shouted Antonella as she pointed to Councilman Rossi's vehicle stopping in front of the house next door.

Vittoria opened the car door and looked to her right at the councilman who was sitting in the rear of the car reviewing index cards; apparently practicing his evening speech. She decided she would breathe in deeply and get this evening over with; she quickly followed her mother's eager hands to come inside. As her mother fussed and tended to her appearance, Vittoria shut off her mind and thoughts. She was just a shell or a mannequin being dressed by an attendant; she was like a beautiful and lifeless doll.

"Absolutely stunning!", announced Antonella to death ears. "Thank you.", she whispered to heaven as she looked to the ceiling. "Go, so you are not late.", instructed the proud mother.

Vittoria walked robotically down the stairs with Antonella coming right behind her with the almost forgotten stole in hand. As they reached the foyer, Antonella quickly draped it over her daughter's shoulders and shooed her out the door.

"My darling, please relax and enjoy yourself.", encouraged Antonella as she smiled with hope.

She was so glad that she always made Vittoria wear heels to church otherwise the poor thing would be a stumbling mess right now, she thought.

Lorenzo nodded at the councilman, who had entered to say hello, as a reminder of what he was tasked to do. The councilman nodded in return at the two parents to reassure them that he knew the plan and would not disappoint.

The Rooster Tail was bustling with guests in support of the councilman and the excitement of dressing up to flaunt their wealth and influence. Ricky and his friends were no different. Ricky had arrived chauffeured in the family Lincoln Town car and dressed to impress anyone with sight. If anyone missed the distinguished six-feet-four-inch frame of Ricky Bianchi, they had to be blind.

His pals greeted him as he walked inside; they were in a huddle as they often were, sharing tales of business conquests. Bernard was dressed dapper as usual in a traditional black tuxedo with a straight leg and Angelo was a little more daring in a black tuxedo with a slightly flared bootleg. Raymond added a little Hollywood flare with a gray velvet tuxedo with a black velvet broad lapel and a grey and black paisley ascot. He was not going to be outdone by Ricky.

Ricky waved at his friends as he walked toward them with his left hand laid on his breast jacket to clearly display his designer watch. He was a magnificent work of art as he glided across the room in his three-piece navy-blue velvet tuxedo. His wavy dark thick black hair seemed to shine as bright as the smile he displayed for everyone to see; one would have thought the party was in his honor. He was very self-aware that he was the center of attention from men and women alike. Drinks were held in mid-air at the lips of the guest as they gazed upon his commanding appearance.

"What's shaking?", asked Raymond as he awaited a thrilling story from Ricky as the others did as well.

Ricky had met Raymond almost twenty years ago and Raymond fit in well with him and Bernard. Raymond was a University of Michigan graduate who had passed up an opportunity to attend Harvard for his bachelor's degree. He had allowed his family to convince him that as an African American, he would be safer if he remained closer to home. Michigan not only provided him with an excellent education but also the confidence to pursue Harvard for law school. Ricky had come to depend on Raymond's law advice and friendship over the years.

"Shid, making that bread! You know how I do!", Ricky said in his Detroit vernacular.

"Sho you, right!", chimed in Raymond as he gave Ricky some skin, their signature handshake and high five when they were feeling playful.

Ricky prided himself on being able to maneuver three worlds, the elite class with Bernard's help, the mob world, and the streets. He felt it took mastery of all three to secure a financially strong foothold in that city and he was determined to maintain it. Bernard and Angelo envied that talent of their friend; Bernard was able to maneuver through the mob world some; but he stuck out like a diamond on display in the streets, an easy prey. Angelo could manage his way easily among the mob and the streets, but he was a fish out of water when it came to the elite. Raymond could have easily fit in all three worlds if allowed, but the elite threw up brick walls in an attempt to block him at every turn.

The alliance the four men developed helped them all to make inroads, establish businesses and make connections to build successful careers. That alliance bound them closer than brothers and like brothers, they teased each other mercilessly. The guys were laughing at Raymond who was spinning around slowly as if modeling his clothes when the councilman was prepping Vittoria for her entrance.

Councilman Rossi didn't understand why the girl was so nervous. She hadn't said a word the whole way there as they were being chauffeured to the event. She just stared ahead with blank eyes. He pitied his cousin that he only had a girl, who was turning into an old maid and no son to whom he could leave the family business. He shook his head at the thought and this girl couldn't do her one part right. All she had to do was marry, thought the councilman as they stood outside the ballroom.

"Just relax. You'll be fine.", he lied as he realized his deceased wife would have known what to say to the poor thing.

Vittoria nodded at the councilman, then he turned on his charm and entered the Palm River ballroom with her a short distance behind. Vittoria felt completely overwhelmed at the immenseness of the room; there were easily 500 guests at the event. It seemed as though every wall was a window that provided a stunning view of the Detroit River and the boats docked outside. There were gorgeous studded globe lights that looked like diamonds hanging from the ceiling. Each table had simple, yet elegant bouquets of flowers with white and red roses. She felt like

Cinderella, out of place among the wealthy elite and local celebrities.

She felt swallowed up by it all, but the more she thought about it maybe that was a good thing; no one would notice her, she thought. She planned it all out in her head before entering; she would find the councilman's table, sit, eat, listen to his speech and then they would leave. She took a deep breath to steady her nerves and then she made her entrance.

Ricky found Raymond hilarious and was about to add to the laughter by telling a joke, but before he could, the most strikingly breath-taking woman entered the room. Ricky swallowed multiple times as he took in the full length of her. She wore a burgundy sheath dress that flowed snuggly down to her ankles; it begged every man to admire the curves it revealed in her body. Ricky took great notice of her full hips, round buttocks and voluptuous breasts that begged to be freed from the corset as they attempted to bubble over. Her long jet-black hair rested gently on her buttocks, my God, thought Ricky as he imagined her tossing it over his naked body as she straddled him in delight. Angelo noticed the desperate look of lust in his cousin's expression and was determined to warn him.

"Ricky, don't do it. That's a complete waste of your time.", warned Angelo with Raymond nodding in agreement.

"Why?", asked Ricky as he sat his drink down on a nearby table as he readied to approach her.

"I believe that's the councilman's cousin, Vittoria. She's a dyke. Fuckable, but a dyke.", cautioned Angelo then he took a sip of his drink.

"A straight-up bulldyker. She even works at her father's meat market for Christ's sake.", explained Raymond in agreement although he wouldn't even bother to have sex with her.

35

"She's what? Fuckable?", Ricky repeated part of the insult that he was shocked to hear his friend and cousin say.

"Yeah, fuckable. That's a compliment, but that's all she's good for. She can teach you some lesbo tricks; you know add another chick in the mix.", laughed Angelo as he dug himself deeper in the hole with Ricky.

Bernard stood quietly as he listened to the elitist and sexist comments of his friends. He was shocked and surprised by their comments; he had no idea that they could be so heartless. He eyed Ricky and was surprised to see that he was becoming defensive.

"You are insulting her! Don't you hear yourself? So basically, you wouldn't bring her around family.", said a shocked Ricky that Angelo would say such horrible things about a woman of such refinement.

"Tell him, Bernard, you don't bring your fucks around friends, family and polite society.", Angelo attempted to educate Ricky as he looked around for support.

"He's got a point.", chimed in Bernard who had been silent thus far.

"Regardless, she's too tall and fat for my taste.", informed Angelo. Ricky looked flabbergasted; did they not see the woman he saw, his mind asked.

"Twiggy has you, all fucked up! I like a voluptuous woman with curves in the right places … hips … breasts.", he said as he used his hands for emphasis, "I can't do anything with a twig; one toss on the bed, she might break a limb."

Ricky's friends laughed at his last comment, but Angelo was steadfast in his opinion and wasn't about to change it.

"She's a brick house. I'll give her that!", Raymond provided his analysis as he nodded lifting his drink to his lips.

"You know what? I've wasted enough time. I need to slide in before someone else does.", informed Ricky as he reached for his glass and took the last swallow before heading to Vittoria.

Vittoria walked toward the front of the room assuming that her table would be near the podium. She tried desperately not to make eye contact with the men that were drooling over her; their lustful expressions made her feel very uncomfortable and unsafe. She found her mind going to her safe place; that protective realm she ventured to, when necessary; when she heard a soothing baritone whisper hello. She was drawn to it and the power of it pulled her mind from the haven her mind sought.

As she turned, she saw the most compelling figure of a man standing before her. Everything about him screamed sex appeal, money and power; the three most dangerous tools a man can have at his disposal, this one had it oozing from his essence and soul. Every one of her senses screamed a warning, don't get close, stay away, but his scent, voice and sex appeal moved her right into the fire.

"Hello.", said Vittoria cautiously in her deeper register; one that led people to stereotype her and create rumors about her.

Ricky smiled at the strength of her voice and imagined how it would sound as it scolded bratty Bianchi children. He could see them stopping in their tracks at her commanding presence. He took note of her height being slightly shorter than himself; he guessed that she was easily six feet tall.

"I'm Ricardo Bianchi. My friends call me Ricky.", he smiled flashing his brilliant smile that made most women swoon, but it made her senses scream warnings even louder.

"Those must be your friends over there.", confirmed Vittoria as she pointed to their obvious interest as they quickly turned their heads.

"Yes, they would be my nosy friends.", chuckled Ricky, a little embarrassed that they would be so obviously nosy.

Vittoria's amusement eased his embarrassment.

"Nice to meet you, Ricky.", Vittoria said his name with surprising familiarity. She loved the sound and feel of it rolling across her tongue. "I'm Vittoria Rossi. My friends call me Vit.", she said as she hesitantly extended her hand to give the firm handshake for which she was known, but he had another plan in mind as he brought it up to his lips.

He allowed his nose to rest upon the top of it first as he tried to inhale her scent so that it could be firmly stamped and sealed upon his brain; then he gently brushed his lips across its surface as his lips parted to plant a kiss as if he were kissing her lips. An unfamiliar and strange sensation fluttered from Vittoria's stomach to the core of her femininity. She gasped at her body's reaction as she closed her eyes and relished in this new feeling as her lips parted.

Ricky's stared at her all the while and was surprised by her seductive display of an innocent reaction. He imagined that she must fool all men with this coy response; either way, he thought, he was hooked and wouldn't ever try to free himself.

The two were entangled in their thoughts of each other and did not realize that the Master of Ceremony had begun to speak so that the event could begin. Everyone had ventured to their seats leaving the pair in the middle of the dance floor. When they had resurfaced from the sea of their newfound desires, they both smiled at their distraction. Vittoria turned in embarrassment and was about to head to her seat when Ricky reached for her hand and entwined his fingers with hers to stop her.

"Please allow me to have the first dance with you tonight.", requested Ricky with his charming smile.

Vittoria nodded in agreement as she gently pulled away to approach her table. Ricky couldn't believe his fortune; he never would have thought he would have met anyone that night, let alone an incredible woman like Vittoria. The fellas were all smiles and couldn't wait for him to sit down. Ricky knew the only genuine smile was that of Bernard; he knew the other two were coming with lesbian jokes and he wasn't feeling it.

"Looks like she's ready to get turned out the right way! If I, were you, I'd tear that ass up!", joked Angelo.

The other two men saw the expression on Ricky's face and they knew to stay quiet. Bernard took note that Ricky was protective of her at first sight and now that he had his antenna focused on Vittoria, he knew to be respectful. He tried to use his eyes to convey that to Angelo, but he was stuck on stupid, thought Bernard. Raymond noticed Bernard's attempt at warning Angelo, but Angelo was too amused by his own joke to notice. Cousin or not, you don't make Ricky angry, thought Raymond; the only one that could stand a chance at doing so, was that crazy Anglo, Bernard.

"Watch your steps.", warned Ricky as his ice-cold stone-grey eyes gave an additional warning that his words did not convey.

Angelo finally got the hint, cleared his throat and drank some water. He knew first-hand, how ruthlessly crazy his cousin could be. So, if Ricky wanted a lesbian, so be it, thought Angelo; it was none of his business and he would keep it that way.

During the councilman's speech, Ricky found himself more entertained by Vittoria than her cousin. He often spotted her stealing a glance at him and then she would coyly turn every time she realized he was looking at her. He wondered how long she would keep up the act because surely a woman as gorgeous knew her way around a dick, thought Ricky. He was eager to see just how well because he was ready to give her everything, his body, his money, his heart and even his soul if she required it.

Vittoria found Ricky totally irresistible and that frightened her; during her cousin's speech and now at dinner she couldn't help but stare at his table. She observed how confident he was and masculine. As he joked and laughed with his friends, it was as if his voice drowned every sound surrounding it; he was all she could hear. As his voice tantalized her ears, the memory of his lips on her flesh tantalized her skin. She found herself desiring his touch once more. Well, Ricky did promise her a dance, she thought as she smiled thinking of his beautiful grey eyes locking on hers as they talked. She purred at the thought of him.

"I agree, my dear, the food is delicious.", said the councilman as he smiled; he was glad that she found something to delight in.

"Oh… yes. It's pretty good.", replied Vittoria; if only her cousin knew what really had her mind captured.

She had barely noticed what she was eating; she was doing it robotically as her mind and eyes focused on Ricky. She was so entangled in her fantasies that she hadn't focused on the reality of actually dancing with Ricky. She had never danced with a man before; she had barely even dated one. The worst thing that she could imagine would likely happen if she even attempted such a folly; she would undoubtedly step all over his expensive designer shoes. There would be no happy Cinderella ending and she would be the joke of the evening; it would be just one more thing to add to her legend. That was a nice way of putting it, she thought.

As the band started tinkering on their instruments in preparation, she started eyeing exits. She planned to convince the driver to take her home; she'd make up some excuse about being sick and maybe fake a tear like most ladies do. Most men are a sucker for that so he should give in easily and take her home, she thought. The staff began removing dishes, so she thought it was a good time to make her exit without being noticed with the extra bodies moving around to mask hers. She quickly tossed her napkin on the table and headed for the exit.

Ricky was getting excited to see the band members preparing their instruments as they would bring him one step closer to touching Vittoria again. He glanced over to see if she was getting excited as well when he noticed that her seat was empty. Maybe she went to the ladies' room to freshen up her makeup, he thought, then he saw her making a mad dash for the exit wearing her stole. The look on her face seemed frantic, he became worried that she had received some horrible news. He felt protective of her and urgency came over him to ensure she was okay. He immediately left his table in pursuit of her. Wow, she can really move fast in those heels, thought Ricky as he exited the building only to find that she was sitting in the Town Car. He was determined that it was only goodbye for now and that he would see her soon.

Chapter 3

It had been one week since Ricky had met Vittoria. He had made several calls to the councilman requesting her phone number and he hadn't returned Ricky's calls. Ricky was quite annoyed that the councilman had the audacity to ignore him. He would have to be more direct and find out the address of the meat market and speak directly to Vittoria's father. He had resolved to ask for permission to court her. Ricky knew very little about Vittoria, but her pull on his essence was otherworldly.

He had spent the night with Giovanna hoping to quell his thoughts of Vittoria, but nothing seemed to work. Maybe another go at it might do the job. He turned over to kiss Giovanna in hopes of arousing her. She awakened to his kisses and his face buried between her breasts. She hoped that his lovemaking would be more passionate this morning than the night before. She felt that he was holding back and that his thoughts were elsewhere. Usually, she was able to make him forget his stress; but none of her tricks seemed to work last night, she thought.

She rolled on top of him to begin their foreplay; she couldn't have him getting bored with her. She had to make sure that she maintained the lifestyle to which she had become accustomed. She bounced as she straddled Ricky's manhood. Ricky closed his eyes as he enjoyed the sensation, but the moment he relaxed, his thoughts drifted back to Vittoria. He pictured her long legs straddled around his body, gripping his torso as she grinded his penis deeper into her; he could visualize her tossing her thick long black mane across his face and her huge breasts bouncing with each pulsation. Ricky gasped at the thought and arched his hips higher as his mouth opened desperate for oxygen.

"Yes.", whispered Giovanna.

I knew I'd get you into it, she thought. She delighted in her prowess to seduce him.

As his manhood burst, he groaned loudly and yelled, "Shit!" as he placed his hands on her hips to pound himself even deeper within her. "Vittoria!", Ricky cried out her name as his body shook with the release of his seed, but his pleasure was quickly replaced with a slap to the face.

"Who is that bitch!", yelled Giovanna both furious and embarrassed that he could possibly be thinking of another woman while inside her.

She had invested too many years of her life into Ricky without anything to show for it; not a ring and not even a baby. He made sure that she took her pills and the one time she slipped up and got pregnant, he forced her to abort it. She knew she was only a kept woman, but she needed to keep it that way; at least until she could meet an even wealthier catch. She raised her hand to hit him again, but before she could say or do another thing, Ricky grabbed her arm.

"Woman, remember your place! I can take all this shit away just as fast as I gave it to you. Don't try me!", said Ricky in a deadly whisper as he was still feeling his orgasm.

He said the words with such venom, like, this Vittoria was the most precious thing to him, thought Giovanna. She didn't know who this Vittoria was, but she was the most dangerous woman in her world at the moment.

Ricky was shocked by his own actions as well; that a woman he had barely touched could have such a hold on his mind. This was an oddity to him and he was now more determined than ever to see Vittoria again. He had to see what could become of this unusual attraction he felt for a woman he hardly knew. He quickly got out of bed and rushed to the bathroom to cleanse himself of Giovanna. As he washed her essence away, it felt as if he were washing her out of his mind as well. As he exited the bathroom, he looked at her as if she were a strange woman that needed to be removed from his life. He left the master bedroom without a word.

Giovanna felt the feelings conveyed by his stare; she knew whoever this Vittoria was, she had put her claws deep within Ricky. It was going to be the battle of Giovanna's life to maintain what she had established, but she had no idea who she was up against.

Ricky had barely dressed as he left the condo; he was buttoning his shirt as he entered the elevator. He used the mirrored walls to assist him in putting on his tie so that he would resemble the well-put-together man, he always was. Ricky stared at his reflection in the mirror, for the first time not recognizing the mature man that stood before him. For the first time, he saw what others might see; a man approaching middle-age, single without a wife or family of his own and empty. He gained physical pleasure from his existence, but nothing of substance; however, something from deep within told him that he could find both pleasure, purpose and a deeper connection with Vittoria. He leaned on the mirror with both hands and looked deeply into his eyes; he saw the void behind his good looks. He vowed to God and himself that he would make Vittoria his and do anything in his power to satisfy her.

"What are you doing? You've been staring at those boxes for who knows how long instead of carrying them to the front of the store!", yelled Lorenzo at Vittoria.

He noticed that Vittoria hadn't been herself since she returned from the fundraiser, but he was afraid to ask either Vittoria or his cousin about it. He had hoped that she would have met a good catch at the ball; she sure was dressed for the part. He was puzzled by the whole thing as Vittoria wouldn't answer any questions about the night at all. It reminded him of a time long ago when she was thirteen; he hoped that it would not be a repeat of that. She had gone weeks without talking to anyone.

Vittoria had been staring at the boxes that her father wanted her to unload for what seemed to be hours. Since the fundraiser, she couldn't stop thinking of Ricky and torturing herself about her decision to leave. She daydreamed every day about what could have happened had she stayed and danced with him as he had asked. With every fantasy, it ended with her telling herself that men like Ricky can't be trusted and that he would only hurt her. She looked around the storage room and noticed how far behind she was in her work, no wonder her father was so frustrated. She reluctantly carried a couple of boxes to the front of the store so that she could stock the shelves.

"Finally! You've got a lot to catch up on. I would help, but I need to check on these accounting ledgers.", said a frustrated Lorenzo as he marched to his office and shut the door.

Ricky finally arrived at work; it seemed the short distance took hours instead of minutes. He stormed into the building past everyone's hellos and went straight to his secretary. She was reading a fashion magazine when she noticed him rush in rudely past everyone. It wasn't like him not to say hello or joke with staff. She was concerned about what might be going on.

"Bettie, get Councilman Rossi on the phone immediately. I don't care how you have to do it. Tell him that I am willing to double my donation if he talks to me!", ordered Ricky as he walked toward his office without stopping to take a breath.

Ricky flopped in his chair and waited to see if Bettie could get through to the councilman. Surprisingly, she must have been able to get him on the line, he thought, when his phone rang.

"Yes?", responded Ricky hoping to hear some good news.

"Sir, the councilman is available to speak to you.", informed Bettie, glad that she was able to make it happen.

"Transfer the son-of-a-bitch.", informed an annoyed Ricky that it took greasing the councilman's palms to get a response.

45

"The son-of-a-bitch is on the line.", responded Councilman Rossi as he confronted Ricky.

"Sorry, Mr. Bianchi.", apologized Bettie before hanging up and ending the three-line conference call.

"I've been trying to reach you all week.", expressed an annoyed Ricky at the greedy politician.

"Well, the work of a councilman is never done ...", Rossi attempted to explain.

"Save the bullshit. Look I need the name and address of the meat market Vittoria's father owns.", demanded Ricky sternly as he held a pen ready to write down the address.

"It's located on Michigan Avenue, 5000 Michigan Ave. That's it I believe; Rossi Family Meats is the name in case the address is wrong. Now about that donation...", said the councilman switching the topic to his favorite subject, money.

Ricky abruptly hung up on the councilman as he got what he wanted and didn't want to waste another moment speaking to him. He yelled at Bettie and requested that she enter his office.

"Yes, sir?", questioned Bettie as she waited to be instructed.

"Send the money to that jive turkey, so I can keep my word. Also, grab one of my clean suits and a dress shirt. I'm going to hop in the shower. I have a very important stop to make afterward.", instructed Ricky as he began unbuttoning his shirt.

"Yes, sir; I'll hop to it Mr. Bianchi.", reassured Bettie as she blushed then quickly turned to leave; the things she could have done to that man in her younger days, she thought with a smile.

Ricky felt butterflies in his stomach as he drove across town to see Mr. Rossi and Vittoria. He couldn't get there fast enough; he had to remind himself to slow down or he might not arrive at all.

He pulled up in front of the quaint store; for some reason, he hadn't expected something modest for the striking beauty. He would have thought they owned a chain of supermarkets instead, as beautiful and refined as she presented herself at the fundraiser. He checked his appearance in the rearview mirror before exiting his well-waxed ride.

Vittoria spotted the side view of the front end of the Lincoln Continental Mark III from the store window; we have a rich customer visiting us today, she thought. She quickly removed the box from the floor and took it behind the counter out of sight. She readied herself at the counter to greet their wealthy customer as he or she entered. She looked down at her wrinkled shirt and tried to smooth it out before the customer entered; then she heard the bells jingle at the entrance. When she looked up and saw Ricky, she wanted to flee and he wanted to run toward her; both were slowed down by fear. However, fear was normally an unknown feeling for Ricky.

"Vittoria! How are you? You look…", Ricky was interrupted by Vittoria.

"A mess!", replied Vittoria.

She was self-conscious of her messy bun, wrinkled clothes and work shoes. All of which she normally felt quite comfortable. Ricky smiled at her obvious nervousness.

"You are just as amazing today as you were when I first laid eyes on you.", reassured Ricky as he took in every inch of her that was visible from the counter.

Here we go with the bull, thought Vittoria, just as expected a sweet talker trying to get sex from her no doubt.

"How may I help you?", asked a defensive Vittoria.

"For starters, you owe me a dance. So, I would like to ask you out so that you can fulfill that promise.", he smiled his words with his devilishly attractive smile dismissing her defensive tone.

Vittoria had never seen a smile so bright surrounded by the most perfect lips just plump enough to feel them cruising over her skin. Her mind immediately went back to the night of their first encounter. She was completely unaware as she stared into his eyes that he had reached for her hand and was holding it moving it ever closer to his lips.

"How about going out with me tomorrow night?", he asked as his lips moved across the top of her hand and up to her wrist.

"Yes...", she whispered then hearing her father's office door open she snatched her hand away.

"Mr. Bianchi, what an unexpected pleasure. Move Vit. How may I help you? Want some steaks?", asked Lorenzo as he pushed Vittoria to the side.

"Actually sir, I'm here to ask your daughter out and to speak to you.", announced Ricky.

He noticed the surprised look in Vittoria's eyes and the bewildered one in Lorenzo's. Lorenzo's confusion turned to laughter.

"Who knew you were so funny? Ok, what cut of beef would you prefer?", said Lorenzo with continued laughter in his voice. It was no way a man of Ricky's statue would want his Vit. "I've got all kinds, even top-shelf." Lorenzo stood waiting for the order.

"I do have a good sense of humor, but I would never make a joke about Vittoria. I meant what I said. I want to court your daughter and I am asking for your approval.", explained Ricky as he walked toward Vittoria to take her hand. "I have never met a woman whose very essence commands attention, respect and admiration. I would be honored to get to know her, sir.", Ricky said with a sincere tone and expression.

Lorenzo was almost speechless and he couldn't wrap his mind around what was happening so he nodded in agreement as he tried to generate the words to respond. Vittoria was stunned as well and simply stood staring into Ricky's eyes as he spoke; although he spoke to Lorenzo, his eyes never left Vittoria's face.

"Well, I guess so... I mean yes, you have my permission.", said a confused and stunned Lorenzo, I guess the fundraiser was a success, after all, he thought.

"Thank you, sir.", Ricky nodded as he spoke the words. "Vittoria, I'd like to take you to the opera tomorrow afternoon and then for dinner afterward. I can pick you up at 2 pm. Is that a good time?", Ricky requested.

"Yes ...", Vittoria said accompanied by a nod.

She decided that a nod would be better than anything else she could think to say. Lorenzo noticed that Vittoria was just as surprised as he had been and was just standing staring at Ricky. He nudged her hand with the tablet and pencil so that she could write their address.

"While Vittoria writes the address, you can ring me up for your most expensive cut of beef. I'll take four pieces.", Ricky instructed the two. He was glad to occupy Lorenzo with a task so that he could speak semi-privately to Vittoria. "I can't wait to see what you wear tomorrow.", Ricky flirted with his eyes.

Me too, thought Vittoria as she said, "Well, you'll just have to wait and see."

She couldn't believe that she was flirting back at the handsome lady's man. Don't start anything you can't finish, she thought remembering the words of her grandmother.

Lorenzo didn't notice the two flirting as he was too busy humming as he packaged the expensive cuts of beef. This was indeed a great sale, he thought, then it hit him that this was indeed a good day. His only child, his baby girl had one of Detroit's wealthiest and most powerful men asking for permission to court her. Most men didn't use the term anymore, let alone ask for permission; they just took what they wanted, he contemplated the significance of Ricky's actions.

"Pappa?", questioned Vittoria to an immobilized Lorenzo standing at the register. "Ricky is ready to pay for his order.", she explained.

Lorenzo snapped out of his thoughts to see Ricky holding his wallet in front of the register. Just wait until we get home and I tell the wife, thought Lorenzo as he told Ricky the total and collected payment.

Vittoria had barely slept; there had been so much commotion in the house, especially from her father. He was so excited that one would have thought Ricky asked him out. Her mother was less excited about Ricky; in her mind, they were heading down the aisle. She was a little trepidatious about a mobster for a son-in-law, but if Vittoria had to marry one, there was no better family than the Bianchis. They were the most powerful and everyone feared and respected them, the Polish, the Blacks and even the Latin American gangs.

Vittoria was overwhelmed with worry and a small amount of excitement that was almost snuffed out by fear. She had no clue what she would wear on her date. A date she thought, I haven't been on one since … Sadly, she couldn't remember.

"Vittoria come down now! I called the boutique yesterday and asked the owner to bring some dresses. We need you to decide which one you like and try it on!", shouted Antonella.

Although nervous about the possible alignment, she felt like she was preparing to hand over her daughter to a prince. She and her husband were willing to pay top dollar for a dress or two for future dates. Oh Lord, thought Antonella, she'd have to buy practically a whole new wardrobe for her daughter; Vittoria owned mainly pants, T-shirts, plain button-down cotton shirts and a few frumpy dresses she wore to church or funerals. She sighed as she waited for Vittoria to drag herself down the stairs like a zombie again.

"You don't have time for pussy footing around. We need to pick out at least two dresses for you.", her mother tried to convince her of the urgency.

"He liked what I wore the last time. I guess something along those lines again.", said Vittoria not knowing what she should wear.

"Well, we don't want to overdo it. Those dresses should be for special and formal occasions only. However, we do want something sexy though.", explained the seamstress and boutique owner.

"Not slutty though.", chimed in Antonella, "Or too short. Too many young girls nowadays show way too much."

"We'll keep it classy.", reassured the seamstress as she pulled one off the small rack Lorenzo had carried inside. "This one is perfect; it's simple, classy and sexy.", she explained as she handed it to Vittoria.

Vittoria eyed the dress without much excitement as it appeared to be plain to her. Her mother noticed her expression and felt the look was warranted.

"That one looks a little plain, Clara. We don't want to bore the man.", Antonella said as she shook her head in disappointment with the dress.

"This dress doesn't require the frills to stun a person; it takes a curvy woman to fill it out. It's the woman who commands attention in this dress, not the dress. Trust me, go on and try it on.", insisted Clara.

Vittoria carried the dress slowly to the powder room off the hallway between the kitchen and the living room. She couldn't imagine the dress looking anything but plain Jane. It was a straight dress with a full sleeve and no waistline that would flow just to her knees. The dress had vertical lines of color and sequins on the lightweight sweater material; its colors complimented her skin. Colors of gold, orange, beige and silver-lined the dress and would hug each curve; which was sure to bring attention to her full hips and breasts. Although they weren't spring colors, Clara didn't think anyone would be criticizing Vittoria's color palette when they were staring at those curves. The high round collar would provide the much-wanted modesty, but those large breasts would demand attention.

Vittoria reluctantly pulled on the dress over her all-in-one shaper; she had a flat stomach, but her mother insisted that a woman should always wear one with a dress so that panty lines wouldn't show. Vittoria stared speechless at her reflection in the mirror; Clara had done it again. This was another stunning dress that would surely cause Ricky and every other man with a pulse to stop and stare. Vittoria hesitantly left the powder room to show her mother and Clara just as her father was in the hall with a cup of coffee. Lorenzo spotted her exiting the bath and immediately choked on his coffee as he saw his stunning daughter.

"Pappa, are you alright?", asked Vittoria who was willing to ruin the dress if it meant stopping her father from choking.

"I'm perfectly fine dear. I'm just so thrilled…", Lorenzo paused as he thought of how excited Ricky will be to see her.

He reached for her elbow to escort her back to the living room for inspection. The two ladies both gasped at the natural beauty.

"That's the one! I told you it's the woman that makes the dress! I have another one by that same designer that I want you to buy. She'll be able to wear it during the latter part of spring and into the summer.", Clara explained with delight as she shuffled through the dresses on the rack. "In fact, I'll just pull these four as well.", Clara informed the family.

"How many dresses …", interrupted Lorenzo as he attempted to add up the cost.

"It's no time for us being cheap or Vittoria being modest right now. We want a son-in-law, don't we?", Antonella whispered to her husband who nodded in agreement. "That's perfect Clara, just let us know the cost. Vittoria, call Anna and ask her to help you with your make-up. We can't afford to hire Kim to come every time you and Ricky go out.", Antonella smiled as she uttered the words; her baby had a suiter, she thought.

"Ok.", said Vittoria as she headed to the powder room to remove the dress.

Anna Bruno was the last person she wanted to talk to right now; despite being her oldest and only friend. Although they grew up together there were things that Vittoria could or would never share with her. In many ways as of late, they were really only acquaintances. In fact, unknown to her mother, she hadn't even told Anna about the fundraiser or Ricky. Anna would have all sorts of views and opinions about what Vittoria should do and frankly, she didn't care to hear any of them. She assumed that they all would require that she be someone other than herself and she wasn't for playing games or being fake.

Now that Cinderella had returned to her rags of old, Vittoria walked to the kitchen to call Anna. The phone only rang once.

"Bruno residence.", greeted Anna as she sat by the phone about to call her guy when the phone rang.

"Hey Anna, it's Vittoria. Look. I need your help with some make-up. I have a date this afternoon. Can you ...", Vittoria was interrupted by screams.

"You got to be fucking kidding me. A date! Finally! I'm on my way.", Anna shouted before hanging up the phone.

"Oh boy!", said Vittoria as she hung up the phone on the kitchen wall.

Antonella saw Anna running down the street toward the house as she did as a child so many years ago. Anna and Vittoria had been thick as thieves growing up and it brought back so many memories of the two girls laughing and playing dress-up. Both had similar fates of being unmarried; Vittoria hadn't dated enough to even dream of marriage and Anna was basically a slut, thought Antonella. Anna considered herself to be a modern woman who wasn't concerned with marriage and dated as many men as she wanted. Antonella would rather have an old maid for a daughter than a slut, she thought as fond thoughts turned to ones of disapproval.

"Anna's here!", yelled Antonella as she opened the door. "Hello, Anna. Vittoria needs your help with make-up, but don't make her look like a slut. So, use less make-up than you wear.", said Antonella not caring whether or not the young woman was offended.

"Ok, Mrs. Rossi. I'll keep her plain as usual, like you.", she said ignoring the intended insult and dishing a couple of her own as well.

"She's in her room.", Antonella informed twisting her lips at the young woman then announced, "Anna's on her way up."

Anna was so surprised that Vittoria had a date. She was intrigued by this sure-to-be nerd that wanted to date her plain friend. Yes, she thought Vittoria was attractive, but nowadays it took more than just a pretty face to attract a man. A woman had to know how to use her body and words to snag one and definitely to shag one, she believed. She couldn't wait to hear about him. When she entered Vittoria's bedroom, she saw a stunning Vittoria in a figure-hugging number standing in front of her mirror. Well, well, Vittoria you are learning, thought Anna.

"Hey girl, looking good! Once I apply a little makeup, you'll knock your date dead off his feet.", said the excited friend.

"Thanks. I really want this to go well, although, I'm nervous.", Vittoria confided as she reached to hug her old friend.

Vittoria moved toward her bed and sat on the side of it with Anna joining her as they used to do so long ago. Anna kicked off her shoes and curled her feet beneath her bottom as she sat ready to unload her questions on Vittoria. She wanted to know who this guy was, where he was from … everything.

"What makes this stiff different from the rest, be they few, that wanted to date you?", asked Anna on edge to find out more about this peculiar man that wanted her friend.

"He's stunning … a man's man … a man that people look up to and even fear. But when I'm around him, I forget about everything, the past … I find myself dreaming of what could be. Despite his reputation, he's so charming, romantic and gentle with me.", confessed Vittoria as she blushed.

She hadn't talked to anyone about her feelings; these feelings were so odd to her.

"Stunning … who is this cat?", asked Anna sure that she would be in for a good laugh shortly.

"Ricardo Bianchi.", Vittoria said waiting for the shocked look to appear on her friend's face.

Sure enough, it did and Anna was at a loss for words. Maybe he knew about the rumors and just wanted to have some wild sex with Vittoria or worst yet, maybe he thought he could break her, Anna thought. She wouldn't share those thoughts with her old friend, she didn't want to come off as jealous or as a Debbie downer, but she was a little nervous for her naïve friend.

"Wow!", Anna murmured again not knowing quite what to say at the moment.

"That's all you have to say?", questioned a now even more nervous Vittoria who had already been asking herself why would he want her.

"Just relax on the date and be yourself… No on second thought don't be yourself. He might think the rumors are true if he's heard them.", said a more serious Anna.

"I don't know why or how those rumors ever got started!", exclaimed a frustrated Vittoria.

'Exactly! Don't they know I wouldn't let those big titties go to waste if you were a lesbian.", laughed Anna as she and Vittoria playfully hit each other as they laughed.

"So, you are a lesbian now?", questioned Vittoria still laughing from their playful exchange.

"No, but I have gotten down with a girl or two.", explained Anna. "Look enough of this pointless talk. Just do whatever you did to draw his interest and things will go well.", explained Anna to a confused Vittoria.

"That's the thing. I didn't do anything special.", explained a perplexed Vittoria.

"Well, if it ain't broke don't fix it. So, do *nothing special* again.", laughed Anna. "Enough talking. Let me apply your makeup. I don't want to be the cause of you being late for your date."

Anna decided to keep the makeup basic and added mascara along with a bronze dab of eyeshadow. She pulled out a brand-new brick orange lip gloss. She was amazed that Vittoria didn't realize just how beautiful she was or maybe she did and purposefully wanted to look drab. Anna always felt it was related to a horrible summer Vittoria had; she was completely different after that summer.

"Ok, I'm done. You can take your rollers out now. I'll help you.", suggested Anna as she began to take the large rollers out and run her fingers through the thick long bouncy curls. "Aww sooky, sooky now!", Anna said as she thought of what she or Ricky could do to Vittoria.

Ricky was truly a lucky man, thought Anna.

"Stop!", insisted Vittoria bashfully as she saw the rebellious look in her friend's eyes.

"Yeah, Vit. Go get that money!", Anna belted out in her deepest register with her head reared back.

"Shush, what if he's downstairs.", Vittoria scolded Anna for her excitement.

"Alright, sorry. My work here is done. Enjoy yourself and don't get in your own way.", Anna attempted to provide a last-minute tutorial as she packed up her makeup.

"I'll try not to.", Vittoria promised as she slipped on a pair of gold open-toed leather platforms with wide straps. She was thankful for once for cute toes that she had polished a burnt orange the night before not knowing it would be perfect for her dress.

Ricky was so excited; he didn't recall ever being this excited about a woman. He hadn't felt this excited since he received his first gun or maybe it was his first kill, he thought, either way, he was anxious to see Vittoria and to touch her again. He hadn't slept much the night before, his mind kept drifting back to her time and time again. Each time he jacked off violently to the memory of her touch and fragrance. The last time he had to laugh aloud because he had been so loud that anyone making their way down the hall would have thought he had a lover inside.

"Damn Vittoria! You got me girl!", he said aloud as he drove to her house reminiscing and realizing that soon he wouldn't have to fantasize about touching her anymore. "Those big titties ...", he stopped in mid-sentence as he felt his manhood come alive.

Ricky didn't want to go inside with his Johnson speaking for him; he realized there would be a more appropriate time to let his imagination run wild. As he turned on the street, he examined the modesty of the neighborhood. He soon spotted her home and pulled in front of the house. He took it all in; it was a modest two-story Queen Anne-style home painted a pale blue, but it looked like it was in need of a fresh coat of paint. It, like most of the homes on that street, looked like they were well lived in by families with kids. They didn't look neglected, just well used and cozy.

As Ricky exited his car, he rubbed down his pants and adjusted his suit jacket. He wanted to make sure that his Johnson was under control. He wore a traditional black suit, a white silk shirt with a black and white houndstooth patterned tie and a white silk pocket square. He eyed his appearance in the side view mirror and was pleased as usual. How could she resist you, thought Ricky, hoping that he and Vittoria would have sex that evening? Antonella heard Ricky pull up out front, so she made her way to the door and opened it. She found herself feeling an old sensation as she stared at the incredibly gorgeous man. Oh my, she thought as she smoothed her hair to make sure her own appearance was presentable. She dotted to the staircase behind her to call Vittoria.

"Vittoria! Ricky is here!", she shouted forgetting she had opened the door and that her voice could travel outside.

She didn't want the family to seem desperate for the pairing, but they were, she thought, they needed Vittoria to get married yesterday. Before she could turn back to be the first one to greet Ricky, her husband answered his knock as Anna ran down the stairs.

"Come on in Mr. Bianchi! Welcome to our home. Please have a seat, Vittoria will be down shortly.", instructed Lorenzo as he pointed to his favorite comfy recliner.

Ricky glanced over the modest living room quickly trying not to appear judgmental, but it was a far cry from what he had grown accustomed. He couldn't imagine Vittoria sitting in the barebones living space as elegant and beautiful as she was.

Really, thought Antonella as she approached Ricky before he sauntered toward the chair, "Please forgive my husband's manners or lack of. I'm *his* wife, Vittoria's mother, Antonella. Welcome.", she said as she extended her hand for a handshake and received a swift kiss on her hand instead.

Oh, yes, our daughter has a fine one; she better not screw this up, she thought, as she blushed from his touch, his smell, his looks … his everything. Lorenzo noticed her response and wasn't pleased.

"Antonella, will you go up and check on Vittoria.", Lorenzo blurted in a jealous tone before realizing it.

He gave an apologetic and embarrassed look toward Ricky who only smiled as he waited for Vittoria, then he felt lustful eyes behind him staring at him from head to toe. He turned and saw

Anna; he didn't know who she was but prayed she wasn't family and he wouldn't have to deal with her often. She gave off a loose vibe to him and he found her utterly unattractive because of it. No man, looking for a wife, finds a woman that spreads her legs across town appealing and he could tell that she had been spread far and wide. He nodded hello and began walking toward the chair.

Anna wasn't used to being ignored by men even when they were with their ladies; they always managed to sneak a lustful eye her way, but not this one. For the first time, she felt disgusting and dirty; that was the look he snuck her way, one that indicated he wouldn't touch her if she were the last woman on earth. She had become quite uncomfortable; she quickly waved goodbye without saying a word and left the house hoping that no one noticed how crushed her self-esteem was at that moment.

For as much as Anna felt inadequate, Vittoria felt the admiration in Ricky's eyes as she walked down the stairs. The surge of his desire vibrated from her head down to her toes as he stared at her. He had never seen a woman more beautiful, elegant and sexy with effortless ability. There was something about her that called to him and made him forget anything and everyone around him. He slowly stood to his feet to greet her and as he walked ever nearer, his throat dried threatening to take away the suaveness of his voice. He swallowed several times to lubricate it so his vocal cords wouldn't fail him.

"Hello, Vittoria. You look breathtaking!", acknowledged Ricky as he smiled while reaching for her hand.

"Hi Ricky.", Vittoria blushed as he took her hand.

She had dreamt of this moment as well as he; he gently and slowly glided his lips on the top of her hand to take in her delicious fragrance before planting a kiss. A kiss that again would have been perfectly suited for her lips. Antonella stared as she held her left hand to her neck as she thought of the sensation that her daughter must be feeling. Lorenzo was less comfortable with the public display of affection and decided to tap his wife's wedding band as a reminder of whose she was. She fanned his hand away, but she was secretly pleased that he was jealous. It let her know that there was still fire between them; she decided to hold his hand and kiss him on the cheek to reassure him of her love.

Lorenzo had seen enough of the budding young couple's affection and he was ready for them to leave. He had started reminiscing about his own first date with Antonella and was getting a little frisky himself. This was the first time in a *long* time that they would have the house to themselves and he had a good idea of how to make use of it.

"Well, you two better get a move on it. You don't want to be late.", he said as he walked to the door to open it, "Have fun. Although, my daughter is a grown woman, I expect you to return her home at a respectable hour.", explained Lorenzo sternly so that Ricky knew to take him seriously.

"Yes of course sir.", promised Ricky although he surely wanted her to stay the night with him.

Ricky held Vittoria's hand and smiled to reassure her that he meant what he said. He would have to wait for a better time for his other plans; after all, he realized she wasn't the type of woman who would actually sleep with him on the first date. He truly felt that she deserved special planning and not just a rumble in a hotel room or a car as he had done in the past with lesser women; she was too special for that despite his strong desire to rip her dress off the moment they were alone.

Ricky exited and held the screen door open for Vittoria to exit and then they held hands as they walked to his car. He wanted to put his arm around her waist, but he didn't trust himself at the moment; he would be too tempted to lower his hand and rest it on the roundness of her buttocks. Vittoria was also thankful that they were only holding hands, anything else would make her feel dreadfully uncomfortable.

Ricky opened the door for his beautiful date and assisted her inside; Vittoria had to be mindful of her long hair that she was used to wearing in a bun. Ricky was aroused by the simplest things she did; he decided that he would assist her with her hair. It was a great excuse to touch it; the soft-silkiness of it felt delightful in his palm and he knew it would feel even better teasing his torso as they made love. He found it hard not to think of sex whenever he thought of her. Perhaps seeing the opera would distract those thoughts, pondered Ricky as he closed the passenger door and walked to the driver's side. As Ricky entered the car and started it, he felt he needed to lay out their agenda for her like a schoolboy looking for approval.

"I have a wonderful afternoon planned; we will see the opera, Otello, first; then I'll take you to Joe Muer's. I hope you like seafood.", inquired Ricky.

Vittoria hadn't been to any fancy restaurants; the closest she came was just some neighborhood diners. She didn't want to admit that he was about to expose her to a world that was completely unknown to her. She didn't know how she could compete with the ladies he was accustomed to; they probably had men taking them to fine restaurants all the time. She had to remind herself to be *herself*; she hated pretentious people and didn't want to start being one trying to impress him.

"Oh, I love seafood.", she admitted although she rarely ate it and she had never heard of this Joe Muer restaurant.

Vittoria figured it must be nice since Ricky thought it was a fitting end to a date. It was gearing up to be an exciting day; she looked around the car with wide eyes as she took in the luxuriousness of his ride. She had never been in anything other than a basic model of a jalopy; this car had everything even a car phone. Ricky saw her wide-eyed expression as her eyes scanned the vehicle. If it would make her happy, he'd give it to her now along with anything else she could dream of asking.

Vittoria felt his attention-drawing her to turn hers to him; the look on his face took her breath away. She had only seen one man look at a woman the way he was looking at her and that was her father whenever he thought no one could see him stealing a glance at her mother. She smiled then blushed and lowered her head, but that wasn't a good move because that brought her attention to his thick thighs and his manhood that was bulging from his pants. She gasped as she turned with an even deeper blush of embarrassment to look out the window.

Ricky wanted to tease her by saying, 'You didn't know I was working with all this.', smiled Ricky as he said the words inwardly, 'I know you can't wait to touch it.', he continued in thought.

The ride from the Woodbridge Detroit community to Mid-Town was a very short drive and went quickly for both for very different reasons; Ricky was lost in sexual thoughts and Vittoria imagined if they had danced together that night at the fundraiser. Vittoria had only seen Orchestra Hall in the newspapers or on television, but all of that paled in comparison to it in person. It was home to the fourth oldest orchestra in the nation, The Detroit Symphony Orchestra. The exterior of the building was modest compared to its magnificent interior. It was built in 1919 in the tradition of Beaux-Arts and Renaissance Revival using rich limestone and yellow brick to create a masterful structure.

Vittoria could only guess how magnificent the inside could be, but as Ricky pulled into the valet area she would soon see. She beamed from ear to ear with anticipation as did Ricky. He was so proud to have her by his side. He felt almost desperate to impress her, although he knew she wasn't shallow and into material things as his past love interest had been.

After handing his keys to the valet attendant, he maneuvered from the car quickly to assist Vittoria. He didn't want anyone touching her. He shook his head in disapproval at the valet who attempted to open the door for her. She noticed that Ricky was dismissing the attendant with a wave of his hand so that he alone could assist her. As she eased her long legs from the car, the attendant nodded in agreement at Ricky expressing that he completely understood why he didn't want any man near her.

'That's a straight-up brick house!', thought the attendant as he backed away with a smile.

As the two walked arm in arm toward the entrance, Vittoria looked up at the brass awning at the entrance with such great anticipation and excitement. Ricky was honored to give her this moment in time and experience this moment through her eyes; her enthusiasm was contagious.

"Isn't this a gem of a building?", asked Ricky proudly as if he had designed it himself.

Vittoria nodded in agreement as he continued with his account.

"My father and I sit on the state committee that petitioned for a submission of the Orchestra Hall to the National Register of Historic Places.", Ricky said with pride. "We hope it will be approved by next year.", he concluded.

He was determined to make a name for the Bianchis in polite society and this along with his other legitimate businesses was doing what he intended. Vittoria was surprised by this news; she only knew of his family as a powerful mob family and nothing else. Ricky could see the questioning in her eyes, so he leaned down a bit to whisper in her ear.

"We have numerous legitimate businesses.", he continued in a normal volume, "My best friend, Bernard, and I have several business ventures together. I'm trying to establish a powerful legacy that will last for generations.", he explained to Vittoria who appeared quite curious.

This was indeed new and foreign to Ricky. Whenever he tried to discuss his hopes and dreams for his family legacy, Giovanna was more interested in discussing a new designer and the latest fashion line she wanted to buy. So, it was refreshing to see that Vittoria was listening and not tuning him out.

"You have to tell me more over dinner. I'd love to hear about your plans.", admitted Vittoria.

This news eased her conscience to know there was some depth to this man; that there was more to him than just drop-dead good looks and the violence of mob life. Just like him, there was more to her as well and she hoped he would come to realize that. She was gifted with a business mind and had a load of plans she wanted her father to implement in the family business, but he wasn't innovative. He had an 'if it's not broke, don't fix it' attitude about the business and wasn't interested in any unnecessary changes. With a man like Ricky supporting her dreams and her supporting his, there was a whole new world of opportunity waiting for her to discover and cultivate.

As the pair entered the vestibule of the hall, Vittoria was overcome with emotion; she knew this was the instant when everything had changed for her. She had no psychic ability to see it, but she could feel it. Ricky noticed the tears in her eyes; he put his arm around her and gripped her shoulder for reassurance. She quickly took her handkerchief from her purse to dab her eyes carefully being sure not to disturb her make-up. Lord forbid; if it were washed away by tears. She had nothing to replenish it nor the skillset required to do so.

Vittoria smiled at Ricky for his attentiveness, but as the usher directed them to the elevator, the beauty of the hall took her attention once more. The couple took the elevator up to their box seats; as they entered the sitting area, she felt as though she would be a part of the performance, they were so close. Ricky attempted to assist her as she sat, but she was in awe and could only stand

and admire the magnificence that was the Orchestra Hall. There was so much brass that shined so brightly one would think that it was gold. Their box seat was encased by an immensely tall arch with thick heavy burgundy curtains seemingly hanging from the rafters they were so tall. Ricky tried to look at things as if it were his first time there, but he was completely captured by Vittoria's beauty; it was indeed unmatched. So, they both stared amazed, delighted and in awe of what was to come.

As the two settled in their seats and the opera began, both were intrigued by the desperate love Otello had for his wife. Neither one had experienced such love and it frightened them both that perhaps they were on the verge of discovering it now. Numerous times, Ricky wanted to touch her but he had to remember that they, too, were on display in their box seats overlooking the stage. He didn't want to bring any shame to her because she was indeed a woman who should be respected and admired. He was just beginning to learn how much so, but for sure her beauty alone should garner that, he thought. So instead, he held her hand throughout the opera. He found himself massaging it often as his mind thought of her other areas of softness just waiting for him to discover.

Vittoria found Ricky's touch comforting and protective. She hoped that she always would find it so and that it wasn't just his best representative making an appearance to make her let her guard down. Behind some of the best representatives are monsters waiting to pounce and take only their pleasures leaving heartbreak and pain in their wake. But for now, she wouldn't let her mind go to any negative places, she thought, she would take his actions at surface level for the time being. If he had any vicious intentions, that monster would rear its ugly head soon, she thought.

After the play, the two made their way to the lower level and for the first time while there, she allowed her attention to veer to the other patrons. She noticed that most of their eyes were on her and Ricky; most nodded their recognitions and some women admired Ricky, then tooted their noses up at her. Most of the men smiled at her admiringly and acknowledged Ricky's prowess in snagging such a beauty as her. For the first time, she actually felt like a woman, elegant, sexy and alive. She hated to admit it, but it was Ricky's intense desire for her that fueled her confidence. For once, the feeling of all eyes on her wasn't frightening; this must be what women like Anna and her mother in her youth felt. It was empowering.

Vittoria glanced at Ricky and smiled; it was the first time she had ever looked at him seductively. He could only imagine what she must have in mind for him that evening, yet Vittoria had nothing in mind but to smile and revel in this new feeling. She had no idea what power her visage had at that moment; she was just naively amazed at the feeling of sensuality that she felt for the first time. Until that moment, she had no idea how to exude her desire for a man; to be honest prior to meeting Ricky, she never had any sexual desire for anyone. She viewed sex as disgusting and only something done to have a baby if done at all.

Ricky strutted proudly with Vittoria by his side to the valet podium outdoors; he knew he was the envy of every single man there and all the women wished they looked half as good as Vittoria. He raised Vittoria's hand to his lips and planted one of his unforgettable kisses as Vittoria's breath quickened. Her voluptuous breasts rose and fell making them appear even larger. Ricky couldn't control his thoughts or his vocal cords.

"Mm.", Ricky sighed audibly as his nose and lips glided across the top of her hand.

He adored her fragrance and was eager to run his lips and nose all over her body; from that look, he knew he would get his chance tonight. Vittoria gasped as she felt that pleasant sensation again rising as if butterflies to her stomach and unknowingly provided the reassurance that Ricky was hoping to receive. The valet attendant smiled and wet his lips as he approached the couple.

"Your ticket sir.", asked the attendant while thinking, I know you gonna do tonight what I would do, sho you right!

He took a quick look at her derriere and nodded as he thought, a straight-up brick house; then strutted to retrieve the keys. He returned with the keys and knew better this time than to even try to assist Vittoria inside the car. You keep a brick house like that under lock and mother fucking key, thought the valet.

During their short ride down to the Eastern Market where the restaurant was located, they laughed and talked. He laid on his natural charm thick and told some of his jokes, but being careful to make them less colorful than he normally would. He was eager to know about Vittoria's hopes and dreams.

"So, tell me what was your plan if you had never met your future husband.", Ricky asked in his playful way hoping she caught the message he was throwing her way.

"Well, my plan is to turn our little meat market into a chain of stores. That is if I can ever convince my father of that.", she said excitedly as no one had ever asked her about her interests or plans.

Ricky couldn't read her; he didn't know if she was really naïve or just being coy. Either way, he was intrigued that she had a mind for business. He was starting to realize there was so much more to this stunning angel. Ricky was engrossed in the way her deep brown eyes lit up with excitement as she spoke of her hopes and goals. However, he was surprised that she never mentioned getting married or having children as a goal like most women would; for a brief moment fear rushed over him, what if the rumors were true. Hell no, he thought to reassure himself, there is no way she could be a lesbian.

As they pulled up to the restaurant's valet section, she noticed the attendants give a wave to Ricky; he must be a regular and no doubt a big tipper. Again, she noticed that Ricky wouldn't allow the attendant to aid her; she found it charming that he was so protective and territorial of her. The men looked at her admiringly but seemed surprised to see her. A hint of jealousy crept in and she wondered who they had grown accustomed to seeing with Ricky.

Ricky and Vittoria entered the well-beloved Detroit restaurant that had become a staple of fine seafood dining. They approached the maître d' to inform him of their reservation. The maître d' greeted them with a welcoming smile.

"Welcome Mr. Bianchi and guest.", greeted the gentleman as he smiled directly at Vittoria.

"Hello, Joseph. My girlfriend and I have a reservation for two.", informed Ricky not noticing the surprised expression on Vittoria's face.

A warmth coursed throughout her body at the thought of being named and claimed as his girlfriend. It was something that was surprisingly comfortable and a label she never thought she would ever be called.

"Oh, indeed sir.", he said as he searched for Ricky's name. Out with the old fox and in with an even foxier model, thought Joseph as he asked, "Would you like your usual table?"

"No. I'd like a different view of the place from here on out.", informed Ricky.

He didn't want any memories of Giovanna creeping into his date with Vittoria. Besides, he and Giovanna had done a lot of freaky shit in that booth, thought Ricky.

"Yes of course, right this way, I have another booth that is just as private.", informed the staff as he ushered them to a secluded booth.

Vittoria smiled at Ricky, but her eyes told him that she realized this was a familiar spot he took his ex-girlfriend. Ricky cleared his throat before leaning over to kiss her cheek; he didn't want her worrying about any past lovers. In fact, he hadn't actually been with Giovanna since she slapped him and he dreaded their next conversation. He no longer desired to touch her, even thinking about her made him feel adulterous. Vittoria didn't know it yet, but he belonged to no one but her.

Joseph extended his hand to Vittoria indicating for her to slide into the booth. Ricky gently swooped up her hair as she slid in and he did as well next to her. She was expecting him to sit across from her as most couples did on dates; as far as she knew, but Ricky had other plans in mind.

Ricky had spared no expense when it came to ordering and he was delighted that Vittoria was comfortable. Some might say too comfortable; she freely ordered her favorites and ate with abandonment. He wasn't used to dining with a woman who could put away as much as he could; most only nibbled or excused themselves to expel any excess that would cause them to gain weight. He attempted to hold back his laughter, but it was impossible.

"Is everything to your liking?", Ricky laughed as he asked the obvious.

Vittoria completely forgot that she was supposed to eat lightly and not as she would at home. Well, too late, she thought, besides she was told to just be herself; and this was her.

"I'm sorry.", she said as she wiped her mouth and continued, "I've always had a huge appetite and an active metabolism."

She hoped that she hadn't turned him off since things have been going great till that point.

70

"It's no problem. I find it refreshing that you are yourself and not pretentious like so many women are.", Ricky confessed, "In fact, I adore everything about you."

Ricky leaned over to kiss her cheek and smell her neck. He wanted to show restraint, but his desire was urging him to do more; so, he kissed her neck and moved his hand from her shoulder down to her waist then up to squeeze her side bosom. Her gentle gasp quickly turned to a stiff body that warned him that he had moved too fast. As he pulled away, he saw blank eyes staring straight ahead like a deer in headlights. He didn't know where her thoughts had taken her, but he was fearful that he had ruined his chances to possess the beauty for life.

"Vittoria... angel ... I'm sorry. I didn't mean to move too fast.", pleaded Ricky as he gently touched her face to turn it toward him.

Could she be a virgin, he asked himself, that's ridiculous that a woman this stunning at her age could be a virgin. At that moment, he realized that he needed to tread very carefully until he found out the truth of the matter. Vittoria returned to the world; she hated that his gentle touch caused her damaged soul to react the way it did. Perhaps one day, she could confide in him and tell him what she had never told a soul. But until then, she had to reassure this wonderful man that they were okay.

"Ricky ... please ... be patient with me. This is all new to me.", Vittoria beseeched him hoping that this worldly man wouldn't tire of her.

"I think the world of you Vittoria and I am willing to take things at whatever pace you want. If you want to take things at a snail's pace, so be it and if you want to run at a marathon's pace; I'll take you straight to my place right now.", said Ricky shocked by his own words on two accounts.

For one, he was used to getting whatever woman he wanted, whenever he wanted and two, he'd never taken a woman to the home he shared with his parents. Vittoria leaned upon his strong shoulder and placed a gentle kiss on his cheek. She was relieved that he was so understanding and he was willing to sacrifice his desires to please her. He was truly a respectable man, she thought.

"Thank you, Ricky.", she sighed as she said the words and continued to rest her head on his shoulder.

She felt so protected, calm and happy at that moment and when he laid his head atop hers, she knew that there was something special happening between the two of them. Is this, what love looks like and feels like, she asked herself. Is this what she had been so fearful of all this time and had avoided? Perhaps, she had been a foolish girl, she thought.

Joseph was about to approach the pair when he noticed the loving and innocent display between the couple. He completely stopped in his tracks at the sight as this was completely different than what he would stumble across with the other lady. He would catch them doing obscene things in a public setting, but this was an altogether different sight. Maybe the young Bianchi was finally in love.

The ride back to Vittoria's home was laughter-filled. The two talked about everything from sports to business and even religion. Ricky felt like the most blessed man alive, much the way Bernard felt when he met his first wife. Ricky didn't think the feelings could actually be real; he thought Bernard was all talk, but now he was a believer that a man could fall in love at first sight. As he was surely hooked from day one. Ricky realized that Vittoria would be a true test of his restraint; he wasn't used to holding back. With any other woman, he'd have her dress pulled up by then or off her shoulders so he could kiss and suck her breasts or even other more sensual parts. He had to pray for strength so that he could kiss her goodnight as a gentleman and not the lust-filled sex fiend he could be.

Antonella and Lorenzo were sitting in the living room waiting to see if Ricky would be a gentleman and bring their baby girl home at a decent hour when they heard his car pull up out front. Lorenzo walked over to the window to check and was pleased to see the couple had returned timely.

Ricky as before walked to open the door for Vittoria; he reached for her hand to steady her. The two walked arm in arm toward the front door, but Ricky decided to stop halfway so that he could steal a kiss. Vittoria looked at Ricky expectedly for what she hoped to be their real first kiss and Ricky didn't disappoint. He took her by the waist being careful to position his hands respectfully and gently pulled her close. He touched her nose with his own and inhaled deeply before planting a gentle kiss on her lips. Vittoria slowly encircled her arms around his shoulders and allowed his lips to linger then they allowed their foreheads to touch.

"How long are they just going to stand there?', asked a confused Lorenzo.

Antonella looked out the window alongside her husband, but unlike him, she thought it was romantic. In fact, she was pleased that the two were sharing an innocent moment; it was very sweet. Who knew the mobster had a sweet side, she thought with a smile.

Chapter 4

Since that first date with Vittoria, Ricky was flying high like the Commodores and everyone could tell there was something different about him. The night saw a difference in him as well; Ricky thought of Vittoria every single night and since he couldn't explore her body the way he desired, he played their time spent together over and over in his mind. So much that he often found himself masturbating multiple times a week; not only could he not control his thoughts, he couldn't control his outburst as he imagined touching and kissing Vittoria. He had no desire to go to Giovanna for a night or morning romp, so he pleasured himself instead.

Bianca was headed down to breakfast when she heard more moaning and groaning from Ricky's suite; she knew that he wouldn't dare bring a harlot to her home. The commotion was really getting to her and she was determined to stop it. She decided to halt her breakfast plans and see exactly what was going on with him.; she walked across the catwalk toward the other half of the house. Ricky was in full-blown fantasy mode and was ready to explode and was getting louder and louder.

"Ah shit!", shouted Ricky.

He threw the covers back to sit on the side of the bed utterly out of breath. At the noise, Bianca's facial expression turned from anger to disgust back to anger as she pounded on the door.

"Ricky! This is getting ridiculous. You better not have a slut in my house!", Bianca reprimanded her only son.

A naked Ricky walked to the door and cracked it enough to see his mother's annoyed countenance yet hiding his nakedness.

"Mother … do you really want to know what I was doing?", Ricky laughed.

He was slightly embarrassed that as a grown man his mother would be eavesdropping outside his bedroom. It's no telling how loud he'll be when Vittoria comes over, he thought with a smile.

"Nasty boy, get washed and come down for breakfast.", Bianca fussed at her cherished son.

"I get it from father. I remember how loud you two used to get.", he laughed as he tried to reach out to tickle his favorite girl.

"Stop! Your hands are filthy!", laughed Bianca as she dodged his hands and continued her original plans for breakfast.

Yes, your father would get even louder, she thought with a smirk as she reminisced about their youthful lovemaking. She walked downstairs then toward the back of the house to the kitchen where Carlo sat waiting. Carlo greeted his wife with a smile as she entered the breakfast room, located just off their huge kitchen, but his smile quickly turned to concern as he noticed her frustrated expression.

"What's wrong dear? Come sit and tell me.", asked a concerned Carlo as he poured a cup of coffee for her.

"Do you know what is going on with Ricky? Did he break up with that harlot he keeps in the condo?", asked Bianca as she added two sugar cubes to her coffee.

"No, I don't keep up with his distractions unless it affects business. Why do you ask?", inquired Carlo.

"You haven't heard him? … He masturbates almost every night! He didn't even do it that much when he was a teenage boy. I'm concerned. He should be finding a wife and making babies, not spilling his seed everywhere.", said an irritated Bianca, but Carlo found it hilarious instead of concerning.

"Well, you can ask him yourself.", laughed Carlo as Ricky entered the room.

"Ask me what?", inquired Ricky shocked that his masturbation was going to be the morning topic at breakfast.

Bianca was embarrassed that Carlo would put her on the spot like that. She tried to be as normal as possible by fixing Ricky a cup of coffee, but Carlo wasn't going to let her off that easy.

"Your mother wants to know if you broke up with that Giovanna girl. Isn't that her name?", informed Carlo to a surprised Ricky.

Ricky never would have thought his father would remember her name.

"It's complicated. I met an incredible woman about a month ago and we've been dating. She's a real class act. If you know what I mean?", Ricky said as his eyes questioned his parents.

Bianca picked up on it quickly and was excited to think that he might have met his future bride. Carlo's attention perked up as well; it was about time, he thought.

"I haven't had the mind or heart to tell Giovanna that it is over although she probably has a feeling since I haven't seen her in weeks. I won't even tell you what happened the last time I did.", Ricky said while shaking his head in disbelief that he had done such a faux pas.

"So, this new girl is something special?", asked Carlo.

"Yes, she is.", informed Ricky all too eager to tell them all he knew about her.

He began to discuss his time with her and how their personalities seemed to mesh. His parents listened intently and were excited about this new prospect as most men Ricky's age were on the verge of having grandchildren. It was well past due, they thought.

Even Giovanna, who hadn't seen Ricky in weeks, knew something had to be up that would cause him not to make at least one booty call weekly. She needed to know who this Vittoria was; she needed to find out more about her competition. So, she made up her mind to visit the funeral home before Ricky arrived. She knew he normally would arrive hours after opening, so she decided to head down the street to pay a quick visit to the funeral home.

As she entered, she was glad that the first person she saw was Lenny in the vestibule; Ricky always used Lenny to drop things off for her. She quickly spoke and motioned for him to come close. He could see that she was up to something so he quickly walked over to see what she wanted. He figured she would ask him to help her get Ricky to have him chauffeur her somewhere; she liked the air of having staff.

"Hey, Giovanna. What's shaking?", asked Lenny eager to hear her scheme.

"I need some information. Do you know a woman named Vittoria?", whispered Giovanna.

"Yeah ...", responded Lenny, but he had heard how protective Ricky was of her, so he wanted to tread very lightly.

"Well ... who is she?", demanded Giovanna not understanding his hesitation.

"She's some gorgeous chick that the boss is into. Some say that she's a lesbian because she's a ten but never is seen with a man; well not with anyone for that matter. So, I guess she's a closet lesbo.", informed Lenny not wanting to say much more and he was glad he had stopped since Ricky was walking in.

Ricky squinted at the two; he believed that the pair had to be up to no good. From the look of Giovanna's surprised expression and Lenny's nervousness, he must be spot on, he thought. Ricky approached the two and before he could speak, Lenny jetted from the vestibule out the door.

"Hello, Gio. Why are you here?", asked Ricky as he turned to walk toward his office.

She knew that she was practically on the outs; there was a time when her very presence evoked his desire and passion. She had been barely able to keep him off, but now it was as if she wasn't even in the room. She hesitantly followed behind him, not sure how to respond as she was not accustomed to being ignored. Ricky sat down and crossed his legs trying not to look as annoyed as he felt.

"Hi Ricky.", Giovanna said in the most seductive way she could in the awkward moment as she sashayed to his desk to sit atop. "It's been a while, Ricky, I miss our time together.", she explained.

"Yeah, about that ...", Ricky began to explain why when Giovanna interrupted him.

"I've been thinking that I shouldn't be jealous of ... Vittoria. Maybe we can spice things up a bit and invite her over. I'm down with a threesome; that would be groovy. I hear that she's a lesbian; maybe she can teach us both some new ways to get down.", Giovanna said as she rubbed his strong thighs.

Ricky's eyes intensified with anger at the utterance of Vittoria's name and he immediately moved his leg away from Giovanna's touch. His annoyance quickly turned to anger at her insinuation that he was only with Vittoria for sex and just wanted a new sex partner. He swiftly stood and dusted his pant leg as if brushing away her touch.

"So that's what this little trip here is about? You're checking for me now? You don't come here unless I send for you.", Ricky said in his deadly whisper.

"I just want to know what's going on with you. You used to come by my place every single night, but now... I haven't seen you in weeks and the last time you were with me, you called out that dyke's name!", whined a nervous Giovanna as her voice cracked.

Giovanna felt her whole world crumbling around her. Ricky walked around the table to confront Giovanna face to face. Fear swept through Giovanna's body with each step he inched closer. She feared what he might do to her despite Ricky not being known for hitting women but there was a deadly cold as steel look in his grey eyes. She slithered from the table and backed away, but too slowly to avoid his grasp of her arm.

"No, you just want to know if you're about to lose all the shit I provide for you. Who did you talk to? Where did you hear these lies!", he said as he took her face in his hand; his long slender fingers reaching through her hair to rest on her scalp. "I know it was loose lip Lenny; I'll deal with him later. As for you, I'm done. I'll let you remain in *my* condo for a while, but *we* are done. Don't come back here again!", Ricky voiced in his deadly whisper.

Giovanna was furious; how dare he throw her out like trash, she thought. Maybe the new rumors about him were true, after all, an unmarried man in his forties was a peculiar thing, she thought, perhaps he needed to know what the streets were starting to whisper about him. She wasn't going to go out quietly, so she mustered up the courage to tell him.

"I get it now. I guess I was just a beard maybe to cover up other desires; now that you have a lesbian masquerading as your woman, you both will be free to do what you want!", Giovanna shouted the insinuating words at Ricky.

He didn't care what rumors existed about him, but he was enraged that she would give life to the hateful and untrue rumors about Vittoria. Vittoria, as far as he was concerned, deserved better than that and if he had anything to say about it, she would be respected.

"Get the fuck out of here, you cheap trick! You aren't even good enough to say her name!", shouted Ricky.

He threw a vase at the doorframe; she had bought it for him years ago to commemorate him taking over the business. Giovanna was humiliated and angry that she was losing the good life and status of being his woman. Her friends and even her mother told her not to get too comfortable; hell, even Ricky would remind her of that from time to time, she thought. It would be damn near impossible to find another on his level as a replacement. She stomped from his office in tears and vowed to figure out a way to restore what she lost.

A whole new world had opened to Vittoria and she knew that it was only a matter of time before she could no longer work in the meat market. She sensed her father realized it too; she would sometimes catch him looking at her as if he were already missing her. She often, as she did that morning, found herself twirling on the floor as she stocked the shelves; Ricky still owed her that dance. She didn't know the first thing about dancing with a man, but she pretended that she was in his masterful arms and he twirled her with expertise.

Lorenzo saw his daughter, who was just now experiencing things that most women did as teens and it brought tears to his eyes. His precious daughter was on the verge of an engagement, he thought for sure since Ricky practically called every single night. The pair would talk for hours and Lorenzo and Antonella loved to hear Vittoria's laughter fill the house. She was happy for the first time in years and it satisfied them to know that she could have the happy ending that they wanted for her.

Lorenzo walked over to Vittoria and took the jar of seasoning from her hand. She was extremely confused by his actions and tried to retrieve it assuming that he was being playful perhaps.

"One day soon, you'll have staff doing everything for you and taking orders from you. Your hands will be even more delicate from being waited on hand and foot.", he informed Vittoria proudly, knowing that she would be the first Rossi to really achieve ultimate success and wealth.

"Pappa! We haven't been dating long enough for anything like that. Give that to me now.", she insisted he stop the discussion and let her get back to *work*.

"I'm a man and I know when a man is in love. Ricky's just like I was when I met your mother. I thought she was the most beautiful woman in the world; in fact, I still do.", Lorenzo said as he smiled thinking, of him and Antonella in their youth.

Vittoria didn't want to admit it, but she was starting to believe that Ricky was in love with her as well; she definitely had *strange* deep feelings for him too. She had never been in love, so she wasn't sure what she felt; however, she knew for sure that she loved his companionship. She also agreed that he did remind her of her pappa in so many ways, he was just as protective to a fault where she was concerned. As a child, she had witnessed her father go berserk on a man who had disrespected her and her mother. Even then she knew, that if her mother hadn't stopped him, her father would have tried to kill the man. She felt that same intensity with Ricky whenever they were together; it was a fierce protective nature that comforted her.

"So, when are you and Ricky going out again?", asked Lorenzo who was surprisingly inquisitive; had he heard his wife asking the same question, he would have called her nosy.

"This weekend Pappa …. tomorrow. Can I get back to work now? Did you finish your shipment order?", asked Vittoria.

Vittoria was slightly uncomfortable talking about her budding love life. The next thing would be him asking if they've had sex and she definitely didn't want to discuss that, she thought. Lorenzo realized that they were treading into unfamiliar territory; they had never even discussed men before and at times he wondered if she was even interested in them. So, he decided to lay off the subject and get back to work. He knew he would have the rest of his life to delight in their union and future babies that were sure to come.

"Ok, sweetie. I get your less than a subtle hint. I'll go back to work.", he said as he turned to walk away.

Just as she thought she was free to imagine her and Ricky on the dance floor, she heard her father's voice once more.

"Maybe you should go to the boutique today and pick up a few more dresses, what do you think?", asked Lorenzo as his eyes calculated the amount of extra money he could splurge on the dresses.

"Thank you, Pappa, I'll keep that in mind, but Anna said she would help me spruce up my wardrobe and even let me borrow a blouse or two. She's coming by tonight.", informed Vittoria then she pushed him toward his office when she noticed he was about to object.

It was no secret that he and her mother did not approve of how Anna dressed, but they had to admit that she drew the men like flies, smiled Vittoria at the thought. She was starting to bubble with excitement at the thought of seeing Ricky in a day. They were going to the Detroit Zoo and she hoped that Anna could help her look casual and feminine at the same time; that was challenging for Vittoria and if left up to her she'd look like she was headed to work.

Ricky's nerves were shot after Giovanna's visit that morning. He needed to find a way to relax; he didn't want to be even more wound up for his next date with Vittoria. He knew he would already be ready to bust a nut and wouldn't be able. Everything was agitating him that day; Lenny had been puttering around, in and out of his office all day saying that he wanted to ensure all the broken pieces were up.

"Bettie!", yelled Ricky as he heard her outside his office. "Lenny, are you still sweeping? Get your nosy ass out of here!", he ordered, figuring that Lenny was hoping to hear some juicy information.

Bettie was glad she didn't witness whatever caused him to throw the vase; there had been fewer violent outbursts since he had been dating his new love interest. She was hoping it would stick because it was the happiest, she'd ever seen him.

"Yes, sir.", Bettie said as she waited expectedly.

"Call the fellas and invite them here tonight for cards. Call the cater to order some type of finger food and booze. You know what to get.", instructed Ricky as he quickly turned his attention from her to his ledger.

"Yes, of course, sir.", Bettie said relieved it was a short order and that his temper had steadied.

Ricky hoped that his friends would be available for the last-minute invite; he was pretty sure he could count on Bernard who appreciated any excuse to stay away from home and Angelo, who was single. Raymond had the most stable and loving relationship in the group; he couldn't always pull away from his wife with such short notice.

Ricky leaned back in his tall black leather chair and allowed his mind to focus on Vittoria as he breathed deeply, seemingly for the first time all day. He closed his eyes and pictured her in some spring number that showed off her figure. He imagined acting as a tour guide at the zoo by sharing his love and knowledge of the animals. He remembered the feel of her silky hair on his fingertips and the smell of her sweet fragrance as he imagined his eyes gliding over her body.

"Sir, all the guys will be able to make it.", Bettie informed Ricky as she wondered if he were awake or not.

"Thank you, Bettie. I really do appreciate you. You put up with all types of shit, my moods and these goons around here.", Ricky said trying to fain one of his-million-dollar smiles.

Bettie could see there was something troubling her young boss, but she felt it was best not to pry as it probably concerned a woman.

"It's not a problem at all sir. I know how to keep all of you in line.", she said with a wink then left his office.

"I can't believe Vittoria has another date with Ricky! It must be going quite well.", confessed Antonella to Lorenzo while drinking their evening cup of coffee.

"I don't know why not, when he calls almost every single night.", Lorenzo chastised his wife then took a sip of coffee. "Today, I told Vittoria that she should pick out a few more dresses.", said Lorenzo proudly in support of his daughter's courtship.

"Oh, Lorenzo, sweetie! That is wonderful! She will need more outfits. Anna's coming shortly to help rehab some of Vittoria's things. God knows she needs help, but we don't want her looking slutty though.", Antonella shared.

"Absolutely, it doesn't take much for Vittoria to fill out a dress in her size. We don't need Anna bringing tight short dresses or blouses. Ricky likes that our daughter is a class act.", Lorenzo bragged on his only child, "Besides our baby girl is still a virgin."

"Women, nowadays, don't know their own power. If they held back, a man would give them the world.", Antonella said as they both nodded in agreement.

Anna knocked on the front door as she opened it to enter. She waved at the pair sipping coffee in the living room then ran up the stairs with a few blouses in hand. She couldn't believe that Vittoria was still dating Ricky; she knew for sure that he would have grown tired of her by then, but for some reason, he remained interested. She was determined to find out Vittoria's secret.

"Hey lady. I can't believe things are still groovy between you and Ricky. Girl, tell me your secret.", demanded Anna not waiting for a hello from Vittoria.

"Hey. I can't even look at the blouses first then you ease into the questions.", Vittoria said as she laughed at her friend shaking her head in disbelief, "If you must know … I'm just being myself."

Vittoria snatched the blouses from Anna and began examining them to see which ones she wanted if any. However, Anna had other plans; she wanted to know the details.

"So, you must have put it on him and shook those big titties in his face. Come on give me details. Does he have a big cock?", asked Anna aroused by her own words.

"No, and I don't know! He's respectful. He knows I'm not ready for that and he's being patient with me.", explained Vittoria, but Anna didn't like what she was hearing.

"Don't make him wait too long. A man like that has the ladies lined up to suck that cock.", Anna advised. "And trust me, those hoes know rule number one when dating a rich man … you get pregnant and lockdown that child support.", Anna schooled Vittoria on the ways of the world.

"Oh, God. Why do you have to be so brash and vulgar about everything? Let's move to the real topic at hand … my wardrobe.", insisted Vittoria who despised sex talk and Anna knew that.

Vittoria walked toward her closet so that she could take some things out for Anna's scrutiny. She needed to give Anna something else to talk about, even if it was her out-of-style wardrobe.

"That's not as much fun to talk about, but okay. Pull out a newer pair of slacks. I'll show you how to dress it up with the right blouse and cute shoes.", explained Anna as she moved to the closet and gently pushed Vittoria out her way. "Looks like you only have like three pairs of cute shoes.", Anna confirmed.

"Yeah, Pappa let me get them when he bought some new dresses for me.", Vittoria explained.

"Well, they will have to be put into heavy rotation and your clothes too; at least until Ricky starts taking you shopping.", explained Anna as she salivated over the money Ricky had.

"Shopping! I am not going to let him buy things for me.", Vittoria explained to Anna shocked that she would even suggest such a thing.

"You better! If he offers, do not turn him down!", shouted Anna as if talking to a child.

These inexperienced women get these rich men and don't even know what to do, she thought.

"Girl! Just match my slacks with a blouse.", insisted Vittoria trying to get Anna to redirect her focus.

Anna continued looking in her closet and found some nice blouses.

"You have a few nice blouses, just don't wear them buttoned up to your neck! Show a little cleavage; a little goes a long way with those big titties.", laughed Anna.

"Ha, ha, ha. I hate yours are small. You really must wish yours were bigger.", teased Vittoria as she snatched the blouse from her friend.

"I know how to use the ones I have, though. If I need to push them up using a bustier, then I will, to give me a sexier look.", Anna said in an attempt to educate Vittoria on how to turn a simple look into a sexy one.

"Okay, I'll be a good student. I admit I need a lot of help with looking feminine.", Vittoria conceded and gave up the fight.

Anna shrieked as she danced and shimmied her shoulders and breast for her friend, who couldn't help but laugh at her silly friend.

"I'll teach you that dance later.", laughed Anna.

"No thanks, I think I have that down.", laughed Vittoria.

"I'd like to see that!", Anna said before a robust outburst of laughter.

'I bet you would.", Vittoria said in agreement as the two laughed.

The guys started filtering into the funeral home for game night. It couldn't come fast enough for Ricky; that day had been such a drag for him literally and figuratively. Bernard was the first to arrive as usual and he brought the good Vodka with him to get the party started. He popped into Ricky's office to announce his arrival.

"Hey! Are you ready to get your ass kicked tonight?", asked Bernard as he smiled broadly waiting for Ricky's sarcastic remark.

"Who's going to do it? Not you unless we're playing Euchre.", laughed Ricky as he stood to greet him with a vigorous hug.

Bernard had known him since childhood, so he knew something was out of sorts with his buddy. He hoped it didn't have anything to do with his relationship with Vittoria.

"Is everything okay with you and Vittoria?', asked Bernard as he was hoping that Ricky would finally settle down.

"Oh, things are great with Vit! It's Giovanna; she came here trying to check me, so it was the perfect opportunity to end things. Granted I haven't seen her in weeks and the last time I did, I called out Vittoria's name during sex.", informed Ricky still shocked by the blunder.

"Oh damn.", laughed Bernard at Ricky who was usually much smoother than that. "Vittoria really has you by the balls.", joked Bernard.

Raymond walked in just as the two were discussing Ricky's ladies.

"Shit Ricky, you are a cold motherfucker.", laughed Raymond, "And Giovanna still wants your ass? Damn, I need to know your tricks; you keep the women hooked.", laughed Raymond as he approached his two buddies.

He gave Bernard a hug and then slapped some skin with Ricky. The three men continued their laughter as they made their way to the meeting room. The three were ready for the much-needed reprieve to have fun and blow off some steam. They hoped that Angelo wouldn't be much longer, so they could get the party started. Angelo entered the room behind the men; they had been so caught up in their laughter they didn't hear their friend.

"Hey fellas! Were you about to start without me?", said Angelo carrying a bottle of liquor.

"What's up with you guys bringing your own bottles? You know I'm still rolling in dough.", laughed Ricky as he took the bottle from Angelo. He noticed it was top shelf. "On second thought…", he added as he took it under his arm to the game table.

"It's been a while since we really hung out.", announced Ricky.

He had really missed the guys and more importantly wanted to brag on Vittoria.

"Yeah, we haven't seen much of you since you started dating that Rossi chick. What's her name?", Raymond agreed as he poured a drink of the scotch Angelo brought in.

"Vittoria.", Ricky said as he smiled brilliantly for his pals.

They all noticed how his face lit up with joy and dare they say, love, at the mention of her name. They had never witnessed this before. They were all treading in unfamiliar territory.

"She must be showing you all sorts of devilishly good tricks.", Angelo joined the discussion hoping to hear every freaky detail.

"She's got him by the balls bad. So bad, he called out her name while fucking Giovanna!", Bernard added, too eager to share that the smoothest cat there, had lost his cool.

"Fuck!", laughed Angelo who hadn't heard the story.

"Yeah, man. That's so fucked up.", laughed Raymond, "If I had done that with one of my chicks back in the days, I'd be dead."

The guys laughed uncontrollably at Raymond and his animated hand gestures. Ricky was embarrassed but realized how hilarious it was and gave in to his own laughter.

"So, dude, is Vittoria the hottest lover you've ever had?", asked Angelo who had stopped mid-motion while he was pouring his drink.

The other two waited to hear one of Ricky's detailed recaps of his escapades. They were expecting a toe-curling tail of orgasms and lust, but they were met with silence instead. Ricky didn't want to admit that they hadn't had sex yet; he had never experienced a woman not begging him to bed them. The guys all paused in anticipation and the longer the pause lasted they joined Ricky at the table to see his uncomfortable smile.

"Shit! You two haven't fucked yet!", Angelo blared his surprised summation.

"Cool it.", Ricky warned as he looked around the room to make sure no one else had entered. "Vittoria is a class act and I don't want to pressure her or frighten her.", explained Ricky.

"Frighten her? You talk like she's a virgin or something. She's damn near a middle-aged woman. Shit.", laughed Bernard as he looked at his crew for confirmation.

"Exactly. We told you she was a lesbian. But no, you just had to have a challenge.", scolded Raymond as he shook his head in disappointment.

"No, she's nothing like the rumors. She's very inexperienced and doesn't know her own power as a woman. If she actually knew her power, I would be even more of a fucked up mother-fucker.", Ricky attempted to explain.

"So that coyness that she displayed at the fundraiser wasn't an act?", remarked Bernard.

"Apparently not ... I'm all fucked up. I haven't had sex for almost a month. I have no desire to touch Giovanna; even the thought feels adulterous. I broke up with her today in fact.", confessed Ricky as his friends looked on with sympathy.

"So, Giovanna is available?", questioned Angelo.

"You know you can't pull that.", dismissed Raymond, "So, Vittoria's really a good woman?", Raymond redirected everyone back to the most important topic at hand.

"Yes, the best. I don't even know how a tramp like me was able to pull a dame like that. She's the most beautiful woman I've ever seen with a heart just as beautiful and kind.", Ricky described Vittoria with glistening eyes.

His friends knew that Ricky had found the one and all jokes about her had to cease. Soon their shocked expressions turned into hopeful and supportive ones. So, they encouraged him to talk more about his new love.

"I like that she appreciates the simple things. I'm taking her to the zoo tomorrow and then out to eat. She's not into material things like my old chicks were.", bragged Ricky as he proudly discussed how Vittoria enjoyed their time together. "We talk about everything from business to politics. She has a brilliant mind.", Ricky further gushed.

"Maybe I would be happier if I had found one like that, but I quickly found out that Eleanor wasn't; like the moment I met her.", laughed Raymond. "There was a time I naively thought all Black women would just be satisfied and content to have a successful man.", confided Raymond.

He realized he had never discussed any of that with them before. He looked at his glass as if to figure out if they were drinking Scotch or truth serum.

"Your wife grew up rich and she's so light, she's damn near White. You might as well have married a White one.", chuckled Ricky as he took a swallow of Scotch.

The men nodded in agreement with Ricky as they drank as well, but Raymond shook his head in disagreement.

"You guys would have treated me differently?", Raymond explained one reason behind his choice.

"We are more open-minded than what you give us credit.", concluded Bernard.

Bernard turned his attention to his glass and swirled the liquor over the ice. His eyes were looking to a far-off place and Ricky knew exactly where his best friend had gone. He wanted to reel Bernard back and get the gathering off to a great start. He didn't want any grey clouds overhead tonight.

"Like I said, we haven't hung out as much as back in the days. It would be a great idea if we all went to The Schvitz one weekend.", suggested Ricky as he attentively eyed Bernard to make sure he returned to their world.

"The bathhouse!", belted Raymond then he got choked on his drink.

"Cool.", Angelo provided his support for the notion.

Bernard didn't respond; he eagerly awaited Raymond's objection.

"What's wrong with that idea?", asked a confused Ricky as The Schvitz was a long-time meeting place for business deals of all kinds to take place.

"I'm not trying to let you white boys see my Anaconda. That's nothing but White boy freaky-deaky shit!", he announced shaking his head in complete disagreement. "I haven't taken a bath with another male since I was six years old when I had to share a tub with my brother. I didn't like it then and I am damn sure I won't like it now. No thank you.", Raymond said definitively.

Bernard and the guys were not disappointed by his response, but Ricky wasn't going to let Raymond get the last funny word in if he could help it.

"Raymond, you're missing out on a lot of business deals. Look, I go there, the fuck! Shit, have you not seen what I'm slinging?", laughed Ricky then he took another swig of Scotch as all the men laughed.

"No, and let's keep it that way!", added Raymond not wanting the visual.

"I have black blood on both sides of my family tree.", Ricky added emphasizing his endowment.

"Well, I'm a hundred percent Nigga; so, you ain't got, what I got. Shit!", Raymond blustered as he pretended to adjust his pants.

Ricky knew he had been bested by the best and could only allow his laughter to vibrate with his boys. This was one fun way to get over his sexual frustrations and enjoy an evening. But tomorrow night, he thought, he might rip his dick clear off his body while jerking off.

Vittoria rose early from bed and even cooked breakfast for her parents. She was extremely excited about her day planned with Ricky. As her parents entered the kitchen, they saw her twirling and dancing around as she set the table for them. Antonella had never seen her behave in such a feminine way before; she almost didn't recognize her daughter. Lorenzo nodded at Antonella that now she had proof of what he had been telling her; he told her that Vittoria was now hopeful and energetic about life. Antonella was almost in tears watching her only child; she knew she would soon be on the verge of having grandbabies. She smiled at Lorenzo as she held her hand to her chest in shock, awe and delight. He too anticipated the future for Vittoria.

"Good morning! I have your eggs, toast and coffee ready for you.", announced Vittoria as she gestured for them to sit and be served.

"This is so nice Vittoria. So, tell us where Ricky is taking you.", requested an anxious Antonella

Lorenzo nodded his agreement while sitting in his chair.

"He's taking me to the Detroit Zoo and out for dinner afterward. And I hope we go dancing or *something*. Don't expect me to rush home tonight.", exclaimed Vittoria as she plopped down on her seat.

"Ok darling, I think we can allow some exceptions.", laughed Antonella as she smiled at Vittoria.

My girl is becoming a woman, she thought. Lorenzo cleared his throat; he didn't want Vittoria to forget that she should continue to be herself because that's what had obviously attracted Ricky.

"Don't be pressured into doing anything.", warned Lorenzo now feeling overly protective.

"I won't Pappa. Ricky's a gentleman; he's not like that at all. You don't have anything to worry about.", explained Vittoria as she reached across the table to squeeze his hand.

"You just make sure you remember those boxing moves I taught you if you need them.", ordered Lorenzo as he demonstrated what she should do.

"Stop before you pull your shoulder muscle. With all the dating Vittoria will be doing this year, she won't have time to fill in for you if you do.", ordered Antonella.

"Yes dear.", agreed Lorenzo.

"And Vittoria, just, make sure you have loads of fun today; that's what you do.", instructed Antonella as she buttered her toast.

"Yes Mother.", said Vittoria all too happy to be obedient this one time. "I'm going to leave you to your breakfast so I can

94

start getting ready.", informed Vittoria after taking one last bite of her toast.

"No, take that plate upstairs and finish it. You know your metabolism will run through that little bit of food. I don't want you fainting on your date. The way he is about you, he'd have you at the hospital all day trying to make sure you are really okay.", insisted Antonella, they didn't come that far for her to mess up, she thought.

"Yes mother.", said Vittoria reluctantly as she shuffled her feet on the wooden floors to the stairs with her plate in hand.

"That's our baby girl.", smiled Lorenzo.

"Soon, she really will be a woman. I'm going to start shopping for a mother of the bride dress.", Antonella informed nodding as Lorenzo's eyes questioned her actions. "Just eat.", she silenced him.

Vittoria couldn't believe how much her world had changed; she was now wearing dresses more and more. She even learned from Anna how to apply make-up. She barely recognized herself in the mirror, but she loved what she saw. She felt alive whenever she was with Ricky and she couldn't wait for him to see her in her sundress. It was a perfect late spring day for a cute and sexy sundress. Sexy, she laughed at the thought; there was a time she never imagined being called sexy, let alone, feeling sexy.

She modeled her navy goddess sundress in the mirror; it had a single strap that draped around her neck that required a strapless bra. She couldn't help but show some cleavage that she was sure Ricky would appreciate. The material was so delicate that one might doubt it was cotton; the softness of it clung to her curves. She paired it with some cute high-heel tan leather mules. She didn't know how comfortable she would be wearing them, but as Anna says, no pain, no gain. Vittoria had made her mind up that she would do things differently now and Ricky was the proof that she could.

Anna suggested that she layer three gold-tone necklaces so that the longest one would always draw his attention to her cleavage, but Vittoria had a feeling that all of that wouldn't be necessary yet she wore them anyway.

"Obviously, Anna doesn't know Ricky, because he loves these!", she said as she shook her breasts for the mirror.

She made herself blush at her own behavior; she just couldn't contain her excitement. She kept her hair simple; she wore a high ponytail and some unruly wisps of hair framed her face.

"Enough playing in front of this mirror. Ricky should be here any minute.", she scolded her reflection and grabbed her purse on her way downstairs.

Sure enough, Ricky had arrived with more flowers for Vittoria; she was becoming quite familiar with different types of arrangements. Soon she would be an expert on bouquets, she thought. This time he gave her multi-colored roses and she was curious about their meaning as he loved to discuss the significance of the colors.

"Thank you, Ricky.", offered Vittoria.

She planted a quick kiss on his lips. Ricky uncharacteristically blushed as he eyed her parents' attentive stares.

"The multi-colored roses represent love and friendship. Of all the women I've dated, you are the most special and not only do we have a love affair, but a friendship also.", Ricky confessed his intimate feelings within earshot of the Rossi judge and jury.

He was pleased to notice their smiles of approval and he was able to slip back into his cool demeanor once more.

"Are you ready Vittoria?", asked Ricky anxious to leave the prying eyes of her parents.

"Yes, I got up ready.", laughed Vittoria as she held tightly to his arm.

As they walked outside, she inhaled his fragrance continuously; it was intoxicating and it was causing such strange reactions in her body. Her body awakened with every touch of his hand on her or hers on him. He was the first to ever stir such pleasurable sensations in her body. Ricky did as was customary for him; he opened her door and assisted her inside. His hands always managed to touch her hair, either deliberately or seemingly accidentally; either way it delighted them both.

The drive to the zoo was much like their other dates; they talked about the latest news locally and nationally. They both appreciated the depth of each other's interests and intellect.

"So, I hear, gambling might become legal in Michigan. How will that affect you?", inquired Vittoria assuming that he and other mob families would be affected.

"It's looking more and more like a sure thing, but I have some legitimate business plans with my best friend, Bernard, that will ensure we continue to make money from numbers. And not just here, but nationwide. We are entering the game by selling the machines, supplies and maintenance for them. We now have several contracts with multiple states.", informed Ricky proudly.

Vittoria was glad that he had the foresight to invest in the opportunity before it could be snatched up by someone else. Vittoria was not only attracted to Ricky's unmatched looks but his business savvy and shrewdness as well.

"People, in general, don't trust the government, so they will still play numbers in the streets. They will trust it more than legal numbers. I know a few men, black and white, who are skilled in playing the numbers and have created a very comfortable life for their families.", Ricky educated Vittoria on the mentality of people on the fringe of society.

Vittoria knew well that people made a decent living outside of the normalized ways of employment. Her father's older brother was one such person in addition to some friends of the family.

"Do you have relatives that work for any of the families?", asked Ricky.

He would be surprised if none of the Rossis got their hands dirty.

"Just one … my father's big brother.", Vittoria ended her response abruptly as she turned the conversation elsewhere. "Is that the Zoo?", she asked in childlike awe.

She had never been to the Detroit Zoo and not even the Belle Isle Zoo. Ricky was opening her world up to so many things; even simple pleasures like the zoo. Ricky savored the childish twinkle she displayed as they pulled into the parking lot. His past women would have been insulted if he suggested such a date; they would have preferred an expensive restaurant or a trip. He planned to give Vittoria all of that and more, but her appreciation of the small things softened his heart and demeanor more than any other woman ever had.

Their late morning stroll through the zoo was magical for them both. As he planned, he shared his knowledge of some of his favorite animals; he was her personal tour guide, though be it a sometimes naughty one. When possible, he kissed her wherever he could, sometimes it would be her shoulder, her cheek and if absolutely no one was looking, a passionate kiss on her lips. He tried so very hard not to touch her as he doubted, he would get past home plate, but her sex appeal and his love for her urged him to kiss or touch her whenever or wherever he could.

Vittoria realized that her decision to take things to the next level was right on time; she was ready to explore another aspect of their relationship. The frightened girl that usually dictated her actions was oddly quiet and less afraid. She found herself being bolder and even kissed Ricky often herself or held his hand close to her heart; which he loved since it rested upon her breast. He could feel her nervous heart beating and he wanted to reassure her that with him she would always be safe.

Just then a gorilla captured their attention; he was putting on a mighty show of strength as he pounded his chest to all the on-lookers. Vittoria laughed at the antics of the gorilla who appeared to love the attention. Little did she know that Ricky felt the same; he wanted to pound his chest to announce to the world that Vittoria was his and nobody better cross into his territory unless they wanted death.

Suddenly the pair heard another noise, a noise that announced to the world that someone was hungry. Vittoria began laughing out of embarrassment.

"I'm sorry. My mother warned me to feed my overactive metabolism. I should have eaten my normal portion this morning.", Vittoria said as she laid her head on his shoulder.

"Well, I guess I better get you fed.", laughed Ricky knowing that she had a healthy appetite; then he pulled her close to kiss her on the cheek. "We have reservations at Amore da Roma. Have you been there?", he asked.

"No, but I know it's located at Farmer's Market. I've been to the market with my family to buy fruits, vegetables or flowers, but never to eat at any of the restaurants.", Vittoria replied feeling unsophisticated again, yet excited for the new experience.

There was so much to her city that she hadn't experienced before Ricky and so much of the world she had never seen. She hadn't even ventured outside of the city limits until that day, yet she knew Ricky would show her the world and she couldn't wait.

'You'll enjoy it. It's world-class Italiano dishes fit for my world-class Italiana beauty.", Ricky bragged as he kissed her hand.

The two drove back to the city limits till they arrived at Farmer's Market slightly southeast of Mid-town. Mid-town and downtown had become their favorite hangout spots. If things went smoothly, Ricky planned to take her to his second home uptown in Palmer Woods. He felt that he was reading her vibes well and it was a safe assumption that she would be comfortable going there with him that evening.

After the couple parked the car, they approached the early 19th century two-story brick style building that was built in 1888. The building was constructed using red bricks and had red and white striped fabric awnings at the windows and entrance. Vittoria thought it had the quaint feel of a family restaurant, but as they entered, she saw historic features that added to its charm and the richness of the atmosphere.

Vittoria admired the polished cherry wooden bar area and the copper tile ceiling, but Ricky, like everyone around them, admired her striking beauty. Giovanna and her friend, Jill, were dining there also; they too saw the remarkable beauty enter. They both took note of how proudly Ricky entered with his new love and they were the center of everyone's attention. Giovanna hated that her eyes were fixated on who she assumed had to be Vittoria, but her friend was ready to gossip about the pair.

"Just look at him. He acts like he's carrying jewels and diamonds in his arms and he's showing off his wealth.", whispered Jill in a jealous disgust.

Giovanna compared that entrance to how he would behave whenever they came together. She thought back to how he'd strut in pointing fingers and laughing like a jive turkey and everyone treating him like a celebrity with her being the one excited to be along for the ride. Her eyes followed their movements as the host ushered them to their table. She noticed

Ricky assist his date with her chair and then carefully helped to adjust her hair that flowed from her long ponytail. Then to make her jealousy rise, even more, he kissed his date atop her head. Giovanna spied Jill smiling as she observed his attentiveness, chivalry and romantic gestures. Jill soon became conscious of her broad smile and quickly turned it into a critical frown.

"It's no telling what type of freaky shit she's doing to get him to act like that. What are you going to do to win him back?", instigated Jill as she waited for a response.

"I don't know.", she confessed her uncertainty.

Giovanna had never been at a loss of how to seduce a man, especially Ricky; she had been with him for a decade, so she thought she knew him better than he knew himself. She didn't know what was going through his head to date and woo a reported lesbian. She thought maybe she should try to imitate this woman's look even if she had to buy a wig. She didn't really know what to do. Jill's voice reminded her that she wasn't alone as she was pulled out of her thoughts.

"Well, at least he let you keep the condo. He's still paying the bills, right?", Jill snooped so that she could take the gossip to some of her other friends.

"Yeah, for now, but who knows how long that will last without him getting ... without us ... seeing each other.", Giovanna said feeling the brunt of people's criticism that she was simply a kept woman. "I'm not hungry anymore. Let's go.", Giovanna informed her friend whose gaze was fixed on Ricky.

Giovanna discretely flagged down the waiter to inform him that they needed to leave. She put on her hat, making sure to pull it down low to hide her face from Ricky's view. Jill on the other hand boldly stared at Vittoria with a hateful glare as they exited the restaurant. Vittoria attempted to smile at the hateful woman who obviously must be miserable, but she was not going to allow such misery to take away from the beautiful outing she and Ricky were sharing.

Vittoria was enjoying everything about their date and was disappointed that it was coming to a close. She wanted to suggest dancing or something even though she had never danced with a man before. She knew the moment required boldness so she became the aggressor.

"Ricky, I'm not ready for our time together to end…", she paused.

She was not sure what to say next, but Ricky's smile reassured her that she didn't need to say anything more.

"I feel the same way. I'd like to take you to my home in Palmer Woods so we can have privacy.", Ricky suggested the destination.

"I thought your family had moved out of the city?", Vittoria asked for clarity as she blushed at the need for privacy.

"it's one of the three homes that I own. Back in my wilder days, I used to host parties there. It's not much use to me nowadays, so I'll probably sell it soon.", he explained to Vittoria who couldn't imagine owning multiple homes.

"That sounds good.", she whispered the barely audible words.

That's all Ricky needed to hear; he snapped his fingers for the waiter to stop so that he could request the check. This is what he had been waiting for since the moment he saw Vittoria; the very thought of what would soon happen aroused him.

"Just put it on my tab.", instructed Ricky.

Shit, I don't have time to wait for your ass, he thought. He assisted Vittoria from her seat and she smiled at his eagerness. She had appreciated his patience with her as she was sure he was accustomed to sleeping with his girlfriends right away. She bubbled with excitement; she couldn't believe she really had a boyfriend for the first time at the age of thirty-two. Yet she felt like a twenty-two-year-old who was about to have sex for the very first time.

Despite being enthusiastic about this new experience with Ricky, the car ride seemed so quick. She didn't know if he had been speeding or she had just been lost in thought; either way they arrived at his home in the gated community of Palmer Woods in no time. They pulled up to the sandy-colored California-style mansion with a grand triangled atrium at the entrance. The height of it could easily be almost twenty feet tall. It was newly built in 1965 and was an impressive 5,000 square feet with five bedrooms and four and a half bathrooms; more space than any bachelor needed. Why would he ever want to sell this work of art, thought Vittoria.

Ricky was pleased that she liked the home; he too, was thinking how it would be sad to depart with it, however, he didn't want any memories from the place haunting a new marriage. He didn't know when, but he knew for sure that he would ask Vittoria to be his bride. He smiled at her animated reaction to the home and he was eager to show her the most important room of all.

He quickly parked in the circular driveway and exited the car, seemingly before it could completely get stationary. Vittoria waited as she always did for him to open her door; as they walked to the massive double door entrance, Ricky fumbled his keys.

"Sorry, I haven't been here in months, but don't worry it's clean. A maid comes weekly to dust and keep it spotless for me.", he explained as he unlocked and opened the door.

The view from the entrance's atrium was a clear one to the back of the house to the sunken living room and fireplace. The fireplace surround ran up the entire wall to the ceiling; it was a remarkable display of marble tile. Her eyes quickly scanned the bachelor pad as he guided her to the bedroom; it definitely had a modern and hip youthful vibe.

Ricky had wanted to set the mood for their first time and not just rush her to the bedroom, but his desperate need for her wouldn't allow him to slow down and plan things out. He directed her into the large master suite then he quickly began removing his shirt. He turned to Vittoria with his shirt opened and pulled from his pants to reveal his black curly-haired physique. She gasped at how manly, strong and virile he was; and she too became desperate to touch him. She immediately began running her slender fingers through his chest hair and his cologne came alive with her touch. She was intoxicated by it and Ricky by her as he began kissing her neck and her long-awaited cleavage.

He was drunk with her fragrance and the softness of her breasts beneath his lips. He wanted to devour them as he quickly freed them from her bra; one nipple then the other was worshiped and sucked by Ricky. His tongue was wild and uncontrollable as it sought to taste every inch of her breasts, her neck and her lips. He was about to strip her standing up then decided that he should at least carry her to the bed first. With that thought, he swooped her up and carried her there. All of his nerve endings were burning and he needed to quench that fire.

Vittoria's mind was whirling; there was new pleasure mixed with fear and confusion. She didn't know what to do, yet her body and mouth knew it must moan and her hands gripped his torso because the sensation felt so good. When he laid her on the bed, he removed his hands to toss his shirt and take off his pants; even for that brief time, she didn't want him to let go. She wanted to keep him in her arms so she could feel the protectiveness of his strength. Just like her hands, her eyes didn't want to leave his body; he had removed all of his clothing exposing his lean muscular body and his manhood. Vittoria had never seen a penis as large and thick as his; she gasped at the thought of it entering her.

Ricky didn't think of how she might react to his actions; his only thought was his pleasure and he slipped back into how he would have approached any other girlfriend for sex. He leaned over her kissing her passionately only stopping when he pulled her dress over her head. He unsnapped her bra so quickly; that she wasn't aware it was off. He buried his face into her breasts and she loved it; then he began pulling her panties off, but he struggled so he used unintended force to rip them from her body tearing them.

Vittoria's new passion immediately turned to panic as her body began to be reminded of a different touch, a different scent and a different time. Her eyes bulged in fear and she had a driving need to push this desperate and rough man off her at all cost. Ricky was so caught up in his own need for pleasure that he wasn't aware of what Vittoria's body was feeling or communicating. Suddenly, Vittoria flung Ricky off her and onto the floor.

"No Tommaso!", screamed Vittoria from the top of her lungs striking confusion and fear in Ricky.

The sound was a heart-wrenching shriek that sounded as if it came from the uttermost depths of despair and fear. A sound that frightened both its listener and wailer; Ricky tried to make sense of it all as Vittoria frantically tried to exit the room.

"What?", questioned Ricky as he stood to see what was going on with her.

Vittoria's eyes were wild, scared and angry. She quickly gathered her things; she was dressing and moving at the same time. She was desperate to flee *that* place and *that* man; she didn't see Ricky and barely was conscious of where she was. The only thing she was clear on was that she had to get out of there; she was running for her life. Tears and makeup blurred her vision as she ran frantically from the house; she managed to remember that she wasn't far from the Woodward Avenue bus line, so she desperately fled the gated community and ran to the bus stop hoping *that* man wouldn't follow her.

Ricky dressed as swiftly as he could and ran to the living room expecting to see her there crying perhaps, but there was no sign of her anywhere. He rushed to the door and looked outside, but she was nowhere in sight. He jogged to his car and drove down the driveway to circle through the community, but she had vanished from sight. Later, he thought about the bus line, so he sped up the road the short distance to Woodward Avenue. There was no one at the bus stop nearby; as a result, he decided to turn back home and call her parents. Maybe they would know what had gotten into her, he thought.

"Mr. Rossi, this is Ricky. Something happened with Vittoria ...", Ricky began his explanation not sure what to say.

"What do you mean? Is she okay?", questioned a concerned Lorenzo, "Do I need to come to check on her?"

"I don't know what's wrong. She's not here; she left. She screamed and then bolted from my home. My only guess is that she hopped on a bus. I'm confused and thought you should know. Do you know a Tommaso?", Ricky asked.

He hoped to get some details from Lorenzo, but Lorenzo didn't have time for questions.

"Yes ... I need to go.", Lorenzo's mouth quivered as he uttered the words.

Antonella was breathless as she waited for him to hang up. Lorenzo walked to her just as confused as Ricky. He repeated the information that Ricky had provided, making Antonella just as confused as the two.

"Do you think he did something and he's only telling part of the story?", Antonella begged for an answer.

"He better pray to God that he didn't. Mobster or no mobster, I'll kill him if he hurt my baby girl!", Lorenzo shouted as his anger boiled turning his face red with rage.

Antonella attempted to reassure him, but how could she really know that there was nothing to be concerned about. Vittoria's actions were so strange; she must have feared for her life for her to risk catching a bus alone in the city at night. A woman that looked and dressed the way Vittoria was dressed, could be in real danger on a bus alone at night, she thought. Her mind thought of every hideous man and the acts they could perpetrate on their daughter. It was too much for her to contemplate leaving her hysterical and in tears.

Lorenzo paced around the living room for what seemed to be hours; he had contemplated calling the police, but he knew he would just sound stupid, telling the cops that his thirty-two-year-old daughter hadn't made it home from a date. The oddest thing about everything Ricky said was that Vittoria mentioned Tommaso. Why would she mention Tommaso's name unless she was truly afraid, he thought? He knew that Tommaso was almost as protective of her as he; perhaps it was because Tommaso was crazy enough to kill Ricky if she needed something done to him.

The pair heard whaling outside that seemed to get louder the closer it came to the door. Vittoria had been a wreck the entire way home. She cried non-stop on the bus rides; after getting off the transfer bus, she had to walk a mile home. She was exhausted, dehydrated, embarrassed, heartbroken and angry; she screamed in her head for thinking that she could have a normal life like other women. She blamed herself for her situation and that she should have known she wouldn't be comfortable having sex.

Lorenzo opened the front door and tried to console Vittoria by hugging her, but she didn't want anyone to touch her or even talk to her.

"Leave me alone Pappa! I'm such an idiot. Why did I even think I deserved happiness?", she whaled her heartache in the self-loathing words.

Her parents tried to reach out to her despite her protestations, but she quickly jotted up the stairs out of arms reach. Lorenzo was going to follow behind her when Antonella stopped him.

"Let me try to talk to her, honey.", Antonella suggested knowing the conversation could become quite delicate.

Antonella walked timidly up the stairs afraid of what Vittoria might disclose to her. She was not only frightened for her child but pitied the stunning young woman who believed she didn't deserve happiness. That was news to her; no wonder she never tried to date or do things other young people did at her age, thought Antonella. The loving mother stood at the closed bedroom door not knowing if she should attempt to enter or just speak from the hall.

"Vittoria ... please tell me if Ricky hurt you.", she said outside the door. Antonella's words were choked with tears and almost remained lodged in her throat.

"No ... he would never ... I just can't ... I'm the problem. I'm all fucked up; I'm not a *real* woman! Go away!", she shouted her last words much as she did with Ricky.

There were terrible cries of pain and screams coming from her room; it was heart-wrenching despair and anger. Vittoria threw her possessions against the walls, her dresser-drawer and then stopped as she looked at her reflection in the mirror. Even more, tears welled in her eyes and her body shook as a buried feeling emerged.

"I hate you!", she screamed at her reflection.

She tossed herself on her bed overcome with pity, self-hatred and guilt as her body quivered like a frightened child. Lorenzo heard her screams and panickily rushed upstairs to find his wife collapsed on the floor sobbing with her cross pendant in hand asking for mercy. The pair sat at the door praying as they worried that their daughter was having a nervous breakdown.

Chapter 5

Ricky had tried unsuccessfully to speak to Vittoria for two weeks; he sent flowers daily to both Vittoria's home and to the meat market. He called nightly only to hear Lorenzo say that Vittoria didn't want to speak to him. Ricky had never been as confused about a woman or as drawn to one as he was with Vittoria. He thought about her constantly; he was often too distracted to focus on his businesses and had to lean on Angelo for mob business and Bernard for their legitimate ones.

Most days he would feign being productive by at least going into the office, that day he wouldn't even be pretentious. He had no plan or desire to go; he'd make other plans instead. He dragged himself out of bed to shower and grabbed something to wear. He put very little effort into his selection; everything about him was uncharacteristic as of late. Maybe, sometime with his boys would help, so he decided to call Bernard to invite him to the Schvitz as he had discussed at their last gathering. He had already confirmed Angelo's interest in going.

"Hampton Inc., office of Bernard Barrington. How may I assist you?", greeted Ester.

"Hey Ester, may I speak to Bernard?", asked a demur Ricky speaking slowly and deliberately.

"Mr. Bianchi? Is that you, sir?", asked a concerned Ester who was used to being agitated by the longtime jokester.

"Yes, ma'am.", responded Ricky dryly.

Ester was shocked and didn't know if she should pry so that she could encourage him or just transfer the call. She decided that it was best to confide her concerns to Bernard instead so that he could uplift his friend.

"One moment sir.", said Ester before clicking over to ring Bernard.

"Yes Ester.", answered Bernard thankful for what he hoped would be a distraction.

"Ricky is on the phone for you, sir and there is something wrong. He's not behaving like himself. Please check on him.", pleaded Ester.

She loved to pretend that she didn't like Ricky, but she was just like every other woman; she found him irresistible. So, she was quite concerned.

"Of course, please transfer the call.", instructed Bernard hoping that Ricky wouldn't deliver any bad news about his family. He couldn't take another family loss; it was too soon. "Ricky, how's it shaking?", asked Bernard trying to set the tone for a lighter mood.

"Not good. I've got some issues with Vittoria. She freaked out on me two weeks ago during our date; she left abruptly and won't return my calls. I've never had to chase a woman before... I ...", Ricky disclosed his novel experience and confusion.

"And you think I have experience?", laughed Bernard acting more like Ricky than Ricky.

"I just need to hang with the guys. Can you pull away from the office to hang out at the Schvitz. I figured 3 pm would be a good time. Angelo will meet us there. Of course, Raymond is out.", suggested Ricky.

"That does sound good. You can count me in.", Bernard paused to think of something encouraging to say to his longtime friend, "Don't give up on her; fight to win her back. And if you need to get laid in the meantime, just hit up Giovanna for a quicky so you can get your mind back in the game.", Bernard added the at one time unlikely advice.

He, being a more jaded Bernard, knew there were times when a man, like Ricky, just needed sex. He surely used his second wife solely for that purpose; she was always ready for a good fuck, he thought.

"You're right; I won't give up on Vittoria. I can't. Thanks, Bernard.", Ricky responded to his best friend's advice.

He would take the advice to heart as he viewed Bernard more as a brother than a friend.

"Good. See you this afternoon.", replied Bernard.

After Ricky's conversation with Bernard, he felt energized to take action. He would call Vittoria at the meat market again. He vowed he would call every single hour of the day if that's what it took to win her back. He quickly dialed the meat market before his doubts had a chance to get a foothold.

"Rossi Meat Market.", answered Lorenzo eager for a sale.

"Hello, Mr. Rossi. How are you?", asked Ricky recapturing some of his usual swagger and energy.

"I'm good, son. How are you?", responded Lorenzo who noticed the hint of hope in Ricky's voice.

"I was wondering if Vit is available. May I speak to her?", asked Ricky then he instantly regretted his call.

"One moment.", informed Lorenzo then he called out to Vittoria who was in the back stockroom, "Ricky is on the line."

"I'm busy.", Vittoria yelled rudely.

She didn't want to hear his name or see him; it only reminded her that she had been foolish to think that she could have found happiness with a man.

"Look, Ricky. I'm sorry, but she said no.", informed Lorenzo.

"I had to try ... you know ... I won't give up. She's too special to me.", Ricky announced his plan to be steadfast.

"I completely understand. I went through the very same thing with her mother. Just like Antonella, Vittoria is just afraid. That's how virgins are. Keep calling.", encouraged Lorenzo surprising Ricky.

"Yes, sir. I will.", Ricky voiced his commitment to winning Vittoria back.

Ricky wasn't expecting to have Lorenzo on his side nor for him to share something so personal. This unexpected alliance ignited a spark in Ricky that had been dimmed since his failed date with Vittoria. It was time for him to take care of much-needed business from which his depression had distracted him. He was ready to set up a meeting with a gang that was rising in power; he had put it off for too long now. He quickly called Angelo.

"Tranquil Rest Funeral Home. How may I assist you?", asked Bettie.

"Hey, Bettie. I need to speak to Angelo.", Ricky informed.

"Sure sir. Just a moment.", Bettie reassured Ricky; she was surprised to hear him sound more like his old self.

'What's going on Ricky?", asked Angelo.

He hoped that his boss, best friend and cousin would be back to normal as he was tired of being the go-to guy.

"Set up a meeting with the Southwest Detroit gang. It's time the Bianchi family makes sure our position is known to their leader.", ordered Ricky.

"Sure thing. We're still on for this afternoon, right?", confirmed Angelo.

"Yes, we are. Hey Angelo, I'll be back in the office tomorrow from here on out.", Ricky informed his cousin who was glad to hear that he could step down.

"Welcome back Ricky.", Angelo said as he looked up as if to God mouthing the words thank you.

"Ciao.", Ricky said as he thought of the next action he would set in motion.

He was determined to get Vittoria back, but now … right now he needed some release, he thought. He hadn't paid a visit to Giovanna since he ended things with her, but he still paid all of her bills so he felt he was entitled to a release. He looked at himself in the mirror and was disgusted that he had thrown on pants and a shirt that he had originally allotted for a clothing drive donation. He quickly entered his walk-in closet to select something more presentable. He put on one of his black suits and paired it with a red shirt and black tie. He reached for a red pocket square from his drawer to complete the look. He smiled at his reflection; he now resembled the man he was accustomed to being. It was time for self-doubt and depression to end, he would claim everything that was his- from Vittoria's love, the mob world and Giovanna's body if he wanted it.

Ricky jogged downstairs eager to start his day. He waved at Nicolas, the head butler, as he walked toward the garage. Lately, he had been driving his Lincoln Continental, but he was feeling more like his Corvette. It was a black 1970 Corvette Stingray convertible with red leather seats and interior. He felt like fire; he was excited for the first time in two weeks. Ricky strutted to his car door as flamboyant as a pimp as he imagined his woman, Vittoria, riding with him; he would make sure that beautiful statuesque woman would ride with the wind blowing through her long silky hair.

As he drove to his condominium he thought of Vittoria's long shapely legs, small waist, full hips and full bosom. He remembered how drunk he was from the feel and fragrance of her soft full breasts in his mouth. His penis swelled and throbbed as he pulled up to the valet. He jetted from the car and threw the keys to the valet. He hadn't made any attempt to call Giovanna; he assumed that she would be home that late morning. As he entered the unit, he didn't hear or see her on that level of the living space. Perhaps, she was still in bed, he thought, so he pressed the button to enter the interior elevator. As he walked down the hall, he could hear music playing and her singing in the master suite.

Giovanna was modeling a new look and checking out her reflection; she was wearing a long black wig that flowed down to her buttocks. She noticed Ricky enter her room and she immediately removed it and tossed it on a chair.

"Ricky, why are you here?", she questioned him.

She was hoping he was there to reconcile or even just for sex. She would take what she could for now and work on the rest later. Ricky's eyes drifted to the wig as his penis throbbed from his thoughts of Vittoria. His expression was intense and striking; Giovanna knew his singular desire whenever he looked at her that way. Oh God, yes, she thought, not realizing that his look of longing wasn't directed at her; she would only be a substitute.

"Put it on!", demanded Ricky speaking of the tossed black wig.

Giovanna was just glad she had another chance to experience the pleasure of his body and if she had to imitate Vittoria's look to get him back, so be it. She quickly retrieved the wig and placed it on her head and she noticed the fire that consumed his eyes. Her body quivered in anticipation for the wild torrid sex he was going to deliver. She had barely finished adjusting it when he grabbed her and started ripping her robe off.

Ricky's moans were intoxicating as he squeezed her breasts in his hand tightly bringing her nipple to his mouth. He devoured it all the while thinking of Vittoria and his mind tricking him into seeing her and smelling her. He effortlessly picked her up and she straddled him and he cupped her vagina from behind as he toyed with her clitoris until his fingers entered her. He thrust three fingers hard and deep within her as he carried her to the bed. With each thrust, he sounded animalistic and desperate for release. Giovanna's cries of passion became that of Vittoria calling his name begging for pleasure.

He laid Giovanna on the bed and he began taking off his clothes in a mindless motion. There was no logic or heart behind his actions, just the need to feel release with the vessel beneath him. He bounced on top of her and took in her fragrance as his lips moved down her body until his face rested on her vagina. All the while, his mind thought of Vittoria and fooled him to believe he was smelling her fragrance that he had come to love so much.

Giovanna wanted to devour his huge penis, so she flipped him over and began sucking him. It had been so long since his manhood had felt the softness of a woman. He smiled as he visualized Vittoria's face and full lips surrounding his penis. He could feel her long hair cascading down his legs.

Giovanna was pleased that she still had a powering effect on him and she looked up to see his reaction. Ricky saw his beauty raise her head, then his fantasy and heart became broken when he realized his longing had caused him to be caught up in a fantasy. Guilt instantly swept over his body and he felt ashamed that he would seek out sexual gratification whereas his focus should be solely on winning his true love back. His body became tense and his penis lost its strength becoming limp.

Ricky was shaken that he was about to commit such an adulterous act against the most incredible woman that he had seen or known. He vowed he would never attempt anything so heartless ever again. Giovanna saw the effect on his body of what must have been happening in his mind, yet she was willing to beg him to set those feelings aside for pleasure's sake.

"Baby, just relax. I've got you.", persuaded Giovanna as she stroked his body in an attempt to regain its arousal.

"No. I can't. I shouldn't have come here. I'm sorry that I was going to use you like that. Vittoria is the only woman that arouses me now. I don't want anyone else.", Ricky explained as he attempted to stand.

As he guided her off his limp penis, he had an epiphany that he had lived his entire life seeking pleasures without finding anything of substance until he found Vittoria. He now realized that his aggressive foreplay must have frightened Vittoria away. Hearing Giovanna's pleas brought his attention back to her.

"I don't mind if you call me her name. It's okay, really.", Giovanna begged Ricky to stay as he stood to gather his things.

"That would be sick and you deserve better than that. Vittoria definitely deserves better than a man that would allow you to do that. I can't … I won't do that. I need to put all of this behind me.", he said as he gestured with his hands, "I'll pay your bills for the next three months. After that, I need you to move out and we go our separate ways.", announced Ricky realizing that he needed to remove any and all temptations from his life to create a clean slate with Vittoria.

Ricky adjusted his clothes and began leaving the bedroom despite her urgings for him to stay. She ran after him and pulled on his arm to no avail.

"No, you deserve better than that and I'm releasing you so you can find it.", insisted Ricky as he entered the elevator.

Ricky's eyes were opened to see that he was destined to live his actions on repeat unless he grew up. To do so he had to acknowledge that he had been acting like a child by being so focused on the physical pleasures of a woman's body when mature relationships are based on something far greater. He realized that he and Vittoria have that and because of the strength of their connection, they would get through this storm and be stronger for it. It was time to set aside childish thinking and build his legacy; he would rebuild and claim his relationship with Vittoria and he would remind Detroit that the Bianchi name is still to be feared.

"Do you think Vittoria and Ricky will get back together?", asked Lorenzo as he looked at the virtual flower shop surrounding them in their living room.

"I hope they do, so he can stop sending flowers every day.", Antonella responded as she looked around at the bouquets of roses, "Why don't we have more than this here?"

"I take them to the market every morning.", explained Lorenzo to his puzzled wife.

"For what? Vittoria doesn't want them. I was going to give them to the nursing home nearby.", Antonella continued in her confusion.

"To sell them of course. Those flowers are top-notch and the bouquets are so big that I can make two out of one. I've made a lot of extra money from them.", explained a proud Lorenzo.

"I can't believe you sometimes.", Antonella said as she shook her head and then sipped her tea, "You are profiting from our daughter's grief.", she scolded.

"I'm just being a smart businessman. Isn't that why you married me?", he said then leaned over to kiss her on the cheek to soften her annoyance. "Besides, it'll be over soon. I talked to Ricky the other day and encouraged him not to give up. I explained that's how virgins are. I even shared that you were the same way when I tried to have sex with you the first time.", Lorenzo announced feeling quite pleased by all of his actions.

"I was eighteen; that was completely different. I had never seen a penis before and knew nothing about sex! Our girl is thirty-two years old!", insisted Antonella not sure why Lorenzo couldn't see there was a reason for concern.

"A virgin is a virgin, no matter the age. Trust me, she'll be fine. She'll realize that there's nothing to be afraid of and our girl will get married to Ricky.", reassured Lorenzo being more hopeful than Antonella had expected.

"I pray so.", Antonella said accepting his optimism.

Since she trusted her husband's judgement, she allowed herself to feel that same hope. Vittoria overheard her parents' discussion while she stood atop the stairs in the hall. She had come to realize that she had to conquer her fears and pain so that her past wouldn't continue its hold on her life; otherwise, she would remain that same frightened girl hidden away in a woman's body. It was time for her to face it head-on and break fear's hold; it was time to heal.

Angelo and Bernard arrived at the bathhouse earlier than Ricky. As the two men waded in the waters, Angelo wished that it was open to women as well.

"Too bad this place isn't coed.", Angelo said with a smirk.

Angelo would have enjoyed seeing them bouncing in the water and discussing their shopping excursions and their sexual frustrations, with him on-site ready to pick one in need of release. With that juvenile statement, Bernard could tell from that distant look in Angelo's eyes that his mind was on some freaky Bianchi shit, he thought, those Bianchis are sex maniacs. He on the other hand noticed a lot of new faces and he wasn't at ease with it, especially with the words he had overheard in the locker room.

"Fellas, the life of the party has arrived.", announced Ricky as he entered the water with his pals.

"I don't see Raymond.", joked Angelo creating laughter with his response.

"That would be a funny sight with him hiding his dick like he was afraid for anyone to see it.", laughed Bernard remembering their last laugh about the bathhouse.

Ricky joined Bernard and Angelo in laughter as he nodded in agreement.

"Ricky, you seem to be in a good mood. Are you and Vittoria back together?", inquired Angelo hoping that Giovanna was still on the market for him to try a hand at getting her.

He wasn't as rich as Ricky, but he could afford to provide for her; unlike Ricky, he would even marry her if she would have him. He had been in love with her since he first saw her with Ricky.

"Not yet, but I'm energized to make it so and I'm ready to set up meetings with the bosses.", Ricky began to explain before Bernard cut him with a whisper in his ear.

"Hold off on any boss talk here. Something's about to go down; the FEDs have been snooping around. We shouldn't come here anymore. I would suggest you tell your men that as well. We don't need to get caught up. If the rest go down, then there's more money to be made by you.", warned Bernard, although Angelo couldn't hear his words, his eyes communicated that caution was required.

"Good looking out.", Ricky thanked his friend.

Ricky was always thankful for Bernard's squeaky-clean appearance that put people at ease. *Good ole boys* often said things in front of him that would never be said in front of someone that looked like him.

"That red hair comes in handy; boy I tell you it pays to have a Barrington on your side.", whispered Ricky to his boys and they shared in a boisterous laugh.

"So, you decided to pass on my advice to see Giovanna?", asked Bernard switching the topic; he would be surprised if Ricky passed up a chance to have sex.

"No", informed Ricky with a shameful expression.

Not surprised, thought Bernard, yet Ricky did all of that talk about wanting Vittoria back; but Bianchis will put their dicks first every single time.

"It was a huge mistake!", continued Ricky, "I finally realized that I need to grow up and not be solely focused on the physical aspects of relationships.", explained Ricky to his shocked friends.

"Huh? She must have turned you down.", Angelo responded to the shocking revelation hoping that she had dismissed Ricky's advances.

"No, the opposite. I turned her down and my penis went limp.", confided an astounded Ricky.

"Damn!", said the two friends in unison as they came to the realization that their friend was truly in love.

"So, what's next? How will you win Vittoria back?" asked a hopeful Bernard who had been eager for years to have his friend settle down and make him a godfather.

"I'll make my move next week; although I haven't figured out how. There's a part of me that wants to go to her job, swoop her up and carry her out of that place.", explained Ricky.

"I don't think that's a good move considering how your last date ended.", concluded Bernard not wanting his friend to make matters worse.

"Yeah, you're right. I'd just make a scared virgin more afraid.", agreed Ricky forgetting he hadn't shared that tidbit with them.

"The hell she is! The fuck!", Angelo said defiantly.

"Oh shit! Really?", asked a bewildered Bernard as he didn't think that they existed anymore.

"They still make those?", laughed Angelo, "She's playing you good."

Bernard threw his head back with laughter but stopped abruptly when he realized that Ricky was getting infuriated and he knew Ricky didn't play when it came to Vittoria.

"Sorry. You know Angelo cracks me up.", Bernard said apologetically.

"Look you little shit", Ricky directed at Angelo, "Vittoria is the most incredible woman you'll ever see and you can't bang a woman half as good as she is.", Ricky defended his love.

"Apparently, neither can you.", insinuated Angelo with a huge grin.

This time, Bernard couldn't control his laughter regardless of Ricky's expression. A smirk was the only thing that prevented Ricky from bashing in his cousin's face; he had to admit it was funny.

"Laugh now. I'll give you this moment since I'm not usually the butt of jokes and you *are* most of the time. You'll see I'm getting my girl back and you can go get my leftovers.", Ricky boasted.

"Oh, I wish to God Raymond had joined us!", laughed Bernard uncontrollably as he splashed water on his pals.

Chapter 6

"Ricky!", called an excited Angelo as he entered Ricky's office.

Ricky looked up from a pile of papers on his desk to see what his overly excited cousin wanted. He hoped it was something worthwhile and not anything frivolous.

"I was able to set up the two meetings you wanted. I set up a meeting with Canto Santana for tomorrow afternoon; the bosses and associates are set for Friday morning.", Angelo said proudly hoping to please Ricky.

"Wonderful. It's time for me to take things to the next level. The winds are changing and the Bianchi family needs to level up in order to ride this thing into the future.", Ricky disclosed to Angelo.

Angelo didn't understand where Ricky was coming from. The only thing he knew was that this Canto was a real son-of-a-bitch that was a different breed of dangerous. One thing he knew for certain, it would not only be a meeting of the minds but that of crazy confronting even crazier; he wasn't sure of which Ricky was.

"Make sure I have my most dangerous soldiers by my side for the meeting with Canto; even the youngbloods need to be with me.", instructed Ricky then he dismissed Angelo to arrange things.

Before coming to power at the retirement of his father, Ricky had been *that* soldier for the family in his youth. Ricky had done a number of ruthless and heinous acts in the name of Bianchi, some of which his father was aware and of most he wasn't. There was almost nothing he wouldn't do for power and money; however, there was a difference between him and Canto. Canto chose an Italian first name for a symbolic reason; he viewed himself as the new mob, the new symbol of power in Detroit. They both shared the Catholic faith, but there were limits for which Ricky would ask absolution; limits that he didn't think he shared with Canto.

Ricky realized he needed to be on his sharpest game and use some of his old tricks as he maneuvered his game plan with Canto. This could possibly be the most dangerous meeting he would ever have as a mobster; therefore, safety was of the utmost importance as he wanted to make sure he lived a long happy life with Vittoria.

"Angelo!", called Ricky from his desk.

Angelo turned on a dime and returned to the office.

"Yeah, Ricky. What do you need?", asked Angelo not looking forward to tomorrow's meeting.

"We've done a lot of research on this Canto over the year, but what's the skinny on his greatest weakness?", inquired a bewildered Ricky.

"Oh, that's easy. I thought you knew.", said a surprised Angelo.

"Spill it!", ordered an annoyed Ricky who didn't have time for guessing games.

"His mother. That's his only family.", informed Angelo again glad to be of help.

"Interesting ... a mama's boy. Your number one task is to find out as much as possible about him. I want to know her name, location and what she looks like. Take a photo of her and create a file; I need as much information as possible. Thanks, I'm good.", Ricky dismissed Angelo for a second time.

Ricky was about to delve back into his work when Bettie stepped into his office with a peculiar look on her face.

"Sir. Sorry for the interruption, but you have a call on the line from a young woman. I believe her name is Vickie or something like that.", Bettie said trying to remember the woman's name.

Bettie normally was better at taking messages, but she was very stunned by the call. She hadn't known any other woman to call him other than Giovanna. From what she had heard, they were on the outs, so what was this about, she thought, not liking that she wasn't in the know.

"Do you mean Vittoria?", asked a hopeful Ricky.

"Yes, that was it for sure.", confirmed Bettie as she stood waiting for instruction.

"Transfer the call!", shouted Ricky.

He opened his desk drawer frantically to check his appearance as if they had video conferencing. He needed to feel confident and the best way was to know that he looked the part and his reflection confirmed that he did. Bettie immediately went to her desk to transfer the call wondering what manner of woman this could be that commanded him to look his best even when she couldn't see him.

Ricky didn't know what to say; should he allow her to maintain control of the conversation or should he beg her forgiveness. He was once again in unfamiliar territory with a woman; Vittoria really kept him on his toes. Most men wouldn't want to entertain a conversation with their woman before a big meeting, but Ricky felt no matter the outcome he would be more dangerous. If she took him back, his confidence would be off the charts making him excited for the meeting; if she crushed his heart then he would be furious with the world and want to see it burn.

"Hello, Ricky. How are you?", asked Vittoria hoping to sustain the courage it took to make the call.

"I'm … it's good to hear your voice. How are you?", asked a tongue-tied Ricky.

"Ashamed … I'm sorry for how our last date ended and you deserve to know why it ended the way it did.", Vittoria apologized to the powerful man that consumed her every thought.

"I'm the one who should apologize…" Ricky began to apologize before being cut off by Vittoria who spoke with certainty.

"Nonsense. I love you Ricky and I want to see you this evening. In fact, let's meet at your home in Palmer Woods. I never want us to go this long without seeing each other or talking to each other ever again.", informed Vittoria with a confidence that surprised even her.

"Agreed on all counts. I love you too!", exclaimed Ricky; it was the first time that either had confessed their feelings, in fact, it was the first time he had ever loved a woman. "Do you want me to pick you up?", asked Ricky still in shock that the call was going in that direction.

"No need. I'll catch the bus there, but you can drive me home in the morning. Meet you there at seven o'clock. Bye Ricky.", said Vittoria as she blushed at her forwardness; she reminded herself of Anna at that moment.

"Bye.", Ricky said almost in a whisper; his mind was in shock and his thoughts in a whirlwind. "Drive her home in the morning?", he whispered the words hoping that he didn't imagine them. "Shit, yeah!", Ricky shouted; he was a hopeful man in love who now knew they had a real shot at a happy future together.

He had to remind himself that despite her reassurance, he needed to tread very carefully so as not to frighten her again. She was after all a virgin, he reminded himself. He gathered up the papers on his desk and tossed them in his safe; he had no focus for work at that point. He already knew the talking points he would discuss with Canto; so now he was ready to get energized. Sex was like his spinach and he would definitely get pumped up like Popeye after being with Vittoria that night, smiled Ricky at the thought. A part of him was already getting pumped as he grabbed his things to head out. Before leaving the building, he stopped at Bettie's desk to give her a couple of directives.

"Bettie, call Pattinson and tell him I need a policy drawn up ASAP with Vittoria Rossi as the beneficiary. Tell him I want those papers delivered to my home. He has an hour to get it done.", instructed Ricky to his attentive secretary.

"That's quite a quick turnaround.", informed Bettie.

"If he gives any push back, you tell him to give me the same expediency he would give a Barrington. Also, contact my attorneys; I want all of my legit holdings to go to Vittoria should anything ever happen to me. Understood?", Ricky remarked as he waited for confirmation.

"Yes, of course, sir. Consider it already done.", replied Bettie stunned that this mystery woman had hooked herself deep into the impenetrable heart of Ricardo Bianchi.

Canto was a little uneasy about this proposed meeting with the Don of the most powerful Italian family. He reassured himself that Ricky was just an entitled prick that inherited a business he didn't know how to run and probably depended on others for direction. He puffed on his Cuban cigar in contemplation then flagged his right-hand man over for a discussion.

"What do you know about this Gringo pup?", asked a curious Canto.

"Well, El Jefe …", he said then swallowed trying to figure out the best way to say what he knew. "He used to be a soldier for the old Don, his father. People used to call him the Reaper.", informed Miguel as he intently waited for the realization to kick in.

"Oh …", Canto said contemplatively.

Things just got interesting, Canto thought. He had heard talks of the Reaper around town when he first moved to Michigan from California; the mere mention of the Reaper made grown men shake. He now understood why so many of the families were afraid to align with him on anything. So, what brings the most ruthless of them to him now, he thought.

"El Jefe ... ", voiced a nervous Miguel; he knew that when his boss got quiet, he was concocting evil plans.

"Ricky is an evil son-of-a-bitch; if he truly is the Reaper. I can't wait to meet him.", concluded Canto as he smiled devilishly. "Miguel ... one last thing. What's his weakness?", asked a curious Canto.

"There's nothing he loves more than women and blood. He has aborted babies all across Detroit.", informed an obedient Miguel.

"Find out who his number one girl is ... his heart. I want her killed if this meeting goes sideways, so he'll know not to fuck with me.", informed Canto with a deadly glare.

"Yes, El Jefe. I'm on it.", Miguel responded then quickly left his boss' presence.

Ricky rushed home to shower for a second time for the day and change into something that would impress Vittoria. He didn't want to overdo it though, he thought, perhaps he should keep it casual. He spent an inordinate amount of time trying to decide, his father often teased, he didn't know who took longer to dress, Ricky or his wife. He finally decided to keep it casual by wearing a pair of brown slacks and a cream dress shirt. He passed on wearing a tie, instead, he would keep it open just enough to reveal his chest hair and gold chain. He applied the finishing touch by spraying on his cologne, the one that Vittoria loved.

Vittoria, like Ricky, put a lot of thought into what to wear for the evening. She decided on a simple off-the-shoulder white blouse and some jeans. She topped off her look with two long gold-tone necklaces and a pair of matching hoop earrings. She wore her only pair of sneakers with the ensemble. She looked at her reflection; she wore her hair up in a messy bun. The woman looking back at her was beautiful and confident. She took several deep breaths for strength so that she wouldn't leave that confident woman behind. She knew that her actions that day would set the trajectory for the rest of her life.

As she walked down the stairs, her parents were stunned by how the slightest thing could enhance their daughter's natural beauty. Hope and anticipation rose in their hearts as they hoped that she had a date with Ricky. Vittoria hadn't spoken to them about her outburst, so they really had no idea what her feelings were concerning Ricky. It was still a very sensitive subject that they were not brave enough to address with her.

"Darling, you look absolutely irresistible. Are you going out with Ricky?", asked Lorenzo hesitantly.

Antonella sat on the sofa next to Lorenzo waiting anxiously for their daughter's response. She and her husband prayed that the couple would reunite and more importantly that their daughter's sanity would remain intact. Lorenzo took her hand as he sat beside her allowing the nervous energy to flow back and forth between the two as they waited.

"Yes, we are.", informed Vittoria hoping that they didn't make too much of a fuss.

She wanted to remain focused on the serious conversation that must unfold and not get caught up in the girlish excitement that was just beneath the surface ready to bubble up.

"Oh, thank Mary, mother of God!", Antonella shrieked as she kissed her cross pendant and bounced on the sofa.

Lorenzo tried to appear less excited, but he probably was more excited than Antonella about the news. He stood to hug his one and only child.

"That's wonderful news. What time is he picking you up?", asked Lorenzo.

"I asked him not to. I'm going to catch the bus.", explained Vittoria hoping that they would let it go.

"Catch the bus? That doesn't make sense if you are getting back with him.", Antonella added with a confused expression.

"We are definitely back together. I just need that quiet time alone to prepare myself for what I need to say. Don't worry. He'll bring me home in the morning.", expressed Vittoria matter-of-factly as she quickly moved past them to the door. "See you tomorrow. Bye."

"Oh my.", Antonella said as she blushed.

"Bye.", said Lorenzo to his baby girl for the last time, knowing that when she returned, she would indeed be a woman.

Ricky paced back and forth in his sunken living room as he waited for Vittoria to arrive. He had rushed over immediately after signing the papers from his attorneys and Mr. Pattinson. He kept thinking what if something happened to her on the bus route or she couldn't remember the address. He vowed he would never agree to allow her to do such a thing ever again; he was a nervous and anxious wreck.

The bus ride for Vittoria was that of a spiritual nature; she exorcised her demons during the ride, leaving behind a clear and resolute mind. She didn't think her mind had felt that light and carefree since childhood. Vittoria's feet walked at a sure and determined pace down his street. She had never been so sure of anything in her life. She felt free and empowered at that moment, much like the feminists who were all over television sharing their philosophies and beliefs. She took several deep breaths as she walked up the driveway and eventually rang the doorbell at the massive entrance.

Ricky almost ran to the door, but he had to calm himself. Calm down boy, you've already popped a nut twice, he said to himself, as he walked to the entrance. He took a few deep breaths and then opened the door. The woman that stood before him ripped the breath from his lungs; she was even more beautiful to him than the first day he had seen her.

"Vittoria … hello. You look incredible. Come in.", he said after pausing to allow her beauty to engulf him.

"Thank you, Ricky.", Vittoria responded.

She could tell that Ricky was unsure of what to do; she found it humorous that their roles had swapped and that she needed to calm him.

"Relax Ricky. Let's take a seat on the sofa.", she suggested as she took his hand to guide him through his own home.

A home that was even more stunning than she had remembered; she blushed as she reminisced of him rushing her to the bedroom. This time, she could take in the full beauty of the fireplace with its marble tile that sored to the ceiling. It was magnificent, she thought. Ricky followed behind Vittoria obediently as he hoped she would maintain control as he was at a loss of words to start the much-needed conversation.

She guided him into the sunken living room where they sat on the huge plush sectional in the living room. Vittoria sat close to Ricky allowing their thighs to touch. Ricky wanted to put on an air of confidence, but he was anything but. He crossed his right leg and pulled Vittoria in close as he laid his arm around her shoulders; so that she rested comfortably under his right arm.

She allowed his strength to comfort her and be her strength as well. She knew the conversation was not only necessary but essential to a healthy relationship; one that she so desperately wanted and even needed. She didn't waste any time, as soon as they sat, she placed her hand on his chest. She began to speak as she gazed into his stony grey eyes.

"You are a greatly strange man of duality; you are both powerful and kind …", Vittoria confessed her admiration for her love, but Ricky couldn't let her go on without him bestowing an apology.

"I don't deserve such kind words. I know you say that I don't owe you an apology, but I do. I should not have been so aggressive with you. I've never been with a virgin before, not even when *I* was a virgin. I've always been with experienced lovers.", confided Ricky to the questioning brown eyes of Vittoria, then she began looking at her hands resting on her lap.

"People think that they know my story and they don't. My father and I idolized his big brother. He was so strong, humorous and viciously protective until one day, it was him that I needed to be protected from.", Vittoria began her truth to a confused Ricky.

"I don't understand.", confessed Ricky.

He wondered what this had to do with her reaction to his foreplay that day. He touched her chin to gently turn her face toward his so that he could search her eyes for the truth that she was about to reveal. What he saw, was a deep pain that frightened him and turned his olive skin pale.

"From the age of twelve to seventeen, that monster, Tommaso, who I once idolized molested me.", Vittoria said with a quivering voice as she fought for the strength to continue. "Every time a man touches me it brings me back to those horrific times when he violated me sexually. That's why I've never dated anyone. And I've wanted to get past the pain … and the fear for so long…

When I met you, I thought I was ready to, but it was all too much at that time.", Vittoria said before bursting into violent tears as her body shook to discharge its burden.

She had confided her worst pain, for the first time and to the person, she loved most of all. She allowed her body to free itself from that pain and fear she had held onto since childhood; once released, her body fell limp into Ricky's arms. As the tears flowed, the relief came to the woman-child laying vulnerable in Ricky's arms; the more she felt relief from pain, the anger transferred itself like a demon and rested upon Ricky.

She raised her head from his shoulder to look into those beautiful eyes of his and she saw the love he had for her shining through his tears. He turned ever so slightly and took her face into his powerful hands as he leaned in so that their faces touched as they had for their first kiss and made a vow to her.

"My sweet Vittoria, I love you and I swear to you as long as there is breath in my lungs, no one will ever hurt you again.", promised Ricky then he gently and innocently kissed her on the lips.

It took a mighty show of strength for him to hold back his tears and vengeance. His mind began to plot and devise schemes. Vittoria pulled back to look at her knight and she could see the vengeance in his eyes, but she didn't want him to be consumed with that … not now.

"Show my body how much you love me. Teach it what love-making should *feel* like.", insisted Vittoria as she removed her blouse innocently; not knowing her own seductive prowess.

Ricky stood and swooped her up and carried her to his bedroom. This time he would take care to be gentle and put her pleasure above his own. He kissed her passionately as he carried her to the bed and laid her upon it. His kisses explored her neck and shoulders as he noticed she somehow had slipped her bra off while laying beneath him. He saw the welcoming mound of softness and her tan nipples begging him to embrace them. He looked back at Vittoria's face for reassurance that she was comfortable and that she felt safe before he made his introduction to her beautiful breasts. Before he uttered a word, she smiled, kissed the top of his curly head and then buried his face in her bosom.

Ricky's body shook fiercely as he finally could rest his face and lips upon her bountiful paradise. He breathed heavily as he moved his face across her mounds of softness; she could have sworn that she felt tears as he reveled in her. His quivering body couldn't resist tasting her any longer as he buried a nipple deep within his mouth; each sucking motion pulling her breast in more and more as his tongue swirled around her nipple.

Vittoria gasped at the pleasureful sensations to which he was introducing her; sensations that she hoped wouldn't stop and be even greater yet. She ran her long slender fingers through his curls as he licked, sucked and toyed with each nipple. Soon she felt a throbbing sensation from her womanhood that she had never experienced before, causing her to unknowingly arch her back and spread her legs in want.

Ricky felt like a nervously excited young lover. This time, he noticed her body language; he was fluent in it and knew she was just as ready as he. He swiftly removed his clothes, not caring what condition in which he left them. Vittoria kicked off her sandals as she watched her soon-to-be lover's actions. When it came to Vittoria, he slowly removed her pants and panties together being sure not to frighten her. He saw her small tuff of curly hair hiding her jewel and his throbbing manhood was begging to explore the treasure.

Again, Vittoria was shocked by the size of his manhood, it had width and length; a far cry from the small penis that had violated her. For a second, she wondered if it would cause even more pain than the wee-size dick of her molester, but she reminded herself that it was painful because it was a violent act inflicted upon her; whereas, this was pure love.

Vittoria boldly spread her legs and looked at him over her large breast that rested under her neck. Ricky was nearly out of his mind with desire and love for the most beautiful woman he had ever seen. He gently rested between her thighs and guided his penis inside her as he kissed her lovingly on the lips and neck. She arched her back once again this time gripping his waist tightly. She moaned at the gentle pressure of him entering her long-sealed vagina.

"It's okay, baby. I've got you.", Ricky said as he began to slowly thrust in and out of the long-sought-after treasure.

Words were unutterable for Vittoria as she experienced Ricky's lovemaking for the first time. A time, she and Ricky both wanted since their first encounter. She, like him, wanted to inhale him as she buried her face in his neck as he continued with his love-making. Soon, an incredible explosion burst from her clitoris and her legs shook uncontrollably as she released a cry of pleasure. Ricky's body fed off the pleasurable quivers from hers causing him to shake in response as he released his seed deep within her. Both of them clutched each other as they gasped and inhaled deeply not wanting the sensation to end, but found acceptance as they realized this was just the first of many more nights of passion and pleasure.

Ricky woke from a peaceful and restful night's sleep only to question if the delights he had experienced had been just the figment of his imagination. Surely, he couldn't be the luckiest man alive to have found such a beauty, an incredible woman and the love of his life. He hesitantly turned his head to see if Vittoria was truly there; he sighed a sigh of both disbelief and relief that she was. Could this be what Bernard had with Josephine and what his best friend had wanted him to experience for all these years, he thought.

His eyes began to explore the exquisite creation he had claimed as his own; he noticed that the cover was at her waist, revealing her sculptured frame, an Amazonian goddess. His mind and eyes were always drawn to her voluptuous breasts, but now there was no need for restraint. He willfully and joyously reached for her breast so that his tongue could toy with its nipple once more.

He thought of their future little one, suckling her milk as he imagined the taste of it as he suckled waking Vittoria from her rest. She giggled and smiled as she buried her face in his curly hair.

"Ricky! Again? We did it twice last night. I don't have it in me this morning.", laughed Vittoria at her enthusiastic lover.

"Actually, it was three times. My feelings are a little hurt that you could easily forget that. I must do better the next time, so you have no doubt how many times it's been.", he teased her and her nipple by pulling it with his lips and shaking it as it dangled from his mouth.

They both laughed knowing that Ricky was only teasing; it had only been twice. How on earth could anyone ever forget the number, she thought, it was way too good to ever forget. Vittoria rested her head on his chest as they cuddled. She couldn't believe that she finally had a boyfriend, a man and a lover. Her body began to quiver as she thought the words and remembered their love-making.

"I thought you didn't have another round in you.", laughed Ricky hoping that she was indeed ready for another round.

"No … no … you are too much.", she blushed.

She remembered his manhood; Ricky, you are just so big, she thought as she kissed his chest and twirled his chest hairs with her fingers.

"Well, I do have a meeting to prepare for. So, we'd best shower and get dressed so that I can take you home.", Ricky whispered in her ear as he planted sweet delicate kisses.

Then he hopped from the bed and headed to the adjoining bath. She reveled in his confidence as he comfortably and even proudly walked before her in the nude. She loved his body, his strength and his confidence whereas, she had always been so self-conscious of her nudity and at times had hated to even look at herself before meeting Ricky. But there she was now, going to his outstretched arm boldly, confidently and securely without fear or shame. She skipped to his embrace and kissed him lovingly and passionately before he lifted her to take her to the shower.

The ride to Vittoria's home constituted one laugh after another. He told her about his dearest friends and their personalities. She wished she could allow herself to be as open and make friends; if she hadn't grown up with Anna, they never would have been friends or even have met.

"Raymond sounds hilarious. Too bad he was too afraid to go to the bathhouse.", laughed Vittoria in response to Ricky's retelling of Raymond's feelings. "If he ever saw what you're working with, he would give you all the props.", laughed a blushing Vittoria who shocked herself that she was openly talking about the size of her boyfriend's penis with her *boyfriend*.

"Exactly, Black men don't have the copyright on big dicks.", laughed Ricky wishing he had thought of that line at the card party.

The two continued in laughter as they pulled in front of the house. Ricky parked the car and assisted his girl out. The house door flew open as if her parents were waiting anxiously by it; the two laughed knowing full well that they probably had been. Ricky didn't have time to go inside as he would have liked, so he kissed her openly for any onlookers to see. This time their kiss was less innocent and more exploratory as he moved his hands over her full hips allowing them to rest upon her buttocks.

Lorenzo and Antonella were not surprised by this public display of affection as they were well aware that their daughter came home a woman; more importantly, that things were back on track for the couple. Vittoria said goodbye to her new lover and rushed past her parents with a huge girlish smile then bounced upstairs to her room.

"Good morning, Mr. and Mrs. Rossi.", Ricky greeted the pair then beckoned for Lorenzo to come outside.

"We are glad to see things are good with you two.", announced Lorenzo thankful that their evening had not been a repeat of their disastrous last encounter.

"No one more than me. You can believe that!", smiled Ricky at his soon-to-be father-in-law, "I want to ask for Vittoria's hand in marriage. I want to be sure to have your permission and approval. Nothing would mean more to us both. I know the deep connection and love you have for your daughter.", Ricky queried as he searched Lorenzo's eyes for his answer.

"Nothing would make my baby girl happier, so yes you have my permission.", Lorenzo delivered the news with a firm pat on Ricky's back. "She's a handful, though. Don't say I didn't warn you. Are you ready?", he teased.

"No doubt, I'm ready for that delicious handful.", laughed Ricky forgetting he wasn't talking to one of his boys as he stopped laughing abruptly.

"Trust me I understand.", laughed Lorenzo, "Her mother was built the same way. I had to replace a lot of bed frames in our younger days; they can only take so much pounding.", laughed Lorenzo reminiscing about their friskier days as he hit Ricky on the back once more.

The two men shared robust laughter and shook hands, but Lorenzo decided formality was no longer necessary so he pulled Ricky in for a tight bear hug.

"Sir, please keep this between us. The women don't need to know about this. I don't want Mrs. Rossi to mention anything out of her own excitement.", suggested Ricky.

"I completely understand. Antonella can have loose lips at times.", laughed Lorenzo.

"Well, sir, I have an important meeting ahead of me; so, I'd better get going.", explained Ricky as he patted Lorenzo on the shoulder.

"Handle your business. We'll be seeing you soon, I'm sure.", responded Lorenzo.

"You can bet on it!", shouted an excited Ricky as he walked swiftly to his car.

He realized his excitement had gotten the best of him and he was louder than he had intended to be when he noticed a nosy neighbor peeping behind her curtains. He quickly waved at the nosy neighbor and hopped into his car so that he could have one more meeting with his men before he met with Canto.

Antonella stood impatiently at the door with her hands on her hips trying to strain her ears to hear the two men, but the only thing she could hear was loud laughter. She was surprised they didn't high-five each other like the young black and hip Italian boys did nowadays, she thought.

"What was all of that laughing about? Sit and tell me.", demanded Antonella as she pulled him to the sofa; she hoped that Ricky was going to propose soon.

"You can relax that tone. He was just telling me how devoted he is to Vittoria.", Lorenzo attempted to avoid providing details.

"He *is* going to propose! I just knew it.", exclaimed Antonella as she beamed with joy and bounced on the sofa.

"Woman, quiet. We don't want her to know that!", Lorenzo whispered his warning.

"Ok.", she began to speak in a more subdued tone, "So what else?", she eagerly prompted him for more details.

"And I teased that she's a handful. He agreed because of her …", he cleared his throat, "curves… and I said you were too and that we broke several bedframes over the years.", he added with laughter.

"Lorenzo … that was because of you being over-excited. Don't put that on me.", Antonella chastised.

"Stop being modest. You know there were times you wouldn't let me out of bed.", teased Lorenzo as he kissed her neck and snuggled his face in her bosom.

She blushed as she knew it was true; after her sexual confidence grew over the years, she often initiated sex as a young wife. Lorenzo recognized that look in her eyes that she remembered their youth. He was starting to feel a little frisky himself; maybe he could show her that her old man could still pull off those old moves. He stood quickly and pulled her to her feet kissing her as he did in those early days.

Antonella was surprised by how quickly that old desire rushed back and she could see that same desire was matched by her husband.

"Let's go upstairs if you can be quiet.", she suggested to her lover.

'Me? You mean, if *you* can be quiet.", laughed Lorenzo as he tickled her while they walked swiftly up the stairs.

Vittoria laid on her bed, the happiest she'd ever been in all of her thirty-two years. It was inspiring to hear that her parents were being playful and that love could remain alive after so many years. That's what she hoped she and Ricky would experience together; a solid love affair with laughter, happiness, passion and a little bundle of joy. She immediately blushed at the thought of being pregnant. She was bound to become pregnant soon if each time they were together they had sex multiple times a night. She squeezed her pillow against her breasts as she imagined Ricky's face buried there planting ravenous kisses all over them. A girlish giggle escaped her lips and she rolled back and forth on the bed, like a young woman who had just lost her virginity.

Chapter 7

Ricky strutted inside the funeral home like he truly ran that town; his confidence was off the charts and his stride reflected it. All of his soldiers and men in his path spread like the Red Sea so that their liege could enter without obstruction. He snapped his fingers at Angelo and the third in command, Enzo, to follow him. The two men followed behind as Ricky led them inside his office for a last-minute check; he needed to ensure that everything was in order for the meeting with Canto. Angelo closed the door to begin the discussion.

"Are we good?", asked Ricky as he pulled out his chair to sit with his legs crossed.

"Everything is in order Ricky. We will have a full squad of your best snipers on rooftops in case anything goes south and of course, your strongest guns will be inside with you.", reassured Angelo, he would never forgive himself if he allowed anything to happen to Ricky.

"I want to add to our plan. Dispatch our guy with the bazooka; I need him and snipers in place ASAP. If we don't come out in an hour, I want that building blown the fuck up! I'd rather send us all to hell than allow that piece of shit to live.", explained Ricky without a flinch or quiver.

Angelo didn't like the look in his cousin's eyes, it reminded him too much of his Reaper days. Ricky's eyes were deadly, cold and calculating at that moment; and when he got like that, he was capable of the most gruesome acts.

"You got it boss, but let's pray that won't be necessary. I'm not ready to die yet.", informed Angelo as he nodded to Enzo.

"I need you to stay here to handle things at the office, just in case. Enzo will go with me.", informed Ricky as he shuffled through some documents.

"Thanks, boss.", replied Enzo, thinking that's what I get for wanting to move up in the world.

The two left Ricky alone in thought. He pulled his crucifix pendent from inside his shirt, kissed it and said a short prayer for protection that he had learned from his nonna; he hadn't come that far with Vittoria to become a dead man.

A few hours later, Ricky and his crew drove their motorcade across town to Southwest Detroit, the headquarters of Canto's operations. Ricky felt oddly relaxed; he was at peace knowing that he was willing to do whatever it took to show Canto that he still ran Detroit. Unlike Ricky, Enzo was anything but at ease; Enzo also knew the look that Ricky got when his alter ego came out to play. The Reaper frightened Ricky's whole crew, it was the Reaper that helped to cement the Bianchi claim to power; God help Ricky if he can't tame that beast again.

Canto's headquarters was located in an old industrial part of town. There wasn't much traffic or activity in the area. It was the perfect spot to do evil in the light of day. They pulled up to the unsuspecting building that appeared to be a warehouse of sorts to the average passer-by and parked out front. Ricky and his crew approached the entrance, there was no need to make their presence known as Canto's crew opened the door as they advanced. Two of them exited the building and remained outside as lookouts.

As Ricky entered, he quickly scanned his surroundings to count the number of men visible as well as those lurking inside seemingly out of sight. He noticed that his men were looking a little antsy; he stared at them quickly, his eyes demanding they be on guard, but not jumpy. Unlike some believed, he didn't have a death wish.

Miquel approached Ricky to frisk him to ensure he wouldn't carry a weapon in close proximity to his boss. Ricky knew the drill quite well and allowed the underling to check him for weapons. The only thing he carried was his trusty sling blade tucked inconspicuously in his shoe along the inside curve of his foot.

"Right this way, Mr. Bianchi.", informed Miquel as he pointed to the large table before them.

Ricky's men remained standing on watch as Ricky approached the infamous Canto Santana. Canto sat with his Tequila in hand as he looked him over to gauge what there could possibly be to fear of the pretty boy. He supposed that he would take Miquel's word that Ricky was the Reaper, a vicious killer.

"Please sit.", requested Canto as they both eyed each other's men.

"Thank you. I won't take up much of your time. As we, men of business, know, time is money, so I'll cut to the chase. The families do business a certain way and we respect boundaries ... each other's boundaries ... the one that was given to you. I need you to respect that and keep your business in this part of town as originally agreed. The families haven't said anything about your other business, like your sex trafficking, but our boundaries are critical.", explained Ricky with eyes of steel.

"Oh, I see ...", Canto replied then sipped some of his drink; seemingly unphased by the request. He looked up ever so slightly from his drink, "I think the boundaries may need to be changed based on the movement. I move a lot of product; maybe more than you do.", explained Canto with arrogance only matched by Ricky.

"That may be true; though be it diluted and polluted.", Ricky paused as his eyes searched Canto's eyes for intention. "Well Mr. Santana, I guess we have to do what's best for our families. Si?", commented Ricky.

"Si, indeed.", replied Canto in agreement.

"Good day.", Ricky said as he stood to join his men to exit.

Canto's face began to boil as the men exited. He looked to his top men to signal that he needed to meet with them immediately. Canto stood to relieve his anger as his rage grew; he slammed his crystal glass by throwing it across the room to the wall.

"How dare that arrogant fuck come to *my world, my territory* and tell *me* what to do! I need you to find his bitch and handle it! Let's see if he'll know better than to come here talking shit the next time.", Canto shouted becoming red with fury.

"But El Jefe …", Miquel wanted to warn his boss.

"Are you questioning me?", Canto whispered as he neared his trusted man.

"No, no El Jefe. I'll get right on it.", insisted a nervous Miquel not wanting his boss' fury upon him.

As the driver drove Ricky across town to his main center of operations, he used the car phone to call Angelo to reassure him that all was well and there were no casualties at the meeting.

"We are heading back now.", informed Ricky as he looked out his car window at the ever-changing landscape.

"Good to hear. I'm not ready to lose my cousin so soon.", laughed a relieved Angelo.

Angelo was only a boy during the last time the families were at war and prayed that they were not on the verge of one now, but he also knew something had to give. Someone had to stand up for decency and the old ways; there was a lack of dignity in this new game. People didn't hesitate to pollute the drugs with other substances that damaged bodies and increased addiction. The Bianchi family wanted to maintain the dignity of old in the business.

"I don't think my message was received well; so, just beef up security around the building and my home. I just don't know how to read that motherfucker.", instructed Ricky, "Now we need to get ready to meet with the old fucks tomorrow.", explained a weary Ricky.

He knew that they would not be pleased that he made an executive decision to meet with Canto. They were more focused on the concerns of their legitimate business partners than on what would directly affect their primary business. The other families were for a lack of a better word afraid of Canto as far as Ricky could tell, but he had accomplished too much to allow anyone to intimidate him. Angelo's question drew him out of his private thoughts.

"Anything else Ricky?", asked Angelo.

"One last thing. I need you to round up Tommaso Rossi; he's a low-level numbers guy and take him to the warehouse. It's been a while since we took anybody there for a little fun. Let me know when you have him.", instructed Ricky.

"Sure thing, but I've never heard of this chump before. Ricky, what did he do? Is he related to Vittoria?", inquired Angelo.

He feared that Ricky was on the verge of unleashing his alter ego, but he had no idea why. He just hoped to God that he was not going to relive that period in his life; especially now that he had Vittoria.

"I don't have the energy to discuss that now. In fact, I'll just plan to see you in the morning at the meeting. Arrivederci.", Ricky informed Angelo then swiftly disconnected the call. "Take me home instead and pick me up in the morning.", instructed Ricky.

He needed to rest his mind; there was a lot starting to pile up on his plate from Canto, the old fucks, Vittoria and the bastard Tommaso, he thought. He would be busy; however, he was good at compartmentalizing things and his skills would soon be put to the test. Despite the weight of his forming burdens, he was still happy and content. It was the first time in his life that he felt good about the future; he had an incredible woman he wanted to marry and he knew that his parents would also be thrilled that their only son was ready to settle down.

Just like so many elders of his day, his maternal grandmother, Elisa, wanted to pass down her engagement ring to him. She adored Ricky until her death; he was the culmination of her dreams and goals. Dreams that she had dreamt decades ago; she was thankful to have escaped the projects in the arms of her Italian knight. Unknown to most, that knight rescued a beautiful bi-racial girl named Eliza from a cruel world and created a background story and new name, Elisa, that none would question allowing her to pass as Italian. Ricky remembered her beautiful jet-black hair that flowed to her waist; he played in it every time he saw her. In so many ways, the women he liked best reminded him of her, but none more than Vittoria. He would get lost in his grandmother's deep brown eyes as he did with Vittoria. Only his grandmother could quiet the demons in his head that made him do cruel things to other children. It was her words that he would remember that kept his rage in check even to that day.

That evening as Ricky lay in bed, he remembered the words of his grandmother, her fragrance and then he allowed his mind to drift to Vittoria. The two women he adored most of all comforted his mind that night by steadying his thoughts. Despite the turmoil brewing around him, his sleep that night was the most peaceful and revitalizing he had experienced in years.

The driver picked up Ricky for the morning meeting as instructed the evening before. Ricky exited his home like the King of the streets he was, confident, suave and handsome. He was dressed to impress as always. He decided to wear his three-piece navy-blue power suit, a paisley print tie with shades of blue; but to show his coolness the pant legs were bell-bottomed. He couldn't wear bell-bottomed pants without a pair of black leather platform heeled shoes. He already towered over most at six-foot-four, so a two-inch platform reminded everyone how far above them, the king truly was.

The driver pulled in front of the funeral home entrance and then he opened the door for Ricky. Ricky could see from the number of cars parked nearby that many of the men were inside waiting for the meeting to begin. Upon exiting the car, Ricky adjusted his suit jacket and sleeves to make sure his grand entrance was done in style. His signature Detroit walk glided him inside the building where he found his buddies waiting in the foyer.

"Hey, hey, hey, my boys are here!", exclaimed an energized Ricky as he tried to give Raymond five down low, but Raymond just looked at Ricky's hands. "Oh, so you just gonna leave me hanging.", questioned Ricky as he looked to Bernard to see if he knew what was up with their friend.

"It's too damn early in the morning for all that laughing and shit. I need a cup of coffee.", Raymond fussed at his friend while Bernard and Ricky laughed loudly.

"Come on let's get you a cup.", laughed Ricky as the two followed behind with Bernard's continued laughter and Raymond looking annoyed.

Ricky and his pals entered one of the viewing rooms tucked in the back of the building. At the front of the room, there always was an empty coffin on display with fake flowers in case some unwanted guest wandered to the entrance of the room. There was a table set up with coffee and a continental breakfast. Raymond left his friends to their laughter with a sigh when he noticed the coffee.

"Finally!", expressed one of the business leaders when he noticed Ricky enter the room.

"Sorry gentleman for my delay, but you don't look this good by rushing.", announced Ricky.

He took a seat in the front row alongside Bernard and Angelo. One of the legitimate business owners stood to get everyone's attention and began speaking as soon as Raymond sat next to Bernard with coffee in hand.

"We need you to do something about these unions!", demanded a frustrated business CEO to the mob families present.

Ricky's expression instantly changed from light-hearted to serious as he listened to the men voice their agreement with the statement. Another decided to stand to speak on the matter in more detail.

"The unions are getting out of control. They are demanding that we offer higher wages. It's bad enough we have affirmative action and now they are forcing us to hire even more Blacks!", shouted an infuriated businessman. Raymond cleared his throat to remind the men of his presence. "Raymond, you are one of us.", he attempted to reassure Raymond.

Raymond glared at his former business partner and others who were in agreement.

"Yeah, right motherfucker.", whispered Raymond.

He threw an annoyed look to his crew. Bernard patted Raymond on the shoulder to reassure him that he would stand to his defense. He stood to redirect the men to where their true focus should be.

"I am not on board with racial discrimination of any kind, but what I do want to stop are these unreasonable wage increases. I'm concerned with my bottom line. It's critical that we do something about the Hoffas and other common folks getting new money.", Bernard stated with intensity as he looked around for support.

Coughs could be heard throughout the meeting room as the "new money" became very uncomfortable with the idea of anyone wanting to take theirs away. Ricky decided he would come to his friend's aid and hopefully do a better job than Bernard did for Raymond. As Ricky approached Bernard, he shooed Bernard back to his seat.

"What I think my generationally wealthy friend was trying to say, 'Is we need to take down the union point-blank.' Can we all agree on that?", asked Ricky hoping to restore the meeting to something productive.

Yes, and here, here could be heard clearly as a collective agreement. Ricky continued to speak as he rode on their supportive wave of this singular goal.

"What we have to do is find the right time to take down their top rank and file man. Until then, we need to convince the motherfuckers that they don't need the union, but let's face it the dumb fucks really need a union. Let's be clear on that.", laughed Ricky glad to see that the men were joining in as well. "So, until then, let's try to turn back time and get some of the employment laws overturned."

Bernard, Raymond and Ricky had already been doing that as legitimate business owners as they were directly affected by a demand to provide higher wages. Despite their support of the civil rights movement, they were rich first and wanted to protect their bottom line first and foremost.

As the meeting came to a close, the mob families signaled to Ricky that they wanted to speak privately; so, the men walked to his office to conduct that conversation. Angelo spotted the signal and followed behind; he knew exactly what the old squad probably wanted to address. After the men entered Ricky's office, Angelo closed the door and stood waiting to hear the drama that would be on display.

"Are you out of your fucking mind meeting with Canto?", shouted Alessandro a senior leader that ruled the day with Ricky's father Carlo.

"Tone.", warned Ricky in his deep baritone as he moved toward his desk chair.

Alessandro gave an embarrassed look to his peers after being chastised. He hated that he had to heed the warning of the young pup, but he was no dummy; so, he obliged.

"We don't need a war in this town. What's coming out of Mexico is a different breed of the mob; it's a gang.", Alessandro spoke less animatedly.

Ricky looked at Alessandro and the others as he spoke calmly.

"I have everything under control. Have you forgotten that it was my father that created our ties to South America and to the Columbian cartel and the Columbian government? It's because of *my* family that your palms stay greased.", informed Ricky as he crossed his legs and leaned comfortably back in his chair.

The old squad hated that the game had changed and even more they hated that they didn't know the best moves to win.

'I don't understand the new ways of your generation, Ricky, but you better know what the fuck you're doing.", Alessandro said pointing at Ricky.

The others knew best to remain silent and be observers of the interaction instead. Ricky smiled in response to Alessandro, yet his eyes didn't match the smile, they were deadly.

"Good day gentlemen.", Ricky dismissed the men from his office.

Anna had decided to swing by to check on her friend and to see the latest display of Ricky's pathetic attempts at getting

Vittoria back. Only to find that the family market no longer looked like a floral shop. She still didn't understand how a worldly man like Ricky was obsessed with Vittoria. Yes, she was beautiful, thought Anna, but she was so boring. As she entered, she assumed that Ricky must have finally gotten bored with Vittoria as she only noticed one stunning bouquet on the back counter sitting on Vittoria's workstation.

Vittoria saw her friend enter the shop and wondered why she visited. It was not like her to venture by unless she was in the area and wanted to brag about something one of her lovers had done. Vittoria waved and greeted her old friend. Lorenzo noticed her entrance as well and wondered the same.

"Hey, girlie. What brings you to the store?", asked a bouncy Vittoria as she neared Anna.

From her approach, Anna knew that things were different with Vittoria; so, her interest was *all the way* peaked to find out why.

"Hey, Mr. Rossi.", Anna waved and yelled across the store at Vittoria's father; he responded hesitantly with a wave and a watchful eye. "Back at you, lady. I was in the area. I had lunch with one of my old boyfriends and his new chick. He wanted me to meet her first before we all hook up tomorrow. So, what's up with this bouncy happy Vittoria in a cute outfit?", asked Anna as she touched Vittoria's arm then looked her up and down as Vittoria turned to model for her.

Vittoria was feeling more and more confident the longer she was with Ricky and now that she had freed herself from the burden of her secret, she felt even more alive. She had thrown out her old tattered tee-shirts, that she often wore to work, weeks ago. She wanted to feel more feminine; so, she had decided that she would wear a trendy pullover; it was a hippy boho tube smock top with stitching on the bodice. Her full bosom made the cute top sexy as she wore it off her shoulders and paired it with jeans. It was a far cry from the look Vittoria usually sported; the only thing that remained the same was her upsweep messy bun and even that now looked sexy on her.

"Ricky looks good on you, lady. What else has he bought you?", Anna questioned as she playfully nudged Vittoria's shoulder.

"He didn't buy this. I went shopping and picked up a few things a bit ago.", Vittoria informed, puzzled that her friend would assume that he had bought the items. "He's not trying to make me over.", Vittoria said slightly on the defense.

"I'm not implying that. Relax girl. I'm just saying a rich guy like that should be springing for everything!", insisted Anna.

Lorenzo had been straining to hear the conversation and he didn't like what Anna was saying. He didn't want any of her advice messing things up for Ricky and Vittoria. He was about to walk over to interrupt when the customer asked about pork.

"Look we just got back together and I'm not money hungry like that. I'm not with him for what he can buy me, but because of how he makes me feel and because he respects me.", Vittoria educated her friend.

"Whatever.", Anna dismissed her friend's sentiments, "I just know you better get that money. Alright!", Anna giggled as she provided her unsolicited advice.

"I know that's how you do things, but Ricky and I have something real, something special. And trust me, there's nothing, *that* man won't do for me.", Vittoria blushed at her bold statement.

"Okay now. You must have given him that punani. Okay, girl! That's what I'm talking about!", laughed Anna at her blushing friend.

Vittoria looked around to make sure no one heard and she was glad to see that the one customer and her pappa seemed to be more focused on the cuts of pork than their conversation.

"Quiet, girlie. I don't need people knowing my business.", Vittoria scolded her buddy.

"I knew it. I knew something was different.", said Anna then she leaned closer to whisper in her friend's ear, "Was it good? Is he big?"

Vittoria placed her finger between her teeth and smiled as she swayed her shoulders gently and nodded yes twice. Then the two young women squealed loudly with laughter catching the attention of the customer and Lorenzo at the meat counter. Lorenzo scowled disapprovingly at the ladies as he attempted to bring the customer's focus back to the beautifully cut tenderloin.

"So, what do you have plans for this weekend?", asked Anna eager to talk about her menage-a-trois planned.

"Nothing yet, Ricky had two really important meetings this week; so, he might be exhausted afterward.", explained Vittoria.

"If you say so. My guys are never too tired for me.", Anna said boastfully.

"Well, your guys just work as waiters or line-workers. Ricky has multi-million dollar deals he has to negotiate.", Vittoria said deliberately taking a jap at Anna.

Vittoria was not about to let Anna get in her head and make her believe that Ricky wasn't really into her. Ricky was a man of wealth and power, not the losers Anna was accustomed to and Vittoria wanted to gently remind her of such. Before Anna could get over the shock of hearing Vittoria's comments, the phone rang.

"Excuse me. I'd better get that since Pappa is ringing up the customer.", informed Vittoria.

She held up her index finger and then walked briskly to her desk area to answer the phone.

"Hello, Rossi Meat Market. How may I help you?", Vittoria spoke professionally.

"Hello, I'm calling to speak to the sexiest woman in the world. Is she there today? Maybe you know her? Her hair is long and rests on that sexy ass of hers.", teased Ricky as he waited for her response.

"Ricky!", laughed Vittoria, "What if I were my mother, you know we sound alike over the phone?", asked Vittoria as she blushed thinking of her mother's reaction.

"She might say, you're speaking to her.", laughed Ricky at the thought of Antonella letting her hair down that he assumed was probably as long as Vittoria's.

"Oh my God.", giggled Vittoria. "You would have a war on your hands for sure if my pappa heard that go down. You might be tall and strong, but I don't think you can go toe-to-toe with an angry possessive Lorenzo Rossi.", whispered Vittoria before laughing freely.

"I think you know what you're talking about. If he loves your mother half as much as I love you, I would be a dead man.", laughed Ricky.

At the name of Ricky, Anna had begun to approach the counter. She didn't want to miss any details. After Lorenzo finished with his customer, he realized that Ricky, his future son-in-law, was on the line with Vittoria, he immediately fanned Anna away as she nosily approached the counter.

"So, sir. I ask again. How may I help you?", teased Vittoria as she twirled the phone cord around her fingers.

"I would love to bring you home, to my primary home, to meet my parents.", Ricky said in his serious tone.

"Really Ricky?", Vittoria whispered her question.

She knew things were serious, but she had never met anyone's parents. Hell, she had never had a boyfriend, she reminded herself.

"Yes, I would be honored if you would join us tomorrow evening for dinner.", Ricky made the invite sound as sweet as a proposal.

"Yes of course. I would love to meet your parents.", she said with each word having a higher inflection than the one before.

Anna and Lorenzo's gazes were stunned; however, for different reasons. Lorenzo was just surprised that Ricky was potentially living up to his word sooner than expected. Anna on the other hand had a tinge of jealousy that longed for this to rack up to be another disappointment for her friend. What joy would she have if the tide turned and Vittoria became the one living an exciting life and she lived vicariously through Vittoria's tales?

"What time will you pick me up?", asked Vittoria as her mind tried to calculate if she would have enough time to buy another outfit if need be.

"Well about that. I can pick you up at five o'clock. But I really need to get you some wheels. Please allow me to buy you a new car.", Ricky offered.

"You want to buy a *new car for me*?", Vittoria purposely said loud enough for Anna's nosy ears.

She saw the envy glisten in Anna's eyes and pride in that of her pappa.

"Yes, please let me do that for you?", pleaded Ricky.

"I can't accept a big-ticket item like that, Ricky.", insisted Vittoria hoping that she didn't offend him.

"Ok, the next option is, picking out one from my garage. I don't want you getting on a bus to go somewhere ever again. So please, baby, pick one from there. It can be the Lincoln, Corvette, Mustang or even my brand-new Mercury Cougar. It's black and has a sports package. You'll look hot in that.", Ricky insisted not wanting to accept no for an answer.

Lorenzo and Anna were looking at her as if to say are you crazy. Lorenzo tossed his towel at her back and stood with his hands on his hips demanding she did the *right* thing. Vittoria picked up the towel from the floor and tossed it back at her father playfully.

"Ok, Ricky. I'll accept the Cougar.", Vittoria said reluctantly, but to the delight of her father.

"Cool! I'll have the staff give it a fresh wash, coat of wax and detailing for you, so you can drive it home after our date. Ok, baby; I need to get off the phone. I'll see you tomorrow. I need to call the cook to make sure they know when to expect you and to prepare something special. Arrivederci.", Ricky said joyously that she had accepted his gift. He didn't want her to do without anything.

"A Cougar? Tell me about it. Is it new? Is it fully loaded?", Lorenzo approached with a million and one questions.

"Pappa.", sighed Vittoria as she went on to answer a couple of questions, "It's a brand new 1970 black Cougar with the sports package. Look I don't have time to entertain either of you. Ricky wants me to meet his folks tomorrow and I need to plan my outfit.", insisted Vittoria as she pushed passed her father.

"Listen to you, planning outfits. You're a long cry away from the girl who wanted to wear new T-shirts when she got dressed up.", Anna added sarcastically envious that Vittoria had the rich catch.

Vittoria ignore the jealousy that was apparent in her old friend's tone and even the excitement that was written all over her father's face.

"Pappa, can you manage without me?", asked Vittoria barely slowing down for a response as she grabbed her purse.

"Sure, I'll manage. Do you want the car?", reassured Lorenzo saying the words to Vittoria's back.

"No, I'll walk a while then get on the bus. Bye!", shouted Vittoria as she neared the exit.

"Yeah girl, get your exercise in now before you're driving *your* man's car around town!", shouted Anna as Vittoria left the store. "I guess I'll leave too.", she announced as she headed to the exit as well.

Lorenzo just stared at the jealous friend, maybe she would have found a good man too if she wasn't passing out her pussy around town like free candy on Halloween, laughed Lorenzo inwardly as he shook his head in disapproval.

Ricky called home to inform his parents of his exciting news; he couldn't wait until he arrived home later that evening. It was a momentous occasion as he had never brought a girl or lady friend home in all those years.

"Bianchi residence.", announced Nicolas.

"Hey Nick, what's shaking?", asked Ricky who loved teasing him.

It made Nicolas so uncomfortable as he didn't know how he should respond; should he joke as well or keep it strictly professional, but he found that difficult with Ricky. Ricky always managed to make him laugh.

"Nothing sir. What can I do for you young sir?", asked Nicolas.

He smiled thinking about Ricky's younger days sneaking into the house in the middle of the night and him covering for the lad.

"I am bringing my girlfriend home to meet the family tomorrow for dinner.", announced Ricky with excitement bringing energy to each word.

"Oh, really sir. I don't mean to be nosy, but may I ask which one, sir?", asked a surprised Nicolas.

He knew Ricky had several throughout the city at one point and had a kept girl in a downtown condominium.

"Yes, you *do*, but it's fine after all the trouble you kept me out of as a kid. It's my one and only new girl, Vittoria.", Ricky proudly informed his secret keeper.

"Wonderful, sir.", said Nicolas, it's about time he thought and then added, "I assume you will want us to prepare a special feast."

"I'll leave that planning to my mother. Is she available?", inquired Ricky eager to speak to her.

"Yes, of course, sir. One moment.", informed Nicolas.

He too was anxious to hear her reaction to this unexpected and wonderful news. He like Ricky's parents wondered if the Bianchi line would only continue with Carlo's nephews. But at the age of forty, Ricky could possibly be on the verge of proposing to a young bride. Nicolas placed the call on hold and walked from the hall to the study where Bianca sat with Carlo drinking tea.

"Madam, Ricky is on the line for you.", smiled Nicolas to a curious Bianca and Carlo.

Carlo looked concerned as Bianca picked up the receiver; he knew that Ricky had a major meeting with the families and business tycoons. He assumed everything went well since no one called telling him that he needed to keep Ricky in line. For the last few months, Ricky had been keeping him out of the loop more and more as he stood firmly as his own man; the families realized it as well and stopped calling him as they used to in the past. He attempted to reassure himself that it couldn't be anything bad since Nicolas was grinning from ear to ear.

"Thank you, Nicolas. Let's see what my boy wants.", Bianca said as she sat her cup of tea on the end table next to the phone. Ricky rarely, if ever, called home specifically to talk to her, she thought as she picked up the receiver. "Hello, my heart. Is everything okay?", asked Bianca as Nicolas and Carlo listened intently.

"Yes, it is, better than it's ever been in fact. I could have waited until I arrived home to tell you, but I was just too excited to.", Ricky paused his announcement for effect.

"Go on! Don't tease me like that. What's the news?", Bianca playfully scolded.

"I am bringing the most incredible woman to meet you and father. I am inviting my girlfriend, Vittoria Rossi, over for dinner tomorrow.", informed Ricky.

"That's wonderful news darling!", exclaimed Bianca as she looked at Carlo not able to contain her bubbling excitement.

"What's going on?", insisted Carlo.

"Wait, Carlo.", she said raising her hand to silence him not wanting to miss any details, "I'll make sure the cook prepares something special, my darling.", Bianca suggested.

"One more thing, mother. I need you to take your mother's engagement ring out of your safe.", instructed Ricky imagining his mother's beautiful face when his request registered.

"Ricky! Oh, my goodness! Yes, I'll get the ring for you. Your nonna would be so happy for you! I have so much work to do to prepare for tomorrow. I must go! Arrivederci!", shouted Bianca.

Bianca jumped and sat on Carlo's lap to hug and kiss him.

"Woman, what is going on?", insisted Carlo as Bianca planted excited kisses on him.

"Our Ricky is in love! He's going to propose and he's inviting her over for dinner to meet us tomorrow evening.", Bianca said as the realization of her long-awaited dream was coming true.

She burst into tears as she collapsed in Carlo's arms. He cradled and rocked his love as he kissed her forehead. It had been a long wait indeed, he thought.

"My love, what is her name?", asked Carlo hoping to stop her tears by engaging her in conversation.

He pulled out his handkerchief and dabbed her eyes.

"Thank you, sweetie. Her name is Vittoria Rossi.", informed Bianca.

"Oh, that's the councilman's niece. But love, I thought she was a lesbian.", Carlo stated as he pondered his son's choice of a love interest.

"That is pure silliness. You know our Ricky knows his way around a woman and wouldn't fall in love with a lesbian. This isn't some sort of bet or game; this is real life we're talking about. He wouldn't play games with us concerning marriage.", insisted Bianca who had become annoyed by her husband that he would even think to mention rumors and lies. "Enough talk, I have planning to do. I'm going to take out the engagement ring and shine it up some. You go talk to the head chef and tell him to prepare Ricky's favorite meal. Go!", ordered Bianca who was not going to tolerate any negativity about her Ricky and the love of his life.

As far as she was concerned, it was practically time to start planning the wedding and a nursery. She didn't have time to give life to rumors and neither should Carlo, she thought. It was the first time in years that the household had something to celebrate; the last was Aurora's wedding, but unfortunately, their daughter was baron so they did not have the joy of little feet running down the halls. Her Ricky, on the other hand, was quite virile from what the rumors suggested. That was the end of that torrid history, her boy was ready to settle down and give life to a precious Bianchi.

Chapter 8

Ricky was beyond excited about his parents meeting Vittoria. He spent the morning checking and even double-checking behind his mother that the staff had everything in order for the dinner. He wanted the best of everything used for the evening; the best China, table settings and decorations. As his parents walked to the study, they noticed him being fussier than his mother ever was over the place settings. They were very intrigued about the young woman they were about to meet; they knew she had to be something special indeed.

"My darling.", said Bianca as she gently pulled her son away from the table, "Relax. Come and sit with us in the study. Tell us something about your love.", persuaded Bianca seeing that her son was extremely on edge.

Ricky was just as eager to gush over Vittoria as he had been double-checking the table décor; so, he immediately stopped his fussiness with the napkins and followed his parents to the study. Neither parent had ever imagined their son would ever be so excited over one of his girlfriends; they assumed that even his future bride would just be another conquest. They were astonished that Ricky had found love; they just hoped that this young woman felt the same and wasn't just after money and prestige.

Bianca immediately started pouring coffee for her two favorite men as they sat comfortably in their favorite seats. Carlo sat with his legs crossed and ready to dive headfirst to the heart of the matter.

"Son, tell us about this girl, Vittoria. Despite being good friends of her uncle, the councilman, I only know about the rumors surrounding her.", Carlo requested.

Carlo immediately regretted bringing up the rumors and he also felt his wife's eyes boring into him like a dagger. Bianca walked toward him briskly with his cup of coffee almost spilling it in her haste.

"Carlo!", Bianca scolded him for even mentioning that rumors existed.

"Yes, I'm aware of the rumors and they are just that. Vittoria has not dated much at all and never had a serious boyfriend until me.", Ricky began to explain without going into detail yet knowing that his parents would then assume she was a virgin.

"Oh my; she's a virtuous woman?", asked a shocked Bianca who knew her son had a reputation for dating loose women; but she was hopeful hearing this news. "Tell us more.", insisted Bianca.

Carlo looked shocked as well but kept his questions to himself; no wonder Ricky had been masturbating like crazy, she was holding out; good for her, thought Carlo.

"If you mean, is she similar to my past lady friends, no; nothing like them. She's completely unaware of her prowess as a woman. She's modest with a level business head. She's a perfect match to keep me grounded, centered and focused.", explained Ricky proudly.

"We can't wait to meet our future daughter-in-law.", said Carlo with Bianca nodding in agreement.

Carlo was anxious to size her up; he'd be better able to tell if she was running a game on Ricky. Ricky's head might be too far up her ass to see anything else, he thought.

Just like Ricky, Vittoria was a mess. Preparing for her first dinner with the Bianchis should have been exciting; instead, Vittoria fussed and worried about what to wear and even more importantly, whether or not his family would like her. She had set several outfits on the bed to choose from, but she doubted the appropriateness of each one. What does a person wear to the home of Detroit royalty? The hour of truth was fast approaching and she didn't feel any more confident about her choice. In fact, she was waiting for the absolute last moment to dress. Her parents noticed that she had been a nervous wreck all morning and afternoon and had barely eaten. Her mother was determined to force something down her throat if necessary.

Antonella and Vittoria sat next to each other on the sofa while Lorenzo sat in his recliner attempting to read his morning paper; it was about the third time he had tried that day. Antonella was beginning to fret herself as she eyed her daughter's nervousness.

"Vittoria, you know you need to eat something before your big evening. You haven't eaten all day. I don't want you fainting.", Antonella paused, "Or maybe, we do…", she said thinking how the family would rush to her aid.

Lorenzo closed his paper to put his full attention squarely on his wife and daughter.

"Stop talking nonsense. Vittoria, go eat some fruit right this minute!", barked Lorenzo not wanting anything to mess up the special evening.

Vittoria reluctantly obeyed her father and left the pair sitting in the living room. Her mind was so focused on every scenario, ones where everything was perfect and his parents loved her, coupled with those of his parents telling him he chose unwisely in front of her. If only she could quiet her thoughts, she reflected as she leaned on the kitchen counter munching on a banana.

"You're right, this is our girl's time to let her personality shine through and impress her future in-laws.", Antonella said being more reasonable.

However, Lorenzo began having second thoughts of his own.

"Well, maybe she does need to pass out.", teased Lorenzo as he and Antonella shared a laugh.

"I can hear you!", Vittoria yelled from the kitchen.

"My darling, I'm only teasing. They will love you just as much as Ricky and we do.", Lorenzo belted his reassurance from a full heart.

"Yes, darling your father was only being silly.", advised Antonella as she tapped Lorenzo on his hand.

He looked at his wife questioning her actions as she was the first to suggest such a *silly* thing, he thought. He reached over to nudge her from her seat.

"Go check on our daughter.", suggested Lorenzo then he opened his morning paper once again to catch up on his reading.

Before her mother could stand, Vittoria returned to the living room to inform her parents that she was fine and didn't need any assistance.

"I'm okay; don't worry about me. It's time for me to get dressed anyway.", Vittoria said as she breathed deeply to settle her nerves.

Any longer, Ricky would arrive with her still getting dressed and that would give her parents enough time to embarrass her or themselves with Ricky. In and out is all the time she wanted him to spend with her parents; anything more without her present would be a disaster. She jogged up the stairs to her room to change clothes.

She had decided to wear a two-piece summer pants suit in a soft orange. The pants were flare-legged hip-huggers that would accentuate her curves and neat waistline. The top was a front wrap halter with a ruffled V-neck collar with a bow tie on the back. She slipped it on and stood in front of the mirror and was speechless;

this was not the look she was going for, did she gain weight, she pondered.

The pants hugged her round hips and buttocks and the halter revealed her belly button. Her taut abs could be seen slightly and her shapely arms were evidence that she lifted a lot of boxes for work. Then there was her cleavage; she couldn't wear a bra because of the cut of the halter so, her breasts were bubbling over pushing the ruffles out of the way. As she turned and modeled, she recalled that the outfit did fit the same way when she tried it on at the store. It was a bold purchase that she knew would drive Ricky crazy but was it the right look for meeting his folks.

She didn't want them to think that she was a loose woman; she could only imagine the type of women that Ricky had dated in the past or was known for dating. She decided she wouldn't be negative though and would wear the outfit regardless. She was tired of covering up and hiding in the shadows; this was what God gave her and if his folks were small-minded so be it.

Vittoria opted for minimal jewelry by putting on a long gold-tone necklace that draped to her navel with a pair of large hoop gold-tone earrings. She slipped on her tan straw platform wedge heels and then applied her lip gloss. The last thing was to take out her rollers and run her fingers through the huge curls. The massive long curls cascaded down her shoulders and back making her six-foot frame look even more statuesque.

She took one more look at herself, sprayed on perfume and then she heard the doorbell ring. Right on time Ricky, she thought as she smiled at her reflection. She grabbed her matching straw purse and left her bedroom.

Antonella stood to answer the door but first paused to smooth her hair in place. Lorenzo noticed and fanned his paper to let her know she could have a seat. He quickly walked to the door and opened it for their guest.

"Hello, Ricky. Come on in.", Lorenzo greeted the much-anticipated guest.

"No need Pappa. I'm ready to go.", Vittoria said as she rushed down the stairs and past her parents, but not without them noticing her appearance.

"Oh, my word!", said Antonella as she marveled at her daughter's stunning look.

Lorenzo's words were stuck in his throat as he stared at his baby girl.

"Bye. Don't wait up for me.", Vittoria informed her folks as she slid by her father to exit while Ricky held the screen door open for her. "Hi, Ricky!", exclaimed Vittoria through her nervousness.

Ricky was all smiles as his eyes devoured every inch of her and inhaled her perfume.

"Looking good baby.", Ricky said as he kissed her quickly on the lips under the watchful eyes of Antonella and the stunned expression of Lorenzo.

The young couple walked down the walkway toward his Corvette convertible. Ricky couldn't wait for Vittoria's hair to blow in the wind; he knew every single eye would be on the stunning beauty and they would know she belong to him. Ricky assisted Vittoria in the car as usual, with one hand holding her curly locks and the other holding her hand. The love birds smiled and looked forward to the evening as they drove away leaving behind a stunned father at the door. Lorenzo felt an emptiness grow and it hit him in the pit of his stomach.

"I've lost my baby girl.", said Lorenzo as he wiped away tears.

Antonella hugged him to reassure him that he hadn't lost her, but he was gaining something more.

"She's finally the woman who we both dreamt she could become. She'll never leave us; in fact, our family is on the verge of growing.", Antonella said then kissed her husband tenderly on the lips.

The wind felt exhilarating as it blew through Vittoria's luxurious curls; she noticed all eyes were on them whenever they passed a car or were stopped at a light. She didn't know whether or not, it was the attention-catching Stingray Corvette or her dashing boyfriend; either way, she felt extraordinary and knew she was indeed on the verge of a new life. Hell, her new life had already started she reminded herself.

Every time Vittoria and Ricky were together, she discovered something new about her city, some hidden gem. This time as he drove her to his home, it was her first time venturing that far east on Jefferson Boulevard. As they drove away from Downtown, she saw the grand apartment and condominium complexes off the riverfront. She thought of how expensive it must be to live in those places with valet attendants assisting its residents and guests.

The farther they drove, the landscape changed once more with the street narrowing. As the Detroit River began to merge into Lake St. Clair and the street began to narrow as it cruised along the waterfront, the homes became stately mansions of the rich and powerful like the Ford family. She was literally driving into her future and leaving her old life and ways behind her. She turned to look back as they left the Detroit city limits and entered Grosse Pointe Park; with each mile traveled, the homes became even more exclusive and stately. They drove through Grosse Pointe, then Grosse Park Farms until they arrived in Grosse Point Shores where Ricky's home was located off Lake St. Clair.

Ricky named each city as they entered; Vittoria found it quite silly that all of the cities almost had the same name. She thought it could become quite confusing, but perhaps that was the plan; to confuse those that didn't belong there. She noticed that police could be spotted every few miles, many of whom nodded at Ricky. She wondered if they were bought cops that his family-owned. Nonetheless, they offered him the respect he was due in the streets and in the business world. It was at that very moment that the realization of his power struck her. She became nervous all over again. Ricky noticed that her expression had become panicky; he knew that look well and hoped that she wouldn't jump from his moving car.

"Baby, are you okay?", asked Ricky.

"Yes of course Ricky.", her words belying her expression, "It might sound silly, but I just realized how powerful you are. Do you think your family will be accepting of a butcher's daughter?", asked Vittoria as all of her newly found confidence blew away in the wind.

"My parents, just like yours, want someone honest to love what they treasure most. Baby, believe me when I say they will be enchanted by you, just as I was months ago.", Ricky reassured her.

Ricky stroked her thigh as he thought of the evening hours when he'd have a chance to touch her skin instead of fabric. The feel of his strong hand comforted her and she too thought of their time alone later that evening when he would once again explore her body and she would shake beneath the weight of his muscled frame. She smiled at her king so he knew she trusted his words, but her smile quickly turned to awe as he turned up the long drive to a home fit for only a king.

The immense two-story Italian Renaissance Revival home was intimidating on its own, but the guards she saw sprinkled throughout the property gave another layer of intimidation. What was even more surprising than the beauty of the home, was the fact she saw the Detroit Police Commissioner, Tim Boggs, exiting the mansion. The guards quickly opened Boggs' car door. As the commissioner drove past them down the long drive, he nodded to acknowledge Ricky; however, Ricky was perturbed that he was there apparently meeting with his father.

"I'm going to pay that son-of-a-bitch a visit and remind him who runs this shit; it's neither him nor my father.", said Ricky with venom. He quickly caught himself and apologized to Vittoria for his outburst, "Please excuse my language darling."

"I completely understand. If someone had a meeting with me instead of my father, they would be totally out of line and would need to be corrected. But there will be plenty of time to focus on that. Today is our special day.", Vittoria co-signed his feelings.

"Thank you, baby, yes you're right.", Ricky expressed then kissed her hand for further appreciation of her understanding.

Ricky was pleased to see that he had her support. That was paramount for a mobster's wife to support his work and decisions. He wanted to be open with her about everything; he didn't want there to be secrets between them. He had witnessed how lies could destroy marriages and even lives.

Ricky's power aroused her; she had never thought that such a thing would attract her, but now she understood why women wanted powerful men. She was sure that her man was wanted most of all and if she had to fight to keep them off him, she would. She was after all the daughter of Lorenzo Rossi.

Ricky pulled up the circular drive winding in front of the massive estate and parked; his guards were about to open the door for Vittoria when he stopped them as was his habit. He burst from the car immediately fanning the men away from her; they made haste to do as instructed. They realized this must be his special girl as he had never brought anyone home before. Ricky noticed one trying to get a clear look at Vittoria, so he decided to toss the keys to him to redirect his focus.

"Have my car moved to the garage.", ordered Ricky.

"Yes, Mr. Bianchi.", the guard agreed then walked to the other guard on the post, "This must be his Ace.", whispered the guard to the other, both nodding in agreement as they stepped clear of their boss.

Nicolas was just as curious about Ricky's lady friend as Ricky's parents were. He wanted to make sure that he was the first to see the young woman and size her up. He thought he had a good judge of character and wanted to test it out. He had overheard many staffers betting whether or not the confirmed bachelor would actually marry his new love interest or not. Nicolas was tempted to enter the pool as well, but he used his better judgment against it; as he was supposed to be the staple of proper decorum among the staff. He heard the guards speak to the pair, so he opened the door assuming he would find a pretty petite number that Ricky could manhandle and toss around, but instead, what he saw, took all of his English words from his brain.

"Hello, Nicolas! I'd like you to meet my girl, Vittoria.", Ricky announced exuberantly.

"Nice to meet you, sir.", expressed Vittoria as she extended her hand to Nicolas.

"Si, senorita. Tocado por Dios!", Nicolas said.

His eyes traveled the length of her; I guess when you've waited this long, you are indeed waiting for the best, he thought as only God could create someone so beautiful.

"Nick, nobody knows what the fuck you are saying.", laughed Ricky.

Ricky patted his lifelong confidant on the shoulder not realizing that he said Vittoria was *touched by God.* Nicolas stood speechless as the pair walked through the massive foyer to the study where Ricky expected his parents were sitting. At that moment, Nicolas hated that he didn't get in on the bet because surely Ricky was going to marry this one.

Vittoria wanted to walk through the home unphased by its beauty, but she had never seen anything as grand other than a museum or the Fisher Theatre; she never imagined people actually living in such fine estates. She knew obviously that people did, but she didn't think of them as *real* people like her; *real* people lived in simple homes, saved up enough money to buy a car from the showroom floor and maybe take a trip to Vegas. This, she thought, was a fairytale.

The massive foyer had a twenty-foot ceiling with palatial artwork meticulously painted to encompass the feel of ancient Rome. There were two split curved staircases that elevated the eye to the second story. Her eyes were also entranced by the colossal crystal chandelier that hung in the center of the foyer between the black wrought iron staircases; making them a sharp contrast to the tan marble floors and tan walls with cream trim. There were expansive paintings hung on the walls along the staircases; some of which she could only imagine being priceless works of art along with a few paintings of parents and grandparents. There were brass wall sconces sprinkled along the wall to light the way up the staircases in the dark.

Vittoria followed Ricky's lead as he walked through a sitting area beneath the chandelier and led her under the catwalk to see other gems. Ricky smiled at her wonderment of his home as they passed by the sitting room to the left and a small ballroom on the right before reaching the study on the left. The hallway continued to an open area that appeared to be the living room, formal dining room and kitchen with a huge fireplace mantel in the living room taking the eye to the ceiling once more. The two could hear the laughter of his parents flood the hallway; his parents had joked about how his nonna Elisa was probably busting her casket lid open with joy that her favorite boy would be marrying soon. Vittoria found their laughter refreshing; it gave her hope that Ricky had been brought up in a loving home with parents who were comfortable showing affection to one another, like her parents.

173

Ricky took Vittoria's hand so that he could proudly introduce his folks to their future daughter-in-law; he had butterflies at the thought as the pair entered the study. Vittoria definitely could see where Ricky got his looks, his mother was incredibly beautiful and elegant; his father was a silver fox who appeared to be strong and confident. Ricky's parents continued in their laughter and flirting not aware that the young couple had entered the room. As they heard footsteps, their attention turned to the entrance and the pair were stunned by the delightful creature upon their son's arm.

"Mother, father, I'd like you to meet my girlfriend, Vittoria Rossi.", announced Ricky not able to contain his excitement.

It had been ages since they had seen him so happy about anything. His parents stood to greet and admire the stunning beauty. Carlo could only stare in amazement while his wife forgave his lingering look and spoke on their behalf.

"Hello, my dear. It is so nice to meet you.", Bianca greeted warmly.

"Hello, Mr. and Mrs. Bianchi.", exclaimed a slightly nervous Vittoria.

"Please call me Bianca.", she advised as she looked over the young woman and nodded, "Seeing you helps us understand why our son had been behaving so strangely.", Bianca said as she approached the young woman to greet her with a hug.

Vittoria reciprocated the warm greeting and felt relief that his mother was so welcoming as Ricky had tried to reassure her that his mother would be. Vittoria leaned into the embrace of the much shorter woman as she imagined her precious Ricky running to his mother for comfort as a boy.

Ricky was relieved that his mother stopped her comment there as he knew clearly that she was talking about those nights he pleasured himself to get rid of his pent-up sexual tension during the early days of their courtship. Carlo eyed Ricky to indicate that he too was glad she hadn't continued down that line of conversation, but now Carlo completely understood the whole picture; what man wouldn't masturbate if he was dating someone that gorgeous and couldn't touch her. Carlo would have done the same, he thought with a smirk. He walked over to the three finally able to speak and greet the young woman.

"Hello, Vittoria. It's nice to meet you. You may call me Carlo. You have made our son a very fortunate man indeed!", he said before leaning in for a polite church hug as he didn't trust himself to get any closer.

Ricky held a steady eye on Carlo as he greeted the beauty as well as Bianca realizing that Ricky got his sexual appetite quite naturally from Carlo's bloodline. Carlo cleared his throat as he ended the embrace with the future mother of his grandchildren then he grabbed his son to give him a firm bear hug. The two laughed knowing that hug and pat on the shoulder from his father indicated pride that he had chosen so well. Bianca smiled as she too knew he had chosen well and the pair would create a beautiful family together.

"I guess we should break up this 'that a boy' congratulatory hugging that's going on. Are you ready for dinner? We had Cook whip up something special for us.", recommended Bianca as she took Vittoria's hand to lead her to the dining room.

"Yes, Mrs. Bianchi … Bianca. I'm starving.", Vittoria informed.

She immediately hated her choice of words; she didn't want Bianca to think that she was impoverished. She decided to add clarification.

"I have an active metabolism and I get faint if I don't eat enough.", Vittoria explained.

"Well, you will be quite at home with us. We don't shy away from eating, not in this household.", laughed Bianca pleased that Vittoria wasn't pretentious like so many girls of that generation could be.

Bianca reflected on how so many of her friends were dealing with issues of their daughters struggling with eating disorders; it was a relief that she wouldn't have that concern and Vittoria had a healthy appetite to support the life she hoped would soon be growing in her womb. The men followed behind the women whispering like school-aged boys.

"Well done, Ricky. She's incredible without even trying.", Carlo whispered his compliments to his already ultra-confident son.

"You know how I do; only the best for me … only the best.", laughed Ricky wishing he and Vittoria could skip dinner and head up to his bedroom suite.

Vittoria could smell the delicious aroma floating from the dining room to the hall as she and Bianca bypassed the elegantly decorated living room to enter the formal dining room. It was quite apparent that no expense was spared to make her feel welcomed and special; there were a dozen floral arrangements in the room on the buffet console, the dining table and pedestal tables. The color pallet continued in the dining room with artwork on the walls with two sculptures resting on the floor of the exquisite room. The dining table was massive, sitting ten easily; it was a white oval Carrera marble pedestal table with viceroy beige velvet chairs to match the veining of the marble with black polished wooden legs capped with silver tips. The look was modern and sophisticated; it matched everything about Ricky and what his parents seemed to be.

Bianca noticed Vittoria's hesitation to fully enter the room; her stare was deliberate as her eyes took in every detail with amazement. Bianca smiled at her and encouraged her to be seated. Ricky rushed to catch up so that he could assist his love with her chair. As he assisted her, she marveled at the touch and feel of the fabric; she had never seen velvet up close and had surely never touched it. She felt like a princess who would soon be crowned Queen of Detroit. Ricky spotted her admiration and kissed her reassuringly on the forehead as he sat next to her. His parent sat across from the pair; neither of whom could stop smiling as they watched their son dote on his new love.

Vittoria's stomach growled with excitement at the delectable feast before her; she had never seen anything like it. Ricky heard it and the two shared a chuckle. On the table being served family-style was Italian wedding soup, potato gnocchi with garlic butter topped with mushrooms and snails, Tuscan style veal chops, rabbit stew with olive and rosemary, tossed salad, peppers stuffed with spinach and sausage, mozzarella with summer squash and olive puree and a variety of bread. Bianca was about to start serving the rabbit stew to Carlo when Ricky stopped her.

"Before, we dine; we need something to celebrate, that is fitting to such a feast as this.", he insisted as he stood to gain everyone's attention.

Nicolas had entered the room to oversee the butler and maid as they served drinks, but they all stopped in motion as they were about to pour the family's finest wine from their basement wine cellar. Ricky had captured their attention along with everyone else in the room.

"For years, I have been selfish and played the field by dating numerous women around town. But *never* had there been one that captured my heart and my thoughts, the way you have Vittoria. Now that I know you and love you, I can't imagine my life without you. You would make me a very proud and happy man if you would do me the honor of becoming my bride.", Ricky said then lowered to one knee, "Will you marry me, Vittoria?"

Ricky opened the antique ring box to display the most uniquely beautiful ring that Vittoria had ever seen. It was a gimmel ring; the top and bottom half of the ring mirrored each other as it could be separated and worn as two rings. It had two round one-carat diamonds inlaid in a square casing with rubies surrounding them with smaller diamonds cascading down the side in a swirled design of yellow gold. She gasped for air not sure if that moment or day was actually real; perhaps she was passed out somewhere at the fundraiser ball and nothing had been real since that night. She looked around the room as if for the first time, seeing the loving couple waiting for her response. She blinked her eyes fearful that she was about to faint until she heard the words, 'breathe my love'; then she turned her attention to the most handsome and kind man she had ever met, Ricky Bianchi.

"Yes!", she said gasping for air as tears flooded her eyes.

Vittoria cried tears of joy, disbelief and relief as she clutched Ricky in her arms. She held onto him for life and strength to keep her limp body from collapsing. Ricky kissed her cleavage, her neck and then her tears away then he separated the rings. He slipped one half of the ring on her long slender finger; then the other onto his pinkie. He was close to tears himself as he began to assume that he would be the confirmed bachelor of his peers, but Vittoria had come into his world and turned everything upside down creating in him new desires for a different life.

"The tradition of this ring is that both wear half of it and upon our marriage, it will be combined for you to wear as your wedding ring.", Ricky continued his explanation, "My maternal grandmother, Elisa, my nonna, adored me and wanted me to propose with this ring someday. It was the ring that her own love, my nonno, gave her."

Vittoria was already overwhelmed by the experience, but to hear the touching story of his grandmother and grandfather almost made her cry an ugly cry. Ricky never stopped astonishing her with his romantic gestures; most people would never guess that he was such a gentle spirit and a true romantic at heart.

Vittoria wasn't the only one in tears; Bianca was smiling and sobbing at the same time as Carlo clutched her in his arms. Ricky was astounded to see his father fighting back tears as he wiped his eyes with his napkin. Ricky stood to walk over to his parents to express his excitement and to tease his father.

"Are you getting soft, old man?', teased Ricky.

Ricky gave his father a fierce bear hug as the slightly shorter Carlo rested his head on Ricky's shoulder and then planted several kisses on his cheek.

It was a much long-awaited hope that Ricky would settle down; it was a day that his parents doubted would ever come. Carlo quickly composed himself not wanting the staff to witness him gushing over his son, but no one doubted how much he loved him; one would say that was the reason behind his display of anger at times.

Nicolas put decorum aside and approached Ricky; he hugged him possessively. He couldn't have been more ecstatic even if he were his own son.

"I'm so proud of you, Master Ricky. You have chosen well. She has a kind spirit about her and is strong too. I sense that.", Nicolas complimented his once young ward.

"Thank you, Nick. That means a lot.", Ricky blushed like a schoolboy receiving recognition from his favorite teacher.

Nicolas patted him on the back and then quickly excused himself, leaving the family to celebrate as the staff resumed pouring the wine. He nodded at the future Mrs. Bianchi before leaving the room. As the evening progressed, there was so much laughter and stories of Ricky's childhood; it reminded her of family holiday meals when her mother prepared a feast and invited her best friend over. Despite the grandeur of the home, Ricky's family was warm, tender and loving; Vittoria felt accepted by them and any fears she once had, were vanished.

As everyone stood from the table, Bianca suggested they retire to the study for the evening, but Vittoria and Ricky had different plans. Vittoria took Ricky's hand seemingly apologetically before speaking.

"It has been an unbelievable evening, but perhaps I should say good night since it's getting late.", Vittoria announced bestowing an apologetic look upon Bianca and Carlo.

She wished the dinner had taken place at Ricky's Palmer Woods home so he could ask them to leave; she was eager to be alone with him, but that would have to wait for another time. The expression of Ricky's parents questioned her words as they had assumed Vittoria would stay the night. Ricky knew it was nothing more than modesty that prompted her words.

"Mother, father, please excuse us. We will meet you there shortly.", Ricky advised as he stayed behind to talk to Vittoria.

"There's no need for modesty my love. You are my fiancée and my parents aren't prudes. You can freely stay the night. Hell, you can even move in with me if you want to.", laughed Ricky, but meaning every word.

"Oh Ricky, they might hear us.", Vittoria blushed as she gripped his shoulder while leaning on his chest.

"Well, just try not to be so loud.", he laughed as she playfully punched his chest.

"I'm talking about you. I can control myself.", laughed Vittoria knowing, that was not at all true.

Ricky was an expert lover and knew all the right places and things to do that would cause her to moan and squeal in delight. Ricky decided he would prove that she was to blame for their loud love-making as he slipped his hand down the back of her pants and kissed her. She instantly moaned as his hands maneuvered to her playland and he picked her up to straddle his tall frame.

"You were saying?", Rickey teased then buried his face in her cleavage causing Vittoria to giggle.

Bianca and Carlo entered the study and sat hoping the young couple would soon follow. Bianca was perplexed that Vittoria would want to leave.

"Do you think there's a problem? Do you think we offended Vittoria in some way?', asked Bianca concerned that the young woman was leaving so soon.

"I hear them laughing, so I'm sure everything is fine.", insisted Carlo as they noticed the laughing coming closer.

Ricky and Vittoria entered the study arm-in-arm when Ricky playfully hit Vittoria on her buttocks. Vittoria sat next to Ricky on the loveseat like a woman eager to be alone with her man and it didn't go unnoticed.

"Dears, Vittoria if you are staying, perhaps you should go on up to Ricky's suite. I'm sure you two will have more fun together than talking to two senior citizens.", Bianca insisted remembering how she and Carlo used to be.

"That's a good idea, sweetheart.", agreed Carlo who had suddenly become eager to spend time with his own bride, "In fact, we'll head up as well."

Bianca blushed as she caught the meaning behind her husband's words. He extended his arm and she allowed him to assist her to her feet as the young couple stood as well.

"Sounds good.", said Ricky then he whispered to Vittoria, "Let's see who's the loudest, you or my mother?", laughed Ricky with Vittoria unable to contain her shocked laughter.

Carlo winked at Ricky and Vittoria as he escorted Bianca from the study. Both couples ascended up either side of the split staircase, each couple going to opposite sides of the home. Vittoria was relieved that their suites were on opposite wings of the house;

she felt it would be quite unlikely that they would be heard. Unsuspectingly, Ricky picked up Vittoria and raced down the hall to his bedroom. The pair laughed all the way much to the delight of Ricky's parents.

"Don't you even try that with me.", teased Bianca then kissed Carlo's cheek.

"Don't worry, but you do need to step up your pace.", laughed Carlo as he quickened his steps.

Both couples' laughter filled the hallways creating excitement for everyone including the staff about what was to come. The night had been a whirlwind of pleasure and laughter for Vittoria and Ricky. Everything was new for them both; now that morning had arrived, Ricky was exhilarated and wished that he had met her a decade ago. But as that crept across his thoughts, so did the wise words of his nonna, that everything happens when it's supposed to. Perhaps, he was a wiser man and more level-headed than he was a decade ago; he might not have been a fit husband for Vittoria at that time. Regardless, they were together now and that's all that mattered to him.

He turned over to look at Vittoria resting peacefully beautiful. She had slipped from beneath the covers to expose her long statuesque frame. Her body beckoned for his touch, his lips and his penis that had begun to swell. He quickly laid atop her and buried his face in the softness of her breasts; he could lose himself there. Her fragrance and softness begged him to taste her breasts once more; he couldn't wait for them to marry so that she could bear children. He imagined how he and their children would feast from her softness.

"Ricky, no.", laughed Vittoria as she squirmed beneath him trying to move, "I'm completely exhausted. I don't know if I even have the energy to work today."

"Well don't.", laughed Ricky as he pinned her more securely beneath his frame.

"That wouldn't be fair to Pappa. He's expecting me to work today. I'll have a late start getting there since I have to go home to change.", insisted Vittoria.

Ricky didn't want her to leave, but he understood she had obligations to her family; time would come quick enough when she didn't have to work and they could make love from morning till dusk.

Chapter 9

The weeks following Vittoria's introduction to his family had been a whirlwind; he had so many projects he was working on yet still had to make time for Vittoria. He couldn't be more thankful for her understanding and selflessness; he wasn't accustomed to dating a woman who wasn't constantly asking for or demanding his time and money. It was truly refreshing and soothing; it freed his mind to focus extensively on his businesses. Everything seemed to be coming along quite nicely.

Angelo was glad that he finally had some helpful news about Canto and was able to deliver news on a more personal front as well. He was eager to show Ricky that his trust in him had been well placed. Angelo briskly walked past Bettie and nodded as he approached Ricky's open office door. He knocked on it and waited for Ricky to acknowledge him; he had learned years ago that when it came to work, he was not a cousin or good friend, but an employee who'd better respect Ricky at all cost.

"Come in. What's shaking?", asked Ricky as he closed his ledger.

"I've got those updates you've been waiting on.", Angelo announced proudly.

"Hit me with it!", Ricky said as he leaned forward on his desk with fingers entwined.

"Well, you've mentioned that Canto bragged about moving the most dope.", Angelo paused for effect.

"Yeah, what about it?", asked Ricky starting to get bored with Angelo fairly quickly.

"His statement was a challenge to the Italian's authority. He's pushing way more dope than what the Italians sell to him. So where is he getting it?", Angelo asked pausing again for dramatic effect.

"You *tell* me, motherfucker!", said Ricky thinking if Angelo paused again, he'd slap him.

"He's buying it straight from fucking Columbia. He has a connection with the cartel that is selling to him directly. If you cut that supply chain, you'll bring him back down to size.", concluded Angelo.

Angelo stood with his hands in his pockets waiting for praise from Ricky but instead received a puzzled look. Ricky thought he and his father had a clear business agreement with the cartel and who they wanted allowed to make deals. This was more than updates; it was concerning and would require Ricky to make an appearance in Columbia to get things back on track.

"Ok. That's not the news I was expecting to hear, but it is definitely something I needed to know. How was he even able to make that contact?", pondered Ricky.

"Your guess is just as good as mine.", informed Angelo who hadn't even contemplated that question.

"Contact Diaz and request a meeting; schedule it for a couple of weeks out. Looks like I have an unexpected international trip planned. Set the date then schedule my jet for a trip to Columbia. Now, can you hit me with something good?", Ricky queried as he crinkled his brow.

"We captured that chump Tommaso Rossi for you. He's at the warehouse, tied up and waiting for you.", Angelo informed knowing for sure he would be adulated.

"Yes, motherfucker! Now that's some good news. Good work Angelo.", Ricky shouted his excitement for the pain he was about to bestow on Tommaso.

"So, when are we going?", he inquired so that he would know what day to get buzzed.

It was the only way Angelo could stomach what he assumed Ricky would do to Tommaso. That warehouse filled with weapons of torture hadn't been used in years and now Ricky was willing to sink back into the shadows of fear and evil to inflict whatever sick device of pain on this poor sap, thought Angelo, his mind wouldn't allow him to contemplate what he might have done to Vittoria. It was quite apparent that this was a personal matter.

"Tomorrow evening will be good. I'll call Vittoria and make sure she will be available to go. I want her to witness this shit!", smiled Ricky sadistically as he contemplated what tools he would use.

My God; thought Angelo, he wants his girlfriend to be there. There was no doubt that Tommaso had done something atrocious to her. Angelo decided it was best to leave before Ricky wanted to discuss some of the possible ways, he could torture Tommaso. Angelo definitely didn't have the stomach to hear about it and then have to witness it too, so he quickly dismissed himself as Ricky picked up the phone to make a call.

"Rossi Meat Market. How may I help you?", answered Lorenzo.

"Hello, Mr. Rossi; it's Ricky. Is Vittoria available?", asked Ricky.

"Sure thing. By the way, thanks for giving our girl that Cougar. It's really come in handy for her. I don't have to worry about her being on a bus.", Lorenzo expressed animatedly.

"It was my pleasure, sir. She's my responsibility now.", informed Ricky proudly.

"Vittoria!", Lorenzo called across the store.

Vittoria could always tell when her father was talking to Ricky; he acted like a groupie at times and hadn't stopped talking about the car Ricky had given her. He had been telling people about it for weeks now as if it happened yesterday. Her entire household was ecstatic; it was like they all were dating him. Ricky had them all mesmerized by his charm and charisma; anyone in his presence seemed to be drawn to him as the saying goes like a moth to a flame. The only way you'd get burned is if you crossed him; other than that, he was a gentle spirit, she thought.

"Coming.", Vittoria shouted as she sprinted to her fiancé.

Lorenzo set the phone down so he could continue his inventory as Vittoria approached the mini workstation behind the display counter.

"Hello.", purred Vittoria knowing no one but Ricky called her.

"Hey, baby. I was hoping to see you tomorrow evening. I thought it would be good to have some quiet time alone together, but before that, I want to present a surprise to you.", suggested Ricky.

"Sure thing. Where do you want me to meet you?", said Vittoria proud of her new ride and newly found independence.

"I think it's best that I pick you up for this.", insisted Ricky.

"Ok, no problem. What time?", she inquired.

"I'll pick you up at four in the afternoon and we can have dinner at the Traffic Jam. Then I'll show you the surprise, then after that, we can go to our love shack in Palmer Woods.", laughed Ricky.

"Sounds good. That's another restaurant I haven't been to.", Vittoria smiled hoping he could feel her love and excitement through the phone.

"See you tomorrow, baby. Arrivederci.", Ricky said just above a whisper.

His voice sent a rush of shivers throughout her body and she fumbled while placing the receiver on the base. She was thankful that the store was empty and her father was off minding *his business*; so that her orgasm would go unnoticed. Most men had to physically touch their women for that effect, but not Ricky. That man, that man, she thought, as she inhaled deeply.

That woman, that woman, whispered Ricky after hanging up. Only God knew what it would take to make him settle down and He must have handpicked her for him, thought Ricky. Ricky decided that perhaps it was time for him to get reacquainted with the man upstairs or at least one of His guys on earth; it had been a while since he went to a confessional. He liked to do things differently; he often went to the confessional before he committed an act versus afterward. Father Luca would be quite surprised by the visit, he thought. Ricky cleared his desk before leaving and advised Bettie that he would be out for the rest of the day.

"Let Angelo and Enzo know I'm headed to St. Mary's for confessional.", advised Ricky to a bewildered Bettie.

"Yes, of course, sir.", responded Bettie.

Bettie thought those days were behind him, especially since he met his fiancée; but apparently not. Ricky tapped the top of her desk and rushed out of the building. Ricky hopped into his Lincoln and drove east toward Greektown to reach the family church. His family had been a member of Old St. Mary's Catholic Church ever since they came to America. Ricky and his father made a point to attend at least twice a year for Easter and Christmas, but his mother attended far more frequently. During his Reaper days, he came to the confessional a few times a week; Father Luca served as a great therapist, much better than the new age or hippie ones that everyone was using nowadays, he thought.

Ricky entered the massive structure and stopped at the bowl of holy water. After dipping his fingers and making the cross of Christ on his chest, he instantly felt remorse for all of the evil acts he had committed over the years and those he was yet to do. He had the growing feeling that Tommaso was just the warm-up act to what he needed to do in the near future. Father Luca was sitting in the enormous sanctuary contemplating how the city had changed when he noticed Ricky enter.

"Hello, Ricky. It's been a very long time since you were here. Do you need to confess, my son?', asked the father fearful of whatever deviant thing the young man had committed.

"Yes, I do Father.", informed Ricky then he began walking toward the booth.

Father Luca prepared himself and met Ricky on the other side of the booth. He said a silent prayer that God would give him the strength to tolerate whatever gruesome tale he would hear.

"Hello, Father. Bless me father for I have sinned and I am about to sin some more. It's been who the hell knows how long since my last confession. I'm about to kill a prick that molested my fiancée when she was a child through her teenage years.", Ricky said forgetting proper decorum for his language.

"I am sorry to hear that your fiancée was tormented during her childhood, but I am pleased that you are settling down. Your mother told me, that Sunday after your proposal.", expressed Father Luca.

"Father, I need you to pray that God gives me the strength I need to kill him and anyone who opposes the way I do business or my family.", asked Ricky.

"That's not how it works. God said that vengeance is His alone.", the priest attempted to educate Ricky on scripture.

"Well, I'm going to be the hand of God on earth because no one is going to come against my family.", Ricky proclaimed fiercely.

Father Luca knew when Ricky spoke that way, there was no reaching him or changing his mind. The only thing he felt could help was to begin reciting the Lord's prayer as Ricky left the confessional. At that point, Ricky was more determined than ever to rid the earth of the scum known as Tommaso Rossi.

Ricky barely slept that night as he envisioned the torture he would impose upon Tommaso. His thoughts aroused him as he pictured Tommaso begging for mercy and his girl, Vittoria, beaming with pride that her man was indeed her protector. The Reaper was alive and well in the house that night, as Ricky masturbated as blood flowed from the wounds of his imagined victim.

A new dawn couldn't arrive quick enough for Ricky and he pushed through his work as he salivated for Vittoria and Tommaso's blood that would be shed that night. His nerve endings were on fire in anticipation of the night's festivities; it had been too long since he felt blood on his hands.

Time hadn't passed fast enough for Vittoria; she was ready to see her man yesterday. She eyed her closet full of new clothes, shoes and accessories. What to wear had become a very important question for Vittoria. She had refused a credit card from Ricky, but he had a way of getting what he wanted so she now shopped at a boutique that allowed her to create a running tab that Ricky paid. She had come to love shopping and trying on the latest fashions, who would have guessed that the tomboy would develop a softer side.

Vittoria would dress ultra-modern for their evening out; she decided to wear a one-piece jumpsuit with a halter top with a button choker collar in red with flared legs. On the front was a cut-out in the shape of a flower with three pedals on the bottom beneath her breasts and two on the top to reveal her olive skin. A disk of rhinestones was placed in the middle of it to represent the pistil of a flower. She decided to wear the same sandals she wore to meet his parents and to pair the look with large filigree dangling gold-tone fishhook earrings and a gold-tone bangle bracelet. The final step was to pull her hair up in a tight ponytail atop the crown of her head and add a touch of mascara and lip gloss.

Vittoria twirled in the mirror as she had now become accustomed to doing before making her way downstairs. As she approached the bottom of the stairs, she noticed that Ricky had quietly arrived and was talking to her folks. He looked dashing as always; he wore a traditional black suit with a straight leg paired with a red cotton shirt and a black ascot. He wore her favorite cologne; Vittoria could smell it ever so slightly as she walked down the stairs.

She was surprised that she hadn't heard them laughing at Ricky's jokes like usual. She wondered what they had been discussing especially since they immediately became tight-lipped when she entered the living room.

Ricky stood to greet her and he hoped she hadn't overheard them talking; he had explained that he didn't want a prolonged engagement and that they would set a date very soon. He had reassured them that they didn't need to concern themselves with the cost and that he would ensure Vittoria's every desire was met by the wedding planner.

"So, what are you three whispering about?", she inquired knowing they had to be up to something.

"I was just saying how much my parents adore you and can't wait for us to marry.", Ricky told a partial truth.

"Oh, Ricky, how sweet. I really like them too.", blushed Vittoria as she bounced over to Ricky to kiss him playfully on the cheek, but that wasn't enough for him.

"I only get that little kiss?", he teased as he kissed her fully on the lips and afterward inserted his tongue boldly in her mouth.

Vittoria blushed and hid her face in his neck as her parents cleared their throats, but Ricky winked at them both then kissed his girl on her forehead.

"Well, we better get going. I have a big night planned for her. I'll have her home sometime tomorrow morning.", informed Ricky as he grabbed Vittoria's hand to guide her out the door.

Ricky couldn't stop staring at Vittoria as they walked down the walkway to his car.

"You look absolutely stunning as always.", Ricky told Vittoria as he helped her enter the car.

"Thank you. You do too.", giggled Vittoria.

"That's a first. Fine ass, is what women usually call me.", laughed Ricky as he closed the car door then pimp walked around to the driver's side.

Vittoria laughed knowing how true that statement was; she knew exactly how fine he was and the eyes of any woman they encountered said as much. He was such a delicious tall glass of water; she could drink from his fountain all day long. And she couldn't wait to taste him tonight for the first time; she would surprise him with that move. She blushed as she thought of her growing boldness.

"I think you will like the Traffic Jam. It's a groovy place with a nice vibe.", suggested Ricky.

"I'm sure I will. You have great taste.", Vittoria agreed.

"Sho you right!", he said as he looked her over then leaned in quickly to kiss her cleavage.

The two had a fun evening laughing and eating a delicious meal; it was another epic romantic evening for the record book.

Unknowingly, Vittoria had been the attraction of the evening and Ricky was her number one fan. He was beside himself in anticipation and excitement for what he hoped would please Vittoria. The two had eaten a feast and now it was time for him to cut a pig.

"Ready?", asked Ricky as he wiped away the residue of the delicious meal from his mouth.

"Yes, I am. Ricky, I can't wait for this surprise. If it's anything as good as the last one, I'm going to scream.", Vittoria's words bubbled out to Ricky's delight.

"Anything for you my darling … anything.", pledged Ricky as he took her hand and kissed it.

Ricky didn't want to waste another minute at the restaurant so he signaled for the waiter who had been attentively watching the pair from afar. Ricky retrieved his wallet from his back pocket and removed a hundred-dollar bill from it, then placed it in the sleeve atop the check. He handed it to the waiter who eagerly reached for it as he had spotted the bill being placed inside. Ricky stood and crossed to the opposite side to assist Vittoria from her seat.

"Thank you, Mr. Bianchi.", beamed the waiter over the excessive tip.

Ricky nodded at the waiter and then escorted Vittoria out. They walked hand in hand to the parking lot across the street in front of the entrance. The warm summer breeze swept over them making Vittoria's long ponytail flow in the wind like the trail of a star. To Ricky, her beauty shined as bright as the brightest star; she possessed a beauty that was unmatched and undeniable. He was bound and determined by love to never deny her anything and tonight would show just how sincere he was. He assisted her in the car and then entered. He decided he should check in with Angelo and make sure everything was ready. After he started the engine, he used his car phone to call the warehouse.

"Yeah.", answered Angelo hoping that Ricky was calling to say release Tommaso.

"Have the pig ready.", instructed Ricky then hung up the phone.

Vittoria pondered why they would be eating again unless it was code for something else, but what that something could be she had no idea.

Damn, thought Angelo, Ricky was actually going through with his plan. It wasn't enough for Ricky to torment or even kill his enemy, he loved to humiliate them first. So, Angelo gave the word to the fellas to strip Tomaso down to his birthday suit, then tie him to a chair to await Ricky.

Ricky drove the short distance to the warehouse that was on the docks not far from the funeral home. Vittoria was very curious as she took note of her surroundings; perhaps, he had bought her a boat, she thought. Think bigger girlie, she thought; maybe he was having one built, but how does a pig factor in? Excitement was building as he parked; she noticed that men were waiting outside and one rushed over to open Ricky's door. She realized that his men were like most that encountered Ricky, they wanted to be him, but those that knew him also feared him.

Ricky assisted Vittoria from the car and put his arm around her protectively. He began to whisper to her in his serious tone that was rich and deep.

"You've captured my heart in a way no other woman has and I'll do anything for you. I'll do anything to protect you and ensure your safety. My only desire is to protect you and make you happy, no matter the cost. Tonight, I'll prove that to you.", explained Ricky.

Vittoria would have expected to hear those words before love-making, not before entering a warehouse; she was utterly confused about what to expect when they entered. The men continued to nod at Ricky as they passed them and entered deeper into the dark warehouse.

"The pig is ready boss.", said one underling pleased to satisfy his king.

Ricky led her to a huge dark room where there was a dozen or so men circled around what she guessed was the *pig*. The men parted way for Ricky and Vittoria to enter; they were stunned by her beauty and that Ricky had brought her there. He had never brought one of his women to the warehouse before. As the men parted Vittoria was able to see the tied-up *pig* in its truest form, raw, frightened and humiliated. Tommaso had once been the most loved man in her life other than her father until he became the cruelest. The mere sight of him once would make her sick, her head pound and her heart race with fear; but her love had brought the beast down to size and now that beast was the one with a pounding heart. Ricky left Vittoria's side and approached a quivering Tommaso whose eyes had become oversized with questions when he noticed Vittoria at his captor's side.

"Tommaso, you hurt the most treasured of everything I have when you violated my woman all those years ago. You killed something within her that just *now* has come back to life.", Ricky explained his position to Tommaso as he removed his blazer, ascot and rolled up his sleeves.

He handed the clothing to Angelo who placed the items out of range of anything that would stain them. Ricky then motioned over to a bench that held some of the most sadistic tools of torture one could imagine, but his eyes stopped on his favorite of all, the straight razor blade. The instrument of pain called to him as he reached for it; the weight of the stainless-steel blade felt good in his hand. He wielded it with precision as he cut through the air with his movements; it was a motion that he had missed.

Vittoria couldn't take her eyes away from Ricky. She watched the muscles and veins of his forearms bulge with each movement. She had no doubt about what her lover was about to do, the crime that he was about to commit; but there was a feeling of vindication and excitement rushing over her. He was undoubtedly her protector, her knight and greatest love; she realized at that moment that indeed, there was nothing in the world he would not do for her.

Ricky turned around and the eyes that stared back were darker, sinister and menacing. Tommaso began to cry and begged muffled unintelligible words through his gag; he saw the Reaper coming to settle a debt that was long overdue. Vittoria decided that she would turn her back to the gruesome scene and only listen to her uncle's howls of agony. The closer Ricky came to Tommaso, the more Ricky's countenance changed as he began to salivate for the blood that would soon be spilled by his hand.

Ricky stopped in front of Tommaso and held the blade up, poised in mid-air as he examined it as if contemplating how he would carve the pig and then ... slash after slash as he masterfully twirled the sharp edge over Tommaso's bare flesh. The blood gushed from the pig's body and splashed on Ricky with each stroke. No one made a sound; nothing could be heard but the wailing of Tommaso and the heavy breathing of Ricky. The sight of Tommaso's blood aroused Ricky to the point of him grunting loudly as orgasmic pleasure surged through his body.

"Angelo, pass me the bowie knife!", yelled Ricky as he dropped the blade breathing heavily.

Angelo reluctantly fetched the weapon as requested and handed it to Ricky. Ricky's eyes looked crazed and bloodthirsty. It was no doubt that the Reaper had returned.

"You'll never hurt my girl or any other girl ever again.", shouted Ricky as he grabbed Tommaso's penis and chopped it off.

The screams of Tommaso could finally be heard as Ricky yanked the rag from his mouth and then shoved the severed appendage into Tommaso's mouth. Ricky dropped the blade and began walking to the bench as he looked at the blood on his hands. His expression was a disturbing mixture of maniacal satisfaction and sexual arousal. Angelo couldn't stomach looking at him at that moment; he stared at his feet instead and prayed that God Almighty helped his cousin. Ricky leaned forward on the workbench as his body shook with satisfaction and he screamed his orgasm from the darkest part of his soul.

That sound was similar to the moan of passion with which she had become familiar. The sound stirred feelings of her own sexual desire as she listened to her lover. Her body shivered with the satisfaction of being vindicated and she was aroused by the sound of her lover's pleasure; for she knew he did it for her and would do it again and again if necessary. The surrounding men noticed her reaction and realized that Ricky had found his soulmate; they pitied any man that would even look at her the wrong way.

Ricky used the rag to wipe away some of the blood before walking over to the sink to wash his hands and forearms. Ricky came back to the world as he cleansed his body of the blood and noticed that Vittoria had her back turned to the scene. He walked toward her and held her from behind then kissed her on the head.

"Send him to hell!", ordered Ricky.

As he led Vittoria from the room, Angelo put a bullet in Tommaso's head to end his suffering.

Vittoria looked at Ricky and smiled; her painful past was now dead and she would definitely never look back. Ricky took her into his office where he began to strip. He walked into the adjoining bathroom to shower. Vittoria decided to remove her clothes as well and join him. Ricky stepped under the showerhead and allowed the warm water to run down his body to rinse away any remaining traces of blood. He picked up the bar of soap to begin scrubbing his body. Vittoria entered the shower and removed the soap from his hand.

She squatted before him and took his long dick in her hand; even his cock displayed power, she thought, as its erection made it stand firm and strong. She would stop at nothing to please her protector, lover and confidante. Something within her, perhaps instinct, guided her actions as she ran her hand up and down the powerful shaft while her mouth covered it in coordination. She starved for his flavor as she moaned loudly desperate to please him. Her actions both surprised and aroused him; she was indeed his soulmate.

He needed more of her; her moans were driving him mad with passion. He wanted his penis to feel the warmth of her womb; so, he stopped her and grasped her into his embrace so that he could kiss her passionately. He lifted her up so that she could straddle him and he thrust himself deep within her. Their passionate moans echoed throughout the building as they reveled in the death of Tommaso. Vittoria gripped her lover's strong arms as he thrust deep within her, pushing her against the shower wall as her legs quivered in his hands. Her pleasure was a mixture of laughter and moans knowing she loved and was loved by the most powerful man in the state.

The following morning was a glorious one, despite Ricky and Vittoria not sleeping much during the night. He didn't feel exhausted at all; instead, he got up early to read the newspaper leaving Vittoria asleep in bed. He decided he would surprise her and prepare a small breakfast instead of having the maid come early. He soon realized that was a mistake when he burned the toast and bacon. The smell of burnt food awoke Vittoria and she came rushing into the kitchen to make sure everything was okay.

"Ricky, is everything alright?", asked Vittoria wearing nothing more than a robe as she checked on her love.

"Well, if you think burnt breakfast is alright then yes, everything is wonderful.", laughed Ricky.

He sat down at the breakfast table with his cup of coffee and studied her morning beauty as he sipped. She looked over the mess he had made and laughed; she found it sweet that he would even try.

"I suggest you leave the cooking to me or a cook; you know, someone who actually knows what they're doing.", Vittoria teased as she threw the burnt food in the trash.

"Ouch!", laughed Ricky.

"Let me cook some more bacon and toast for us and we'll be good.", she informed as she pulled the meat from the refrigerator.

Neither one had spoken of the acts that had occurred, but he felt it was necessary to discuss it in part at least. The whole experience was new for them both.

"I've never allowed a girlfriend to see into my world.", explained Ricky as he sipped more coffee.

"That's understandable, but I'm your fiancée. So, I'm different.", said Victoria as she looked over her shoulder and smiled then placed her attention back on the bacon.

"Yes, and a straight stone fox.", he said then leaned forward to smack her on the butt, "But all jokes aside, I need to open up a little more to you about me and my childhood."

"Ricky, you can tell me anything. I'm here for you, just like you were for me.", informed Vittoria.

She removed the bacon from the skillet and the toast from the toaster. She fixed their plates and set them on the table. She sat next to him and waited attentively for his confession of sorts.

"You know we all have issues of our own.", said Ricky then paused as he reached for her hand. "Blood has fascinated me since I was a boy. My parents were scared to allow me to play with other children once I started cutting them. In my mind, I didn't cut them to hurt them; I just wanted to see what their blood looked like. My parents stopped letting me play with other children and my childhood became quite lonely until I met Bernard.", Ricky exposed his plagued youth.

"What changed their minds?", asked a curious Vittoria.

"They hadn't, but Mr. Barrington made a surprise visit and brought Bernard with him. My parents didn't want to admit why I couldn't play with him; that would have been too embarrassing, so they allowed us to go outside together. I was thrilled about it and was glad that I always kept a pocket knife on me.", Ricky explained.

"Oh my God. What happened after you cut Bernard?", asked Vittoria.

"I tried to cut him, but he told me if I did, he'd kill me.", laughed Ricky, "He's been my best friend and brother ever since. In fact, he took the knife and cut our hands so that we could be blood brothers. He's the yin to my yang, my main man. I love that dude."

Although she hadn't met Bernard, the story explained how an upstanding elite businessman like him could be best friends with Ricky. She figured that Bernard had to be just as fearless and ruthless in order to be friends with Ricky and from how Ricky spoke of him there seemed to be no one that Ricky respected more.

"When I became a young man, my father used that same bloodlust to his benefit and I acted as the family muscle. His men started calling me the Reaper and the name stuck. It's funny how

200

it was acceptable then.", Ricky expounded and looked at her expression to see if there was any recognition of his alter-ego.

"I already knew baby. I used to hear my father and uncle speak of the Reaper; so, I already knew about your past reputation. You are very similar to my father; he respected you and still does. Like you, he used to be the muscle for a mob family before he met my mother, but his brother never got out of the life.", Vittoria disclosed.

"If it hadn't been for my nonna, I probably would have allowed that dark desire to overtake me. Thanks to her, I learned how to control those urges and only give them life when needed. She centered me, much the same way you do, baby.", Ricky described the mental state of his formative years.

Vittoria reached for his other hand this time and raised it to her lips.

"Ricky, I completely trust you. You've successfully influenced and run your family's business; I believe you know what you're doing. So, you don't have to explain your actions to me; but I'm glad you trust me enough to do so. I'll stand by your side 100 percent.", Vittoria extended her support.

Ricky stood and picked her up then he showered her with kisses.

"God knows, I don't deserve you.", Ricky whispered in her ear then he carried her back to bed.

"Again?", laughed Vittoria.

"Yes, you know this cock don't stop!", laughed Ricky then threw open her robe to devour her nipple.

Chapter 10

Ricky, Angelo and Enzo had been up to their necks for weeks with ideas, trying to determine how to stop Canto; but nothing was clear cut. All he had was a file on Canto and his mother, but no plan. Ricky decided he would still visit Columbia even if he didn't have a plan to put in motion; often he got his best ideas while under pressure and this was adding up to be the same. In addition to that, Ricky still had another very important task that remained lingering undone. However, the Canto situation was the heavier of the two and he knew that he would need a getaway afterward. Bernard had been suggesting for months that Ricky join him and Vanessa at their cabin up north. Ricky had started thinking that perhaps that was a good idea after all; it would offer an opportunity for Vittoria to meet them. Ricky thought it was a good time to set things in motion so that Bernard would be able to plan things for his return.

"Hampton, Inc. How may I assist you?", asked Ester.

"Good morning, my love!", teased Ricky.

"Hello, Mr. Bianchi. How would your lady friend feel about you flirting with me?", Ester surprisingly reciprocated his flirtation.

"Oh, so loose lips Bernie told you?", joked Ricky then added playfully, "Just so you know, she is stunning and knows I don't give a damn about being with another woman."

"That's what I heard and yes of course Mr. Barrington told me. Congratulations on your engagement. He's so glad you are settling down. Plus, I hear and know everything you boys do.", informed a lighthearted Ester.

"I knew it. I knew you were nosy! Thanks for the confession.", laughed Ricky, "Is Bernard available?"

"For you? I guess. One moment.", teased Ester genuinely pleased by Ricky's news.

Ester placed Ricky on hold and buzzed Bernard's office.

"Mr. Barrington, Mr. Bianchi is on the line for you.", informed Ester.

"Go ahead and patch him through.", instructed Bernard, then his phone rang, "Hello, Ricky. What's shaking?", asked Bernard.

"Look at you trying to be cool.", laughed Ricky.

"Well, if I hang out with you long enough, you are bound to rub off on me.", laughed Bernard.

"You ain't lying.", laughed Ricky, "Look, I've been thinking about that cabin trip you've been wanting to plan. I think now is a good time. I'd like for you and the guys to get to know Vittoria.", provided Ricky.

"The guys? So, you want all three couples together?", inquired Bernard.

"It's four now. Angelo has a serious girl, finally.", added Ricky.

"You've got some nerve.", laughed Bernard at his friend's arrogance.

"I have to get in a dig or two with my cousin. You know me.", laughed Ricky.

"Yes, I do and yeah, you do.", chuckled Bernard, "Ok, I can set that up. When is a good time?"

Ricky became more serious, "Why don't you see if the fellas can make it this weekend? I have a quick international business trip I'm doing this week and I'll need to decompress afterward. You know what I mean?", informed Ricky.

"Definitely, I've been a jetsetter lately myself as I work on our joint business ventures and Hampton, Inc. business. It'll be nice to switch things up a bit. I'll schedule one of the maids to come and cook as well as tidy up for us.", concurred Bernard.

"Out of sight! That sounds good. We'll talk later. Arrivederci.", said Ricky.

Ricky quickly switched gears and grabbed his keys along with a folder. It was time to pay a visit to the commissioner so that he didn't think that Ricky had forgotten that he had spoken to his father out of turn. He knew that Boggs was a man of habit and always had a late breakfast at a coney island restaurant near his home; so, he planned to swing by to surprise the commissioner. There was no room in his business for looking weak or even being perceived as such. He waved at Bettie as he headed out.

"I'll be back.", informed Ricky never slowing down until he exited the building.

The young men that stood watch nodded at him as he passed. He remembered being like them just starting out in the game and he liked to encourage them when he could.

"Great job youngbloods! Keep it up!", expressed Ricky as he opened the car door and hopped inside.

Lorenzo could barely breathe; his face became red and Antonella rushed over to see what news could have possibly caused his reaction. She prayed that his sister hadn't called about their elderly mother; she didn't know if either of them would be able to keep it together if that were the case.

"Lorenzo, what's wrong?", asked Antonella as she rubbed his back.

"That was Tommaso's wife. She said the police found his naked dead body on the railroad tracks in Southwest Detroit. He was murdered...", cried Lorenzo.

"Oh my God.", whispered Antonella as she took her husband in her arms.

"The sick bastard cut off his fucking dick and shoved it in his mouth.", Lorenzo choked on his words and quickly dashed over to the trash can to vomit.

Unknowingly, Vittoria had entered the kitchen and had overheard and seen her parents' reaction. She immediately displayed a look of horror and shock as her mother noticed her presence.

"Vittoria, we didn't want you to find out like this. Oh my God.", cried Antonella as she walked to the doorway to comfort her child.

Antonella embraced Vittoria as she buried her face in her mother's shoulder. Antonella knew how much Tommaso meant to Vittoria as a child, she couldn't bear to look at her daughter's face at the moment; Vittoria's heartbreak would be too much for her to witness.

"We will get through this together, sweetie.", promised Antonella as she watched her husband rush past them.

"I got to get out of here. I need something else to think about; I'm off to the market!", said Lorenzo as he grabbed his keys to leave.

"We're going to be alright.", reassured Antonella as she kissed the crown of her daughter's head.

Vittoria had no words; anything that she might have said at that moment would be an obvious lie. So, the only thing she allowed herself to do was nod at her mother's words, but she couldn't stop her lips from smiling so she buried her head deeper in her mother's embrace.

Ricky drove to the little hole in the wall diner, where he found the commissioner sitting alone. As he entered the restaurant, he noticed Boggs stuffing his face with a slice of pie.

"An odd choice for breakfast.", said Ricky as he sat at the table across from the head of police.

"I thought I'd eat an early dessert.", said the commissioner trying not to choke on the sweet treat, "This is a surprise ...".

Boggs looked around and noticed the place was empty except for the waitress and the cook. He became very uncomfortable as Ricky had never talked to him outside of the funeral home or the Bianchi family home. The commissioner cleared his throat so that he could swallow the remaining remnants of pie in his mouth.

"Why the visit Ricky?", he asked nervously.

"Boggs, enough of this Ricky shit! It's Mr. Bianchi. I think you know why I am here. You had a misstep when you talked to my father instead of me.", informed Ricky as he waved the waitress over.

She quickly made her way to the table as she could see it was a very important meeting that required discretion.

"Yes, Hun. What can I get you?", asked the nervous waitress.

"I'll take a cup of black coffee. ", informed Ricky then he waited for the waitress to depart to continue, "I need two things from you, Boggs. One is for you to come down hard on any of Santana's men; even if you aren't sure, even if they *look* like they could be, you better go hard. You get my drift?", asked Ricky.

"Yes, Mr. Bianchi.", the commissioner said again needing to clear his throat, this time by drinking some coffee.

The waitress picked that time to quickly deliver a mug and poured the coffee for Ricky. She didn't know who he was, but it was obvious to her that he meant business and he was not the type to annoy as evident by the uneasiness of the commissioner.

"Thank you, my dear.", Ricky told the waitress as she scurried away, "Boggs, it will be very prudent for you not to forget who owns you. I'm the one that pays for that mansion in Palmer Woods not your chump police salary or my father.", Ricky informed Boggs coldly as he eyed him over the rim of his cup.

"Sir, okay; there won't be any need for a warning in the future. I swear to you.", reassured Boggs as he went into another mild coughing fit.

"Oh, I know, because this *is* your warning. Do it again, I'll make you regret it. I'll take your job away and everything you hold dear!", Ricky whispered the threat, "You have a horrible *tell*; anyone with half a brain can tell when you're nervous. You should work on that cough.", advised Ricky as he sipped more coffee while he leaned back in his seat with his legs crossed.

"I swear on the life of my wife and kids, I'll do whatever you tell me to do.", vowed Boggs.

"Oh, I'm counting on it. In fact, I have some insurance papers for your signature.", Ricky chuckled as he continued to explain what was funny, "These papers will ensure your compliance and they also insure the lives of you and your wife. Should you fail me, I'll have to call in your number and get paid as your beneficiary. Sign.", ordered Ricky as he pulled a pen from his breast pocket and offered it to Boggs.

Boggs signed the documents with shaking fingers as Ricky watched; Ricky kept a straight face, but inwardly he was laughing hysterically. Ricky amused himself more by adding another piece to the puzzle.

"I'll deduct the cost of these policies from your monthly stipend and place that money into an account established in your name. That money will be used to pay the insurance company. That's a good deal, don't you agree?", Ricky inquired as he sipped on his coffee.

Boggs simply nodded, he forgot that Ricky was a sadistic bastard; only Ricky could think of a way to make a person pay to screw themselves. He reluctantly slid the papers across the table to Ricky. Ricky smiled at the commissioner with an arrogant smirk as he placed the papers back in the folder. I bet you won't forget now motherfucker who runs this shit, thought Ricky, as he stood.

"Good day, commissioner.", Ricky said as he pushed the chair under the table. "Hun, add the coffee to his tab.", he instructed the waitress.

Ricky strutted to his car and decided to call Vittoria during the drive back to his office. He wanted to make sure she knew their weekend plans so that she could pack a few things. He called the meat market assuming that she had arrived there to start her workday; he'd be thankful when they married so she could quit.

"Rossi Meat Market, how may I help you?", answered Lorenzo.

"Hello, Mr. Rossi. How are you this beautiful morning?", asked Ricky excited that he had put Boggs in check.

"Not well. We got news this morning that my brother's body was found dumped in Southwest Detroit on the railroad tracks.", Lorenzo informed fighting back tears.

"Oh wow! I'm sorry to hear that. How is Vittoria handling this?", asked Ricky only concerned with Vittoria's reaction.

"I thought it best that she stayed home today. The sick bastard that killed my brother mutilated his body; the sick fuck cut off his cock and shoved it into his mouth. She overheard me telling her mother, but I'm not sure how much she heard. I couldn't stomach telling her the details. Please keep *that* to yourself; she's much too delicate to hear that.", pleaded Lorenzo.

"Of course, sir; I would never want to do anything that would offend her. I'll give her a call at home to check on her. If you need anything, just call me. In fact, please let me handle the funeral arrangements.", reassured Ricky.

"Thank you, Ricky; that would mean the world to me and my brother's widow, Isabella.", Lorenzo said then cried after disconnecting the call.

Ricky almost felt sorry for his soon-to-be father-in-law to have loved such a worthless piece of trash. Ricky quickly set those thoughts aside as he called Vittoria to make sure she was fine.

"Rossi residence.", answered Antonella.

"Hello, Mrs. Rossi. I just spoke to your husband and he told me what happened. I wanted to check on Vittoria.", informed Ricky.

"That's a good idea. She hasn't spoken about it not once all day. She must be in shock because she's been going about her day like normal. She even begged me to allow her to go to work and when I refused, she insisted on preparing dinner. She's prepping the ingredients now. Please speak to her. If anyone can get her to open up it's you.", pleaded Antonella.

"Of course, she owns my heart.", explained Ricky.

"Vittoria! Ricky is on the phone for you.", called Antonella to the kitchen.

Vittoria needed a distraction to help her get through the day and perhaps even the week. It was quite evident that her parents were going to worry and fret over her and she surely couldn't tell them that she was there when her uncle died. Perhaps Ricky has something planned, she thought.

"Hello, baby, how are you?", whispered Vittoria not wanting her mother to hear the joy in her voice.

"I'm fucking great. I've had a good morning. I set that prick Boggs straight and then I called the meat market to talk to the sexiest woman alive just to find out she was at home grieving.", joked Ricky.

"Shame on you trying to make me laugh.", whispered Vittoria, but she laughed anyway assuming her mother would be pleased that Ricky had lightened her mood.

"Vit, I need to take a trip to Columbia in a couple of days for business. When I come back, I figured we could do a weekend getaway; we could go up north to Bernard's cabin. All the guys and their gals could hang out and everyone can get to know you. How does that sound?", inquired Ricky.

"That sounds *exactly* like what I need right now. Should I pack anything special?", asked Vittoria.

"No, just the sexy stuff you normally wear.", laughed Ricky, "Although, it won't take much to make you the sexiest woman there."

"Stop! I can't imagine your friends being with ugly women! You are all too competitive for that if they are anything like you.", laughed Vittoria, "Look, I better get off. You have me laughing too much. I'm in mourning remember. Bye.", Vittoria whispered.

Vittoria disconnected abruptly when she noticed her mother returning to the kitchen.

"Looks like our Ricardo brought a smile to your face.", expressed Antonella.

"He always does; plus, he wants to take me up north this weekend with his friends and their gals. He thought it would be good for me to get away.", explained Vittoria.

"That's an excellent plan. We'll probably spend the weekend planning the funeral at your aunt's house and that might be too much for you.", sighed a relieved Antonella.

It had been years since Ricky traveled to South America and he was regretting having to go. The cartel was not a group that one wanted to meet with frequently and when it was necessary it was always due to a problem. Ricky studied the landscape outside the window as the plane lowered in preparation for the landing. It was at these times, that he was reminded of his power, reach and the amount of wealth his family had amassed. He brought Enzo and his deadliest crew with him; he truly wanted Angelo by his side, but he couldn't chance something happening to them both. One had to remain to control the family legacy; he didn't admit it often but Angelo had a good head on his shoulders and there was no one better to take over if Ricky could no longer hold the title.

Upon landing, Ricky saw their car and that of the guide who would lead them to the Diaz compound; Diaz was the most ruthless of all the cartels and he respected Ricky's father Carlo tremendously. Carlo and Diaz partied hard, back in the forties and made each other very wealthy men. Ricky had to see what had changed their agreement; perhaps he didn't know that his father, Carlo, had left things in very capable hands, thought Ricky.

It seemed that the ride to the compound was taking forever and it was hot as hell, thought Ricky. His men were sweating bullets and getting quite repugnant whereas Ricky remained as cool as ice. Enzo looked at his boss in amazement and thought Ricky truly was a cold bastard; the bulletproof vest was adding to the heat making Enzo feel scorched. Having Black heritage truly came in handy at those temperatures, laughed Ricky inwardly as his crew continued to stare at him in amazement.

The cars made their way up the drive to the impressive compound; the mansion sat on a hill and was hidden by trees. It was breathtaking even to Ricky; one couldn't help but be

211

impressed. The mansion was an architectural beauty built using the palest of sandstone; it was almost white. The massive two-story British Colonial home featured four fireplaces, a water fountain in the middle of the circular drive and iron fencing surrounding the home. There were cameras mounted at multiple points along the perimeter of the property with men visibly on guard and just as many hidden out of sight. Ricky assumed that the poor local peasants believed Diaz was truly a god. Who could touch him? Who had his wealth and power? No one did and Diaz, Ricky was sure, reminded them of that daily.

Ricky's most astute soldier exited the town car and scanned the scene before opening the door for Ricky. Ricky exited and stood tall and proud after he adjusted his suit jacket. As always, he was dressed to impress; he wanted Diaz to see that he was a modern man. Detroit was always on the cusp of the latest fashions before the world followed suit. He wore a double-breasted navy-blue pinstripe mod suit with a paisley shirt comprised of shades of blue with a white ascot and pocket square. A pair of patent-leather tuxedo slip-on shoes finished the look.

Ricky's men walked in front and behind him as a shield, they all wore bulletproof vests under their suits another reason his men were shocked that he was so comfortable without a drop of sweat. Diaz's men led Ricky and his crew inside the massive entrance to be greeted by Diaz.

"Is this Ricky? I remember when you were a teenage boy learning the business.", asked Diaz shocked that this man with model good looks was actually the Reaper.

"The one and only in the flesh.", laughed Ricky.

"Welcome to my home. Come this way.", Diaz guided Ricky and his crew to a sitting area.

The men entered the study; it was rich and masculine with cherrywood bookshelves and a fireplace with black tile surround and a cherrywood mantel that reached the ceiling. There was an authentic bear rug in front of the fireplace. As a complement to the look, there was an ornate desk of cherrywood with a matching chair; it was clearly not designed for comfort but for flare. There was an oversized plush brown leather sofa and two matching chairs that sat around the fireplace with another ornate piece of furniture, the coffee table. Everything in the room represented his wealth and sophistication.

Diaz motioned for Ricky and his men to sit. Ricky sat on the sofa and Enzo on one of the plush chairs, but the other three opted to remain standing.

"If you don't mind, my other men would prefer to stand.", responded Ricky.

Diaz shrugged his hand to acknowledge that he did not mind as he walked to his desk and opened a cigar box.

"Gentlemen, would you like a Cuban?", offered Diaz.

Ricky and Enzo reached for one as Diaz came to each with the offer and lit them; however, Ricky's standing soldiers declined. He sat on the sofa with Ricky and passed the box to one of his men.

"So, Ricardo, what brings you all this way?", asked Diaz as he puffed on the Cuban cigar.

"There is a gang that the Italian families have allowed to do business in Detroit, but their leader is smelling himself and he's found a way to purchase dope from your people directly.", explained Ricky.

"Really? That's a problem if he's been able to do that. Who is he?", inquired Diaz as his eyes bored into that of his men.

"His name is Canto Santana and I need to bring him back down to size.", Ricky said between puffs of the aromatic cigar.

"And you want me to cut off this deal? I definitely can do that out of respect for my old friend Carlo, but more importantly, I need to find out who has betrayed me. No one should think that they can make a deal behind my back!", declared Diaz then he paused, "However, I will require something of you first."

Ricky nodded in agreement, "What might that be? Keep in mind I've helped you by exposing a crack in the system.", said Ricky.

He then waited for Diaz to disclose what he wanted in exchange for the favor; but instead, Diaz began reminiscing by telling stories of old and the fun he shared with Carlo. Then he poured drinks for him and Ricky.

"As I get older, I think about the wild times I had as a young man. I need to feel that alive again. There was only one woman that made me feel that way and it wasn't my wife. God bless her soul.", Diaz said as he made the cross and kissed to heaven.

Ricky glanced at Diaz with a puzzled look as he continued discussing his past wild times; the new Ricky was so removed from that life. He no longer yearned for wild exploits; he desperately desired his fiancée and none of the perversions that used to drive his desires. He was glad when Diaz got back on track.

"Maria was insatiable; she brought my wildest fantasies to life. The memory of her haunts my mind nightly ever since she went to America. I missed the things she did to me and the pleasures I found in her body. I want you to find her.", Diaz explained as he walked to his desk to remove a picture of her. He tossed the picture to Ricky as he continued, "Her name is Maria Santos. You bring her to me and I will cut that greedy fuck off completely!"

Ricky looked at the picture and a devilish smile spread across his lips; he couldn't believe his luck. Ricky stood in shock at how easy it would be to deliver this one little thing to Diaz and there would be no more competition from Canto. Ricky burst into a loud wicked laugh that made the skin of his own men crawl with fear and uneasiness. Diaz's men looked at their leader with trepidation to take their cues from his response; however, they noticed that he was not fazed by Ricky's reaction.

"I take it we have a deal.", concluded Diaz to the Reaper who had revealed himself again.

"Yes, you can get ready to fuck.", added Ricky as he extended his hand to Diaz.

The two men shook hands on the deal and Diaz couldn't contain his excitement. He started laughing along with Ricky as he put his arm around him. Both sets of men were disgusted by the perverse excitement of their leaders.

Chapter 11

Ricky had developed a strategy on the plane ride home and had assigned tasks to Enzo. In the days following that trip, he informed Angelo what was expected of him. The weekend would be the cherry on top of a near-perfect week; he was thrilled that his meeting with Diaz had gone so well. Subsequently, he felt even more unstoppable and he couldn't wait to pick up Vittoria for their weekend getaway. However, he wasn't accustomed to driving long distances; the ride to the cabin in Roscommon, Michigan was almost a three-hour-long drive from Detroit. He was glad that Vittoria was still excited about driving, so maybe he could convince her to chip in; he simply didn't have the patience for it.

Antonella was so glad that Vittoria displayed so much excitement for her weekend getaway. Oddly, it was almost like her uncle hadn't been murdered, thought Antonella, but perhaps that was just Vittoria's way of coping. Lorenzo remained in shock; the only normal thing he had done since finding out, was to go to the meat market every morning.

Ricky knocked on the door for Vittoria; he had thought about calling from his car as he realized he would have to pretend to be sympathetic to the loss of a child pedophile. Antonella set her morning cup of coffee on the coffee table to answer the door. She knew Lorenzo wasn't up for it as he stared blankly at the newspaper.

"Good morning, Ricky.", Antonella greeted him as she motioned for him to enter.

"Good morning, Mrs. Rossi. I'm so sorry for your loss. Please don't hesitate to ask anything of me.", informed Ricky as he hugged Antonella.

216

"Thank you, Ricky. You are doing plenty by paying for the arrangements.", informed Antonella then she looked at her heartbroken husband.

"It's the least that I can do. Just so you know, the funeral home has the body prepared and dressed. All of the burial arrangements are made. Vittoria provided the name of the family cemetery. All that is left for you to do is to decide on the format of the program and what you want to say.", Ricky informed Antonella then he noticed the distraught look of his soon-to-be father-in-law.

Ricky swiftly walked to Lorenzo to give his condolences as Lorenzo stood to receive a hearty hug.

"I'm here for whatever you need, sir.", Ricky said.

Ricky's words were sincere as he realized that he had done exactly what Lorenzo would have done had he known of the perverse actions of his brother.

"Thank you, Ricky. I ... thank you.", Lorenzo said stumbling over his words as he attempted to speak through his grief.

From her room upstairs, Vittoria had heard her sweetheart enter and the muffled sounds of him talking as she gathered her bags. She rushed down to rescue him from what she assumed could only be an awkward moment. Had her parents known the truth, they would have been celebrating Tommaso's death and exalting Ricky as the hero that he was. Ricky heard Vittoria's footsteps coming down the stairs, so he stepped away from Lorenzo to assist her.

"Vit, allow me.", Ricky said as he reached for her bags and kissed her quickly on the lips.

"Thank you, baby. Well, Pappa and Mother, I might be gone a few days longer than originally planned. I might stay with Ricky for a few days into the week.", explained Vittoria.

She hadn't discussed it with Ricky, but as she packed, she realized that she was in no hurry to return to the house of mourning; she was sick of hearing how great her uncle was. She could no longer stomach that lie; she had heard it enough while she was being abused and during the times she was trying to recover from that abuse.

"I agree with Vittoria; I think it's best for her to stay with me during this difficult time.", explained Ricky.

"That's understandable. No one can comfort her, but you.", Lorenzo agreed as he sipped on his lukewarm coffee.

"Thank you again for everything, Ricky. You two have fun and have a safe drive.", encouraged Antonella.

Ricky held Vittoria's hand as they walked to the car; Antonella smiled at the two from the doorway. She didn't know what Vittoria would have done without him during that time. Now, it was time for her to tend to her husband; he was flustered and a shell of himself, she thought.

Ricky decided to drive his Lincoln Continental instead of the Corvette to make sure Vittoria was comfortable during the long ride, but he sure did miss seeing her in the convertible with her long hair blowing in the wind. He couldn't wait for his friends to get to know her and put their doubts aside. Once they saw her up close, he thought they would truly understand why he pursued her so aggressively; he pitied them that they didn't have a woman as sexy and desirable as she.

"A penny for your thoughts?", Vittoria teased.

"I was just feeling sorry for my dudes that they don't have a woman like you.", laughed Ricky.

"Stop, I keep telling you that can't be true.", laughed Vittoria, "Honestly, I'm looking forward to meeting the ladies. I've only had one female friend my entire life and it would be nice to know women who can relate to this new life I have now.", expressed Vittoria.

Vittoria realized she had outgrown Anna and the longer Anna remained her only friend she was bound to be more jealous of her new life. She realized that there were many things she would have to put behind her as she moved forward with this wonderful life that Ricky and she were creating. It was scary for her at times, but growth was always uncomfortable and she realized she would be the better for it.

The long drive to the cabin was refreshing, Vittoria had never been that far north. She knew wealthy folks loved going up north to their vacation properties, but she never knew anyone who actually owned a vacation home or even any land up north. Vittoria found the views breath-taking; to think she might secretly be a country girl at heart. She could tell that the ride was not refreshing for Ricky; he was getting tired, but his ego wouldn't let him ask for help.

"Sweetie, you seem a little tired? I can take over.", suggested Vittoria.

"I had planned to ask you, but the more I think about it I know my friends would rag me about letting you drive. I can't show up like that!", laughed Ricky.

Vittoria laughed at the idea of his friends teasing the powerful Ricky; she couldn't wait to see them banter back and forth.

"Oh, that's funny?", laughed Ricky, "You know I can dish it right back at them. We're almost there anyway. This is our turn, Barrington Lane.", informed Ricky as he turned on the narrow road.

Vittoria's eyes widen as they began their ride on the property; it was peaceful and majestic, the exact image of what one would think a country landscape would be. She noticed a small creek that ran alongside the road with beautiful white wildflowers along the water's edge. The closer they came to the property the road surface turned to gravel and she could see the cabin afar off, but it was not a small cabin, like the ones she had seen in childhood stories or on television. This cabin was designed in the mid-century style with an asymmetrical exterior design. She had never seen anything like it before. Ricky noticed her awestruck eyes and he loved showing her things and experiences she had never seen or done before.

"Maybe I can build us a retreat somewhere. Perhaps someplace warm like Miami or somewhere in California, how does that sound?", asked Ricky.

"You know that's not necessary. I'd be perfectly happy living with you in a small little shack...", Vittoria began to laugh.

"A shack? Really? Good to know, I can stop spending my greenbacks!", Ricky teased as he laughed with her.

"Well, no; I am starting to get used to fancier things if I'm being honest with myself. You have spoiled me. I can't go backward.", laughed Vittoria.

"I didn't think so.", laughed Ricky as he removed his eyes from the road quickly to kiss her cleavage.

Ricky pulled up the driveway alongside the other cars that were parked. As usual, he was the last one to arrive. He knew they always assumed he did it purposefully to be the star attraction, the man of the hour; but there always seemed to be something that required his attention at the last minute. Well, that was the story he was sticking to at least.

Vittoria noticed the fancy cars of his friends; they were indeed like Ricky; they liked the best and had the flashiest of tastes. She tried to guess which was owned by whom and would later ask Ricky to see if she was right. There was a brand new red 1970 Mercedes-Benz 280SL convertible owned by Raymond, but that would not be outdone by Angelo. He drove a hunter-green brand-new Jaguar XKE Series convertible. It appeared that Ricky was the only one who bought American and didn't come in a sports car; for which she was very thankful. The other men were more into showing off than the comfort of their women, but more than likely their wives were short, she thought. Ricky in true fashion assisted her from the car and grabbed their bags. As they walked closer to the front door, they passed the most expensive car of them all and she knew it had to belong to Bernard. It was a sparkling light grey 1970 Aston Martin DB6 MK2 Volante convertible.

Suddenly, she fidgeted with her purse; what if she wasn't good enough to be accepted by his friends. Surely, the wives of these rich men were elitist or snobby as well. She didn't attend the finest of schools and she had only graduated from high school; although Ricky hadn't graduated from college either, he had attended the best schools. Vittoria couldn't turn back, so she took several deep breaths much to Ricky's amusement. He put his arms around her for reassurance.

"Just relax and be you; you will enchant them just like you did me.", Ricky said lovingly as he whispered in her ear.

Bernard heard Ricky's car pull up the drive. They had started pouring drinks and snacking without the pair; they had looked forward to the weekend for too long to prolong it anymore. Bernard walked to the door with his drink in hand to greet his good friend. He opened the door as he took a sip of his drink and began choking on the liquor as he took in the beauty of Vittoria Rossi. As she stared at the vaulted ceilings, Bernard and everyone else in the room took in the truly stunning feature, Vittoria. She wore a striped boho pants set with what seemed to be her favorite colors of late, gold, burgundy and turquoise; the top was a strapless mid-drift tube top with a mock tied sash that brought every eye to her full cleavage. Her hair was in a high ponytail and she wore just a hint of lip gloss and mascara. She wore brown leather clogs that added to her tall frame; her statuesque stance commanded their attention.

221

Ricky sopped it up; the stares fueled his ego and he reveled in the praise their eyes bestowed upon her. However, as they stared at her, Vittoria stared at the beauty of the cabin; the great room had wooden planked ceilings made from bamboo. It was such a beautiful day and the sunlight beamed through the massive windows. She noticed the light bouncing from wall to wall, but Ricky and his friends only noticed how the light shined upon her showcasing her beauty. Bernard cleared his throat a few times before being able to utter a welcome to his late guests.

"It's about time we met you, Vittoria. I'm Bernard Barrington and this is my wife, Vanessa.", Bernard pointed haphazardly to the pretty brunette sitting on the sofa in the great room.

Vanessa waved from afar and then immediately began smoothing her hair and expensive Gucci blouse; she like Vittoria was feeling self-conscious. Ricky took over the introductions while Bernard closed the door behind them, still trying to clear his throat.

Ricky escorted Vittoria to the great room; he held her hand as they stepped down to the sunken area where everyone was sitting.

"Now that you've met my main man; these are the other cats you've heard me talking about. This is Raymond Brown and his wife, Eleanor.", Ricky introduced the couple.

Raymond nodded at Vittoria and before he could stand to speak, Eleanor cut him off as she spoke from her seat on the sofa.

"Hello, dear. I'm Eleanor Washington-Brown. It's nice to meet you. We ladies do as much together as our men. So, I do look forward to getting to know you.", Eleanor informed Vittoria who was surprised by her stiffness.

"Yes, it's nice to finally meet the woman who tamed our Ricky.", laughed Raymond as he stood to hug Vittoria under the watchful stare of his wife.

He instantly regretted the gesture as he awkwardly hugged her trying not to get close to her breasts, but all the while hoping that he would accidentally brush over them. Eleanor cleared her throat signaling to Raymond that he needed to sit down swiftly.

Ricky moved on to Angelo in hopes that he and his girlfriend's personalities would be more informal and friendlier as he noticed Vittoria's expressive eyes showing discomfort yet again.

"This is my cousin and good friend, Angelo Bianchi and his girlfriend, Martina.", announced Ricky.

"Welcome to the family, Vittoria.", Angelo greeted her warmly and gave her a hearty hug.

This time she didn't feel evil eyes boring into her; it felt genuine and even Martina seemed glad for a new significant other to be added to the mix. She was glad that she at least had one woman with whom she might be able to connect.

"Jewel!", Bernard called the maid to the great room.

"Yes, Mr. Barrington.", Jewel said after jogging from the kitchen.

"Please show Mr. Bianchi and his fiancée to their room. After that we can finally eat a meal and get this weekend started!", ordered Bernard.

"Yes of course. Right this way.", Jewel instructed the couple.

Ricky walked to the entrance to grab their bags and the pair followed the maid to one of the suites on the north side of the house. They passed by a unique wall of wooden blocks before walking through the kitchen to reach the other side. The wall consisted of different-sized wooden blocks that had been pieced together forming an artistic display of ingenuity. This vacation home was no cabin at all, to Vittoria it was a mansion and to think

Bernard considered this just a vacation home. Vittoria wonder just how grand his home must be.

Despite things getting off to a rocky start with the women, the group settled into a fun evening. Everyone sat around the great room as they shared a jovial time. There were plenty of jokes, laughter, good food and drinks to go around. The couples were spread over the expansive U-shaped leather sectional in front of the fireplace; it could seat twelve easily. Ricky noticed that Bernard was partaking of the alcohol a little too much.

"Bernard, maybe you should lay off the sauce.", laughed Ricky making light of a serious request.

"Don't stop him. He's getting geared up for tonight. He can't let you guys be the only ones getting your kicks off later. Bernard only touches me if he's high or drunk.", explained an exacerbated Vanessa as she sipped her wine.

"Give me a fucking break! You're making it sound like I'm a dope fiend! Jesus!", barked a tipsy Bernard.

Vittoria was immediately shocked and concerned by Vanessa's confession. She looked to Ricky for some clarification; surely Bernard wasn't a dope head. Ricky deepened his embrace around Vittoria and leaned toward her ear.

"It's a long story. I'll tell you later.", Ricky whispered.

"For fuck's sake, we know you don't use that shit! Relax, this is supposed to be a fun gathering.", insisted Raymond.

Raymond was not interested in hearing a drunk Bernard and Vanessa fight over nothing; he wished they would leave the past in the past and just try to be happy in the bed they had made for themselves. Otherwise, what was the point in even marrying, he thought. Ricky felt the same and any more arguing would be a complete buzz kill. Perhaps it was time for the couples to depart to their rooms and get their own private parties started.

"Maybe, we should call it a night and retire to our rooms.", suggested Ricky.

"Good idea. Fellas don't forget we're getting up early to go hunting.", Bernard reminded the group.

"It's not hunting season though.", Angelo commented.

"I don't give a fuck. I own this land.", said a drunk Bernard.

"Great.", Ricky said sarcastically.

Raymond and Angelo laughed; they knew how much Ricky hated hunting wild game. After everyone voiced their agreement, they headed to their respective bedrooms leaving a mess behind for Jewel to clean up. Vittoria had assumed that Bernard had a loving marriage, especially in light of Ricky's love and respect for him. She was utterly confused by the exchange between Bernard and Vanessa. Once she and Ricky entered their suite she looked to Ricky for an explanation.

"So, what's the deal with Bernard and Vanessa?", asked Vittoria as she took down her hair in preparation for bed.

"You want me to focus on their foolishness while I have the sexiest woman alive getting even sexier for me.", remarked Ricky as he watched Vittoria take out lingerie.

"Yes.", laughed Vittoria, "I need to know what's going on."

"Well, Bernard had experimented with a drug the night they met and had sex for the first time. He's never touched that shit again. He was under a lot of stress and pressure during that time. That's it, but now he still drinks a little too much after going through that shit.", explained Ricky.

He hoped that explanation was enough for Vittoria; he hated discussing the most painful time in his best friend's life. He wanted to change their focus to a more pleasurable pastime. He motioned over to Vittoria who was standing in front of the dresser eyeing her lingerie. He stood behind her and began kissing her shoulders.

"I don't think you'll need this little number.", he whispered as his lips moved up her neck to her ear.

"No?", teased Vittoria as she slipped her tube top over her shoulders revealing her breasts.

He slipped it over her head and she stood boldly as she smiled at their reflection. Ricky began cupping her breasts in his hands and she leaned her head back to rest on his shoulder as his lips explored trying desperately to inch closer to her soft bounty. His kisses made her skin feel alive and she giggled at his touch.

"I don't want them to hear us.", Vittoria giggled as she turned to face her lover.

She knew the only way that would be possible was if he didn't touch her and there was no way she could be in his presence without either of them touching the other.

"The only way that's possible is if I'm on a ventilator because if this cock won't work, I have these lips.", laughed Ricky as he picked her up and carried her to the bed.

The cabin hadn't seen that much laughter and life since its construction was completed five years prior. Each couple ended the night on a positive note and was energized for a full day of fun. Bernard planned a hunting excursion for the men and left it up to the ladies to do whatever they would decide to do. Ricky was not used to getting up early and he was even less excited about going hunting. However, he resolved to put a pep in his step; he couldn't let his boys see him off his game. He'd let Raymond be cranky enough for all of them.

Jewel had the breakfast laid out for the men; that was one highlight of the morning. The smell of the delicious breakfast enticed the men to enter the kitchen and they were all too eager to bring their large appetites with them. Ricky strutted inside the kitchen and saw the guys sitting and standing around the island.

"Bright-eyed and bushy-tailed. Well, we know at least one man that got some last night.", laughed Angelo.

"You *heard* her!", affirmed Ricky with a smirk as he continued strutting toward the island., "I guess I was the only one."

"A true lady doesn't make noise.", admonished Raymond to the laughter of his friends.

"If she's being *fucked*, she does!", laughed Ricky, "I don't know what you call what you do, but I *fuck*!"

The guys laughed uncontrollably and even Jewel giggled as she quickly excused herself from the men so that she could laugh freely. Raymond wasn't going to let Ricky get the last word.

"You always act like your dick is so big and brag that the ladies love Italians.", Raymond snapped as he slammed the banana on the island.

"You're a little touchy aren't you. Fellas, you know what that means.", laughed Ricky as he egged on the guys to join in the laughter.

"Shit, it doesn't mean that!", barked Raymond as Ricky continued teasing.

"Hell, I'm six-foot-five, it just oughta be!", laughed Ricky as he stacked up the evidence.

"Six-foot-four. See, Niggas always be adding inches!", Raymond corrected Ricky.

"I can't help you are five-seven.", laughed Ricky.

Bernard and Angelo could barely eat or drink without stopping to laugh.

"Motherfucker, you know I'm five-ten.", corrected Raymond.

"Really? What did you say about adding inches?", teased Ricky thinking that perhaps he had pushed Raymond too far, but still loving every minute.

"I got a big dick. I'm tired of the fucking jokes.", insisted Raymond as he stood and started unbuckling his belt.

Bernard and Angelo choked on their food laughing. Angelo protested the loudest and tried to pull at Raymond's hands to stop him as Ricky sat watching. Raymond stopped and then noticed that Ricky was staring at him expectingly and not even Bernard tried to stop him.

"See I thought you and Bernard were on some freaky shit! This is the second time you've tried to see my junk!", Raymond accused as his eyes went from Ricky to Bernard.

"Don't pull me into that lie!", warned Bernard as he shook his head in denial.

"Correction, that's the second time you tried to show me your junk. So hell, I was waiting.", explained Ricky as he sipped his coffee.

"What the fuck? No.", laughed Raymond, "Don't deflect by lying. Let's talk about you and Bernard; you two have known each other since childhood. It's no telling what type of shit, y'all have done.", fumed Raymond as he fixed his clothing.

"Why are you trying to pull me into this shit? I don't fuck men or play with dicks. Let's get that crystal clear.", clarified Bernard as he ate his toast.

"And if I have one in my hand, it's because I'm about to cut that motherfucker off.", laughed Ricky.

There was so much laughter they could barely hear each one banter back and forth.

"It's a little too much bravado for me. What do you think, Raymond?", laughed Angelo as he and Raymond gave each other five.

"You see what I'm saying.", Raymond said to Angelo acknowledging that they were on the same wavelength.

"As for me, I breathe, live, eat and sleep in pussy!", laughed Angelo as he high-fived Raymond with that statement.

"Real quiet pussy; it don't even purr.", laughed Ricky, "Bernard, did you hear Martina last night?"

"Not at all and I for sure didn't hear Eleanor Washington-Brown!", chuckled Bernard as he threw a banana at Raymond.

"Motherfuckers!", laughed Raymond as he broke the banana in half and threw the pieces at Bernard and Ricky.

The laughter of the men awakened Vittoria; she wished she had been able to hear what they found so amusing. She knew that Ricky had to be the center of it all. Normally, she didn't have any problem rising early, but any time she spent the night with Ricky, he completely drained her. She barely had the energy to shower and dress; a night with him was a serious workout.

The delicious aroma of frying bacon floated to her bedroom suite; she was surprised that the maid was preparing more food. She had just assumed that she and the ladies would be eating a lukewarm meal, but she had to remember the rich did things differently. Vittoria thought she would wear one of her more conservative outfits that day; then she realized that Eleanor Washington-Brown would think anything she wore was *unbecoming*, she thought with a smirk. After showering, she slipped on her white wide-legged satin palazzo pants and a matching satin blouse with ruffles at the wrist. The blouse had a mid-square collar with an unusual V-dipped neckline with a cinched waist with ruffles. Vittoria looked at her appearance in the mirror and there was sexy Vittoria again revealing cleavage.

"Too bad, Eleanor. I enjoy my new sexy image.", she whispered to her reflection.

Afterward, she searched for a necklace to accentuate her cleavage even more. She pulled a few gold-tone necklaces to layer and gathered her hair up in a messy bun so that her fish-hook earrings would show. She decided she would keep on the white-furred high-heeled mules she had worn with her lingerie. She wondered what the other ladies would be wearing; they just like her were determined to impress.

Eleanor had been first to arrive and she sipped coffee at the breakfast table while Vittoria and the other ladies entered the kitchen one after the other. She wore a beige linen pantsuit with an orange silk V-neck camisole; additionally, she donned a beautiful and bold necklace of large genuine pearls with matching stud earrings. She let her hair down a little; so, to speak instead of wearing a tight bun, she wore her hair down allowing her long black loose curls to cascade over her shoulders to her back. She looked the part of the refined lady of breeding and culture that she claimed to be.

"Good morning, ladies.", Eleanor greeted everyone as if she were the hostess of the home.

Vanessa pranced in the kitchen wearing a one-shoulder asymmetrical cobalt-blue dress with a peacock surrounded by flowers. It had a choker collar with a flared sleeve; the hem of the dress and sleeve were trimmed in four straight lines of color. The colors were gold, red, green and white. She looked quite stunning; she too wore her hair in a messy bun with oversized hoop earrings and on the bare arm she wore the matching bangle bracelet. She polished off the look with a pair of flesh-tone lace heels with the straps wrapped to her mid-calf.

"Good morning!", Vanessa greeted everyone pleased that she received the unofficial notice to try to outdress everyone else.

"Good morning, girls! The food smells delicious and I am starved after last night.", announced Vittoria as she walked to the island to fix her plate.

Her remarks were met by a raised eyebrow and frown from Eleanor and a laugh from Vanessa.

"Yes, same here. I barely felt like getting out of bed. Thank God for alcohol; otherwise, I'd be sexually frustrated.", laughed Vanessa.

Jewel listened intently as she washed some of the dishes, hoping to actually hear what happened last night; it would be funny to find out which one of them was lying or had embellished their story. Just as Vanessa was about to delve into her tale, Martina entered.

"Hey ladies!", Martina greeted the well-dressed women.

She too was thankful that she had planned well for the trip; she had gone shopping the week prior and bought a few things. She wore a conservative mini-Go-Go dress if such a thing existed; it had cuffed long-sleeves with a patchwork design of patterns of orange, black, red, white and mint green with a sash on the choker collar. The look would not be complete without her knee-high white front-zipper leather Go-Go boots. Topping the look, Martina wore her hair in a simple ponytail and allowed her dress to do the talking. Eleanor took notice and didn't like what it was saying.

"Oh my …", Eleanor said quietly then sipped on her coffee.

Raymond had warned her to be nice, but the ladies were making it quite difficult from the looks of things, she thought.

"Jewel, thank you for the breakfast. Everything looks and smells wonderful.", Vittoria complimented the hard worker.

"Thank you, ma'am.", beamed Jewel.

"And ladies, you all look so stunning and refined.", Vittoria complimented her new acquaintances.

She figured Ricky had been exaggerating about their lack of looks and it turns out he had. What Ricky couldn't exaggerate was how miserable he was on hunting trips. He was awkward in the stiff and scratchy camouflage gear and his feet were getting hot in the boots, but his friends appeared to love it. Also, it was difficult for him to sit quietly, he was used to joking and laughing whenever he was with the guys; he was becoming quite restless, especially since he didn't carry a rifle with him.

"I don't know how you three aren't bored out of your minds.", Ricky brooded as he looked around at the foliage.

"This is a time to become one with nature and get in touch with your inner self.", Bernard philosophized.

"That sounds like new age mumbo jumbo to me.", laughed Raymond in a whisper.

Angelo and Ricky laughed in agreement. Angelo lost focus quickly as he began swatting flies away.

"Exactly! I know you need this to make you feel like real men, but I don't. I only get off killing evil bastards. I'll leave Bambi to you guys.", laughed Ricky.

The men laughed at Ricky's comments knowing full well that he was serious about every word.

"Well, the rest of us are not able to walk freely outside the realm of law and order. So, this is all we've got!", laughed Raymond.

He wished he had the power and muscle backing him as Ricky did; he would have killed many men if he had. Bernard released a shot, but missed and blamed the men that their laughter had frightened the deer. However, Ricky reassured Bernard that was all him and his bad rifleman ship.

Vittoria glanced at Eleanor and Vanessa; she could see how Elanor had won Raymond's heart so many years ago. As for Vanessa, she seemed like a new person that morning; it's amazing what a little sex can do for a woman, thought Vittoria.

"Vanessa, it's good to see you so happy this morning. I was starting to wonder if maybe you and Bernard were headed for a divorce.", confessed Vittoria.

Eleanor and Vanessa started laughing at the remark while Martina and Vittoria stared at each other wondering what could possibly be funny about an unhappy marriage.

"Please forgive me, if I overstepped my boundaries.", pleaded a confused Vittoria.

"No dear that's not it at all. Divorce in our circle would be the kiss of death. It can be very complicated with dividing assets; besides, it's quite unbecoming.", explained Eleanor.

"I don't give a damn about our circle; I just refuse to give him that satisfaction. I'd much prefer that he's miserable versus me. I can't give up my shopping trips to Paris and Italy.", laughed Vanessa.

"Oh, yes, we had so much fun on our last trip. With Ricky's wealth, I'm sure you will start going with us, Vittoria.", Eleanor informed as she fixed a modest plate of food.

"You might not know this, but Ricky is almost as rich as my husband. I'm not sure about Angelo.", Vanessa stated looking sympathetically at Martina.

"Well one thing you said is true, the Bianchis are very rich. Before coming to America, they ran the Italian mob and they still do. In fact, Angelo's father is the Don and Angelo is slated to take over soon if he doesn't take over for Ricky when he decides to focus solely on his legitimate businesses.", Martina defended her boyfriend.

"Well, I guess since he has divulged all of that information, we'll hear about another engagement soon. Speaking of marriage. Vittoria, will you and Ricky build a new home once you are married?", asked Eleanor attempting to change the subject fast.

"No, we haven't discussed it.", replied Vittoria.

"Raymond and I hired an architect to design a new home for us. We purchased a few acres in Franklin and plan to build there.", informed Eleanor.

"Really? Bernard would never move out of the family home. So, instead, we are going to buy a home in Miami to get away during the cold winter months. I can't wait to be in the middle of the party scene there.", explained Vanessa not to be outdone by Eleanor.

"Oh, wow! That's exciting. I'm just so glad to be with Angelo; I haven't given any thought to where we would live.", Martina provided her feelings on the matter.

"Same here. Like I told Ricky yesterday, I'd be happy living in a shack as long as I'm with him.", smiled Vittoria as she fixed another plate of food.

The women were surprised by her appetite and boldness concerning it. Martina decided she would follow suit; she had practically starved herself yesterday trying not to look greedy in front of Eleanor and Vanessa who obviously had smaller appetites.

"May God forbid! Raymond knows better; the day that happens is the day I would leave him. The circle be damned! I come from money; my family has been wealthy as long as the Barringtons. My parents only allowed someone like Raymond, being very dark, to marry me because he's Harvard educated and well connected to the Barrington family. Otherwise, he would have needed to pass the brown paper bag test. As you can see there isn't much of a difference between the four of us.", announced Eleanor as she tossed her long silky hair.

Jewel had heard enough; she had wanted to hear their gossip, but as a black woman, she had no time to hear an uppity high-yellow, damn near white black woman flaunt her paleness and talk about paper bags. She tossed her dishcloth on the counter and left the kitchen.

"Ladies, I have a great idea; we should cook for the guys.", beamed Vittoria thinking she had come up with a great gesture.

Vanessa laughed as she shook her head in disapproval while Eleanor looked insulted.

"Oh no, dear. I'll leave that up to the maid. I don't know the first thing about cooking.", Eleanor said as if cooking were a despicable act.

"And I purposefully forgot what little I knew about it.", giggled Vanessa as she sliced an apple.

"I'm an excellent cook.", added Martina.

"Me too.", smiled Vittoria, glad they had something else in common.

"Darlings, you probably had to be.", chuckled Eleanor as she poured another cup of coffee.

Vittoria ignored the slight dig and chalked it up as something to which she would have to get accustomed.

"Eleanor and Vanessa, you can be our sous chefs.", suggested Vittoria as Martina nodded in agreement.

"Dear, I will *never* be the help! Moving on.", Eleanor dismissed the entire idea.

The door to the cabin flung open and the men roared in with laughter as they returned from the hunt.

"Thank God the men have returned. We don't have to listen to talk about ingredients and measurements.", sighed Vanessa as she glanced at Eleanor.

The men continued their laughter into the kitchen and immediately stopped on a dime behind Raymond as he stumbled in his tracks. He was flabbergasted when he spotted his wife; she hadn't worn her hair down in years. He thought she looked amazing; after bringing everyone to a standstill, he rushed to Eleanor's side and began kissing her. She began playfully pushing him away not being used to public displays of affection.

"Stop Raymond, you smell like the outdoors. Go shower.", Eleanor fussed as she playfully pushed him away.

Raymond obediently left to shower and dress for the day. The other three guys greeted their ladies as well with playful kisses without protestation. Even Bernard and Vanessa shared a passionate kiss. Eleanor attempted to exit the kitchen while everyone seemed distracted, but Ricky noticed her leaving.

"Where are you going, Eleanor?", questioned a curious Ricky.

"Excuse me, I need to check on Raymond.", Eleanor provided reticently as she scurried away to her bedroom.

"Yeah, Raymond! Cat daddy!", Ricky cupped his mouth as he shouted and he high-fived his boys.

"Right on, Eleanor Washington-Brown!", laughed Martina, right before Angelo picked her up and jogged to their bedroom.

The cabin rumbled with laughter from the couples; it was the start of a great day and the rest of the weekend ended on the same note. Ricky was thrilled that Vittoria was enjoying herself and felt comfortable with the ladies. He knew Eleanor was a handful, but he was confident that Vittoria had handled her own with her. He anticipated many more outings like that one and couldn't wait for Vittoria to have happy news of wedding plans; it was high time that they had that discussion.

Chapter 12

Vittoria was relieved that the weekend getaway was surprisingly very festive, but she knew that the environment at her home was the polar opposite. Subsequently, the best choice she could have made was to stay with Ricky following their return. She could imagine numbness in her father's eyes and her mother doing everything within reason to snap him out of his grief. It would have been too much; all the while she wanted to leap for joy that the evil bastard was dead. She had barely slept during the night and when she did, she dreamt she was at the funeral and in the midst of everyone's tears, she was laughing and celebrating. After lying in bed for hours trying to force sleep; she finally resolved that there was no way she could bring herself to attend the funeral and pretend to grieve. She turned over to face Ricky expecting to find him asleep, but instead, he was propped up quietly watching her assuming she was also.

"Good morning, darling. Sleep well?", he asked then kissed her on the forehead.

"Far from it. I've tossed and turned all night.", Vittoria said as she reached for his chest.

"You look worried. What's wrong baby?", asked Ricky as he pulled her in his arms.

"I do *not* want to attend the funeral. I can't fake it.", Vittoria sighed as she buried her face in his chest.

"I understand. I'll have the maid call your folks and explained that you are too distraught to attend.", suggested Ricky with a smirk.

"Oh, thanks. So, we'll have the help lie for us.", teased Vittoria.

"Yes, that's one perk of being rich; it's easy to pay others to lie for you.", laughed Ricky as he rolled on top of her.

Ricky kissed Vittoria's neck then he reached over to press the intercom button on the nightstand along the bed.

"Sally.", called Ricky.

"I'm the only one available, sir. How may I help?", informed Nicolas.

"Please call Vittoria's parents and tell them she is too overwhelmed to attend the funeral.", instructed Ricky as he kissed Vittoria on the neck.

His kisses were too light and they felt like feathers running over her skin, before she knew it, she giggled loudly. She quickly covered her lips like a schoolgirl caught laughing while playing hide-and-go-seek.

"I thought I heard the young miss laughing.", Nicolas pointed out.

"No, that was the television.", Ricky lied to his confidant as he grinned.

Nicolas always knew when Ricky was lying, but he'd play the game along with him.

"I'll get on it right away.", Nicolas promised.

"Thanks, Nick.", Ricky said quickly before Nicolas heard his own laughter.

He was unable to hold back his laughter as he rolled to his back.

"You are so naughty.", teased Vittoria as she ran her fingers down his torso until she reached his penis.

"Now, who's being naughty.", Ricky smiled as he tossed the covers off them.

The Rossi family packed the Bianchi's funeral home; her loved ones were still shocked and perturbed by the events surrounding her uncle's death. No one questioned Vittoria's absence as they knew how close she had been to him growing up. Family members shared their condolences with her parents and they hugged all who came to share in the memory and love of her uncle. As the attendants closed the casket, the waling of the women was deafening bringing the men to tears; all the while, Vittoria moaned in the throes of passion as Ricky savored the sweet flavor of her treasured jewel.

Every time he performed oral sex on her, she was amazed by how much she enjoyed it. Each flicker of his tongue brought her to greater heights of delight and her voice to a higher octave of pleasure. She felt sneaky and found pleasure in her deception. She wondered if Ricky often felt that high when he sealed a deal or got vengeance on his enemy; then she remembered the night he killed her uncle and the satisfaction they both shared.

Her body shook as her arch concaved toward him as he buried his face in her vagina and she squeezed her thighs tightly locking his head in place. Ricky knew she was close to her orgasm and it fueled his insatiable desire for her; he needed to hear her cry out from the core of her essence. He decided that she wouldn't be the only one to orgasm as he stroked his stiff penis while his tongue toyed with her clitoris. He intensified his pursuit of her pleasure; he shook his head swiftly so his tongue dragged back and forth across her clitoris and tugged it until she arched backward and released a wail that echoed through the halls causing him to release a deep animalistic moan from his diaphragm.

Bianca and Carlo were drinking their second cup of coffee when she heard Vittoria's cries. Her hand nervously held the cup and her hand trembled almost spilling its contents.

"Carlo, I should check on the poor thing.", Bianca said concerned about the unbearable grief Vittoria must have felt.

"Bianca, sweetheart, you don't recognize that sound?', Carlo laughed at his wife.

She looked puzzled and genuinely concerned for the young woman. He then realized that Ricky hadn't confided in her and she was completely in the dark.

"What? She's grieving …", Bianca started to express her confusion.

"They are making love, dear.", explained Carlo.

"Instead of going to the funeral?", questioned a confounded Bianca.

"Yes, Ricky told me that Tommaso molested Vittoria for years during her youth. So, he handled it.", explained Carlo matter-of-factly as he sipped his coffee.

"Oh, my …", Bianca whispered.

She had experienced firsthand that the love showered from a Bianchi man upon his woman was fierce and protective. It was no doubt that her son was the most vicious of all Bianchi men, so that was that, she thought as she sipped her coffee.

It was Vittoria's first week back home and in the market since her weekend getaway and stay with Ricky; she had been gone more than a week. She was glad to see that her father had the closure he needed and he seemed to be slowly bouncing back to his old self. Despite that, she wanted to pitch in any extra help she could; so, she arrived early and stayed late since she and Ricky didn't have any plans. She had explained to him that she needed to be present for her parents a little bit more, but they talked multiple times during the day which served as a good break and distraction.

She heard the market phone ring again while she was in the back storeroom taking inventory. Then she soon heard her father's footsteps approaching the room, so she knew it had to be Ricky.

"Our boy, Ricky, wants to speak to you. Don't let him keep you too long so you can finish up. I don't want you dragging that task into the weekend. You need to be free in case he has plans for you two.", instructed Lorenzo.

"Yes, Pappa.", Vittoria said obediently.

She kissed him on the cheek and ran to the front to speak to Ricky.

"Hey there, handsome!", Vittoria flirted.

"What's got you so out of breath? That's *my* job.", Ricky teased as he crossed his legs and leaned back in his leather office chair.

"Oh, I just ran to the phone.", laughed Vittoria.

"That better be all. You better run to me this weekend and jump on this cock!", whispered Ricky with a seductive smile.

"You are so nasty.", she whispered hoping her father didn't hear.

Her imagination kicked in as did her arousal at the thought.

"You know you like it, girl.", Ricky teased before he decided to become a little more serious, "I think it's time to set you up with a wedding planner. It won't plan itself.", suggested Ricky.

"Yeah, you're right. When would you like to get married?", inquired Vittoria.

"The day I met you!", chuckled Ricky, "Seriously, I figured a couple of months is enough time to prepare."

"It will be … for some reason, I hadn't given an actual date and planning much thought …", Vittoria professed.

"It's all copacetic. That's what the planner is for. I was thinking she could meet with you at your folks' house tomorrow. It'll give them something happy to focus on. How's 2 pm; is that cool? You can jump on this cock another day.", Ricky teased as he made the suggestion.

"I think that's a wonderful idea and jumping on your cock is not bad either.", laughed Vittoria.

Ricky laughed with her; he didn't know if he was laughing more at her joke or he was just so eager to be her guy. Either reason didn't matter, she brought happiness and peace to his world; even with threats all around him thinking of her steadied his mind. Suddenly, Vittoria stopped laughing; she felt it was necessary, to be honest about her feelings. She didn't ever want there to be secrets between them.

"Ricky, I'm so ready to move forward with the wedding, but whenever I think about actually making plans, I get nervous.", confessed Vittoria.

"Why, baby?", questioned Ricky hoping she was not headed back to the days of taking flight.

"I get scared that it won't happen because I want it so badly.", Vittoria whispered so scared that if she gave voice to it, it would happen.

"I swear to you, *nothing* will keep us apart. I'm ready to make you my wife and put a little Bianchi in that oven.", laughed Ricky.

Vittoria noticed that her father had approached and was eavesdropping as he often did when Ricky called. She covered her mouth and the receiver to whisper her goodbyes.

"I want that more than anything too. I gotta go, love you.", affirmed Vittoria before quickly disconnecting the call.

"Is everything okay?", pried Lorenzo.

"Everything is wonderful. Ricky is scheduling the wedding planner to meet at our house tomorrow at 2 pm. He thought it would be good to have you and mother involved.", beamed Vittoria as she eyed her engagement ring.

"Wonderful! I was hoping you'd get the planning started soon. He had mentioned to me and your mother that he didn't want a long engagement. This is exactly what we need now; especially your mother. I know it's been tough on her looking after me.", Lorenzo sighed happily.

"Pappa, I'm sure you weren't a burden at all. Mother loves you so much.", reassured Vittoria.

Lorenzo had no doubt that Antonella loved him, but he knew that he had been a handful. He was glad to see that some things were still going right for the family. He was overjoyed that Vittoria had stopped being her own worst enemy and hadn't botched things up. He truly had come to love Ricky like the son he didn't have and Ricky's thoughtfulness was one of the reasons why he had grown so fond of him.

The clock on the wall indicated one fifty-five in the afternoon, Antonella's eyes had gone from the wall clock to her wristwatch all Saturday morning until even then. She paced the living room floor like she was an expectant grandmother; she seemed more anxious and excited than everyone else, even the bride-to-be.

"Mother, please stop; you are starting to make me nervous.", Vittoria pleaded for her mother to sit down as she tapped the sofa cushion.

"You are going to make yourself be in a tizzy if you keep it up. Sit down!", Lorenzo ordered his nervous wife.

As soon as Antonella sat down, they heard not one, but two car doors close. She immediately tried to jump up, but Lorenzo gently pushed her back.

"I'll take a look.". informed Lorenzo as he walked to the screen door. "There are two ladies.", stated a confused Lorenzo.

The ladies walked up the stairs to greet Lorenzo; they both looked like cover-girl models instead of working professionals. Leave it to Ricky to hire the sexiest women in the industry, thought Lorenzo as he opened the door.

"Hello, ladies. Welcome. I'm Mr. Rossi, Vittoria's father and this is my wife, Antonella.", Lorenzo provided an introduction as he pointed to each one respectively.

"Nice to meet you all, I'm Samantha Langston. Vittoria, I'll be your wedding planner. And this Is Gigi, your bridal gown designer.", announced Samantha.

"Please sit, ladies.", Lorenzo insisted as he pointed to the sofa.

Vittoria and Antonella's thoughts were right in the gutter where Lorenzo had been; they wanted to know their connection to Ricky. Vittoria hadn't really been jealous since she and Ricky were an item, but now she wondered how did Ricky know these two beauties. Before Vittoria could even think to ask, Antonella had to get the facts.

"Ladies, how long have you known Ricky?", Antonella bluntly asked.

Lorenzo glared at his wife for being so forward; he thought she knew how to be sneakier than that. Samantha laughed at the question as she knew his reputation.

"Oh dears, I have known that silly man since he was a teen. I've worked with his mother and aunts to plan numerous parties, fundraisers and weddings.", reassured Samantha.

"And I am his mother's personal seamstress and designer. She only wears customed pieces to major events. I'm not as old as Samantha so he was not a boy when I first started making dresses for his mother.", laughed Gigi.

"She's lucky that we are best friends; otherwise, I wouldn't let that slide.", laughed Samantha.

The ladies saw the relief in the eyes of the family. Samantha was very surprised that his intriguing fiancée would have any doubts or jealousy.

"This will be a very special wedding in the community. No one ever thought Ricky would find a woman who could capture his heart; but here you are, a truly uniquely beautiful and captivating woman. Now, let's talk weddings. How grand do you want it?", Samantha advised guiding them to the important job at hand.

"We want it like a fairy-tale or a dream …", Antonella spouted her fantasy.

"No, *I* want it elegant yet small. I only need people there who truly love me and Ricky. I'm not trying to make headlines in the socialite magazines.", Vittoria corrected.

"Wonderful, so let's get to it. I need to know your likes and dislikes. I am so excited.", shrieked Samantha as she and Gigi bounced and giggled on the sofa.

Vittoria started out a nervous wreck that Saturday morning, but after meeting with the ladies she felt very confident in their ability to create the perfect wedding day for her and Ricky. With a successful meeting behind her, she could catch up on some things she had been putting off. Anna had been asking to hang out with her, so Vittoria reluctantly agreed and promised to go shopping. It would be a nice way to spend a Sunday afternoon. She realized it was likely to be their last time together; it was bittersweet, but for the best. Anna suggested that Vittoria meet her at the store as she would be leaving a new lover's home. Vittoria was so thankful that she didn't feel compelled to jump from bed to bed; Ricky satisfied all of her desires.

Miquel had been searching and digging around for weeks to discover who Ricky was dating. He was surprised that Ricky was more private than he would have assumed and didn't flaunt his lady all around town. Subsequently, Miguel had to make more inquiries than expected, but he had successfully found a name. He had been casing out her place for over a week now and had noticed her pattern. He decided that this task was too important to leave up to anyone, but himself.

Miquel trailed the sporty car to the downtown shopping district. He noticed that she parked off the beaten path on a side street; so, he followed suit to be able to trail her as she shopped. He passed ahead of her car twenty or so feet then parked. He used his side mirror to see when she exited the car. He then casually exited his and trailed her. He was hoping that she would be alone allowing him to do the job quickly, but instead, she met up with a friend outside of a store.

"Hey, Vittoria! How are you?", asked Anna as she hugged her old friend.

"I'm wonderful. You?", provided Vittoria.

"Not as good as you apparently.", Anna said as she grabbed her hand to eye her engagement ring.

"It's been like a dream!", exclaimed Vittoria as she smiled at Anna.

"I bet it has. I can only imagine.", sighed Anna.

"Where do you want to start shopping?", asked Vittoria hoping to keep things on a light note.

"Well, it depends on if you want to stay near parking. Where did you park?", inquired Anna.

"On the street as usual, so it doesn't matter.", explained Vittoria.

"Ok, let's hit up one of my favorite stores, so you can spend some of that Bianchi money on me.", laughed Anna.

"Girl!", laughed Vittoria as she playfully hit Anna on the arm.

Miguel followed the pair from store to store as she spent Ricky's money. If only his girl could flaunt his money like that, but Canto would have to pay him more than chump change for that to happen. But here he was doing the bidding of his boss like a faithful soldier. He decided to pretend that he was looking for a gift for his girlfriend. He asked a clerk for assistance to keep up appearances as he watched the pair.

"So, lady, are you still in the condo?", asked Jill as she sifted through the clothes rack.

"Yeah, it's like he's forgotten all about me. He hasn't said a word about me moving and he's still paying all of the bills.", bragged Giovanna as she held a blouse to her body for Jill's opinion.

"That's cute. You'd better find a place before he has your stuff boxed up and thrown out!", Jill whispered not wanting the nearby shoppers to hear.

"He wouldn't do that! He'd give me a warning.", rationalized Giovanna.

"Not the way he's into that new chick. All it takes is for her to want a fancy place; he'll kick you out and move her right on in! Don't fool yourself.", warned Jill in a whisper.

Jill didn't understand why her friend was being uncharacteristically naïve; Giovanna knew the game. Jill had seen the game played wrong like this before when another friend of hers held on too long to a dead relationship then her guy threw her out on her ass on top of all of her stuff on the curb. It was not a good look and one she didn't want for her best friend.

"You really should request the store owner close the shop down for you, so that you can have privacy.", suggested Anna.

Who even thinks of such things, thought Vittoria as she shook her head in disagreement?

"I'm not into that. I don't need a bunch of material things to make me happy.", Vittoria chastised her friend.

Miguel wanted to hear their conversation, but if he got any closer it would be quite apparent that he was following them; so, he'd have to be satisfied with just keeping them within sight.

"You haven't landed another rich guy yet?", Jill questioned her good friend.

"No, they all think I'm still with Ricky and trying to step out on him.", Giovanna vented her frustrations.

"Oh, wow! That's messed up!", Jill sympathized.

"Tell, me about it. I don't see anything I want. Ready?", Giovanna asked frustrated that her retail therapy hadn't resulted in any good picks from that store.

"Yeah, it was a bust for me too. Where did you park?", Jill asked as they walked to the exit.

"I parked on the street a few blocks from here.", provided Giovanna to her puzzled friend.

"Why would you do that? It's safer to park near the store, the cost couldn't be the issue. I know you have the money.", scolded Jill as she looked to her friend for a story that made sense.

"I'm going to another store closer to where I parked.", she explained.

"Okay, well, be careful; we are downtown after all. I'll call you later.", advised Jill as she hugged her friend goodbye.

"Will do, see you later.", informed Giovanna.

As Giovanna began her walk toward the other store, she decided perhaps it would be better for her to spend her money more sparingly; especially since she didn't know when Ricky would pull the plug or if she could find another high roller to replace him soon.

Vittoria didn't enjoy herself as she would have in the past; every chance Anna got, she asked Vittoria to foot the bill for a purchase. She didn't like being used and she could see that's how things would be in the future if she continued to hang out with Anna. It was indeed time to part ways, she thought.

"Anna, sorry, but I need to cut it short. I forgot I need to pick up some clothes I left at Ricky's Palmer Woods mansion.", informed Vittoria as she looked at her watch.

"Wow, it's usually me, ending our outings. I thought for sure we'd spend the entire day together shopping on the Avenue of Fashion.", Anna voiced confused by Vittoria's actions.

"Sorry, I really need to go. I'm going to head around the block to his house.", explained Vittoria awkwardly.

She was over it; Anna's actions confirmed that she was making the right choice. It was over. She hugged Anna knowing it was for the last time.

"Ok, well talk later.", Anna said hesitantly.

"Take care.", Vittoria replied with finality as she began the walk to her car.

Miguel finally had his chance when he saw Ricky's girl had decided to walk back to her car; there were fewer pedestrians as the parking spot wasn't near any major stores. Miquel maintained a shorter distance and pretended to count coins in his hands when she looked back. Once she arrived at the car, she opened the trunk to toss her bags inside and then turned to find Miguel behind her with a gun.

"Don't make a sound.", he whispered the deadly order.

Giovanna nervously locked eyes with her assailant as he gripped her tightly by the waist so that anyone that happened to see the pair would assume they were a couple. Miguel held her tightly and leaned closer to her ear.

"Canto will destroy your man.", Miguel vowed as he pointed the handgun equipped with the silencer to her belly.

"I'm not ...", Giovanna uttered as he pulled the trigger six times.

He quickly pushed her backward causing her to fall partially into the trunk then he swiftly dodged out of sight through the nearby downtown alleyway. Then he circled around on foot for a block then ventured back to his car to make it appear that he was just arriving in the area. He quickly hopped in his car twenty feet in front of her vehicle and took off.

Canto will be pleased to hear that he had successfully completed the task; he was desperate to break the great Ricky Bianchi. Miguel knew that his boss would give him the accolades that he so impatiently wanted. As he drove away, he heard passers-by scream when they spotted the bloody beauty; such a waste, he thought.

Chapter 13

Samantha, the wedding planner, was thrilled about the progress she had made laying out plans with Vittoria. She had insisted on meeting with Vitoria at least twice a week and they had met four times thus far. Samantha called him that morning to provide an update; she had reassured him that everything would be ready for the wedding day scheduled for two months out. She went on and on with Ricky about the beautiful bride Vittoria would make and how gorgeous their children will be. All of it satiated Ricky's ego with pride; he too couldn't wait to proclaim to the world that she was his and he was hers. He leaned back imagining placing the matching ring on her finger and Father Luca proclaiming them man and wife when Enzo and Angelo interrupted his thoughts.

Ricky was taken aback when he noticed Angelo crying and Enzo looking uncomfortably somber; his mind started reeling with all sorts of horrible things running through his thoughts.

"Canto killed ...", Angelo choked on the words.

Angelo knew he had a crush on Giovanna, but until her death, he realized that he actually had been in love with her.

"Who the fuck did he kill?", demanded Ricky as the blood drained from his face and his eyes took on the look of an insane beast.

"His men killed Giovanna thinking she was still your girlfriend.", informed Angelo as he wiped his eyes.

There was relief in Ricky's eyes and face, he slowly resumed the façade of a sane man as he began to contemplate his next moves.

"I want Vittoria under 24-hour surveillance. I don't want anything happening to my girl!", shouted Ricky as blood rushed to his face, "I don't care if you and Enzo have to take turns. The fuck!", shouted Ricky as he slammed the desk with his fists.

He had immediately ventured back into a panic state the more he thought of Vittoria being killed.

"What about Giovanna?", asked Angelo fearful Ricky wouldn't give a damn.

Ricky looked momentarily confused by his question.

"Contact a realtor and put the condo on the market along with the Palmer Woods mansion. Her condo can be sold fully furnished. Contact her folks to pick up her things. Let them know that I'll take care of the funeral expenses, but I do not want it held here.", Ricky coldly advised the plan.

Anger and fear consumed Ricky's eyes; this was new to Enzo; he had never witnessed Ricky unhinged. As they left the room, Ricky began muttering to himself. Enzo turned to look back at his boss to make sure he was stable.

"God help me, I don't know what the fuck I'd do if something happened to Vittoria. Trust me Detroit doesn't want to see me nut the fuck up!", he spit as he said the words while his head began twitching. "Nonna …"

The rest of Ricky's words were unintelligible as he tried to steady his thoughts by calling on his grandmother. Enzo closed the door to provide privacy as he noticed that his boss was not well. Angelo noticed as well, but his own grief wouldn't let him react.

"We think a sane Ricky is ruthless; a grieving one would be psychotic!", Enzo said to Angelo's deaf ears.

He took Angelo by the shoulders to make him focus on his words.

"I'll handle things. I'll contact Giovanna's mother and set up a patrol to watch Vittoria. Go be with your woman; let Martina help you get through this.", informed Enzo.

The Bianchi family needed a clear head working on the matter and from the looks of it, he was the only one in the position to do so. There was no way the Bianchi dynasty would fall on Enzo's watch.

Miguel had been avoiding Canto all day until Canto was unavoidable. Miguel had been summoned and there was no way out of doing what he knew was expected. He dragged his feet and slowly entered Canto's office. He inched closer to his liege and was halted by the steel deadly voice of his boss.

"Did we break that pretty boy?", demanded Canto with a smirk as he lit his marijuana joint.

Miguel was petrified to tell him the news and hoped Canto's joint would relax him. Surprisingly, word hadn't made it to Canto yet. Perhaps, that was a good thing, thought Miguel; that gave him an opportunity to grovel and come up with another plan.

"El Jefe, I found out the girl we killed was an ex-girlfriend.", Miguel paused as he noticed the furious look in Canto's eyes. He forced up the words that threatened to choke him. "I found out who his new girl is; they are actually engaged to be married soon.", informed Miguel.

"I'm listening.", Canto whispered in his deadly tone.

"I've got men tracing her patterns, but it'll be a little tougher now that Ricky is hip to our plan. But don't worry, we'll get it done.", Miguel reassured his boss.

"Oh, my friend, I'm not worried because if you don't, I'll have your head.", Canto threatened.

"Si, El Jefe.", Miguel swallowed his words.

The sunlight glared through Ricky's curtains like a solar flare burning his eyes. His head was pounding from worry and fear; in all the years he had been in the family business, he had never been terrified. Now that he had Vittoria, he had someone to protect and value; she was his future and family and it made him determined to shake off the throbbing pain so that he could handle the much-needed business at hand, securing Vittoria's safety.

After downing a quick bite to eat and a cup of coffee, he drove to the meat market. It was necessary to warn Vittoria and convince her to move in with his family for safety. He wanted to keep her close and perhaps it was time that she stopped working there as well. He used his car phone to make sure Angelo and Enzo were at the office; he left word that he needed to meet with them after he saw Vittoria.

Ricky was glad to see a few of his men on the lookout when he arrived at the market. His men knew that if anything happened to her on their watch, they were as good as dead. Ricky was not dressed in his finest clothes or sported a dapper look. He wore jeans and a cotton shirt; that day his only concern was securing his and Vittoria's future.

Lorenzo almost didn't recognize Ricky when he entered. He paused before speaking.

"Ricky?", questioned a still uncertain Lorenzo.

"Hello, Mr. Rossi. How are you?", asked Ricky however really not in the mood to converse.

"I'm good, but you look like you've seen better days; no offense.", responded Lorenzo.

"Who are you telling? I sure have. I don't mean to be abrupt, but I need to speak to Vittoria.", informed a somber Ricky.

Lorenzo didn't know what was going on, but a serious Ricky gave him pause and created concern.

"No problem, she's in the back. You can go there to speak to her in private.", suggested Lorenzo then later regretting the offer.

Lorenzo decided that he would wait and see if Vittoria voiced any concerns. He just prayed that nothing interfered with the wedding plans. He knew the life of a business owner could be stressful, so he could only imagine the magnitude of issues Ricky had to address.

"Knock, knock.", Ricky said playfully as he entered the stockroom.

He hoped that Vittoria wouldn't see that his countenance had been worn down with worry the day before. He decided to rush in and grab her from behind and plant light kisses on her neck. Her scent calmed him and gave him the strength he would need to carry out the acts he would soon undertake.

"Ricky, what a surprise! What brings you by so early in the morning?", Vittoria surveyed her love as she turned to face him.

"Baby, I don't want to alarm you ..., but my men found out yesterday that my ex-long-term lover, Giovanna was killed. We believe a low-level want-to-be mob boss had her killed while she was shopping.", Ricky explained then paused to gauge her reaction. He saw her calmness so he continued, "I have men watching you 24/7 now, but I'm thinking I should do more."

Vittoria looked puzzled, "What more could you do?"

"Well, all night I was thinking about you ... about us. I was thinking I could move you in before the wedding to ensure your safety.", suggested Ricky as he kissed her forehead hoping she would agree and not argue about it.

"Ricky, I don't know about that. These weeks leading up to the wedding are important and I think I should spend them with my parents. Besides, it didn't happen at her home. You may not realize it, but my father taught me how to protect myself.", reassured Vittoria as she playfully punched Ricky in the stomach.

"So, I'm engaged to Wonder Woman or Supergirl? Which one?", laughed Ricky as he tickled Vittoria.

"They don't have the powers that I have.", Vittoria said seductively as she kissed his ear.

"Oh, I know! Your superpowers are here …", he said then kissed her lips, "They control whatever they touch… and here …", he kissed her hand, "They make a strong man weak. And here …", he placed his hand between her legs.

Vittoria giggled and pulled away as she playfully protested.

"What if my father comes in?", questioned Vittoria.

"I think he'd wink at me and leave me to it.", laughed Ricky then he chased her around a table until she surrendered.

"Vittoria, please promise me you'll be careful.", Ricky pleaded.

"Always. Enough worrying about me. I'm sure you have other pressing matters to focus on.", she said dismissing his concern with a kiss.

"Yes, dear.", Ricky said like a hen-pecked and love-struck man.

Vittoria was right, he hoped, that she would be fine as he did have two pressing matters that required his immediate attention. Ricky walked briskly from the stockroom, waved at Lorenzo then dotted out of the market. Ricky immediately called Bernard while he drove to the funeral home.

"Hello, Ester. May I speak to Bernard?", inquired Ricky.

"This is Bernard.", he informed.

"What happened to Ester? Are you downsizing?", laughed Ricky.

The world truly would be coming to an end if both of them were facing turmoil.

"No.", laughed Bernard, "We are having some weird issues with the phone system."

"Thank God, there's no time for both of us to have issues.", sighed Ricky.

"What's going on?", Bernard asked surprised by Ricky's tone and mood.

"A low life, I'm going to be taking out soon, killed Giovanna thinking she was still my girl. So, I put my men on the watch to make sure Vittoria is okay. He's forcing my hand and I'm going to do something beyond anything I ever thought I would. Just like you a few years back.", explained Ricky.

Bernard knew just about every devious act Ricky had ever committed over the years as his friend and confidant; so, he couldn't imagine what this act could be.

"Whatever you do, don't let it eat away at you as it did with me. I don't think I ever truly recovered. Tell me, is there anything I can do to help?", offered Bernard.

"Actually, there is. I need to ensure I break this Canto bastard ...", informed Ricky.

"Since you have law enforcement in your pocket and I have the judicial and legislature in mine, I can talk to the District Attorney and suggest that he goes hard on any of Canto's men. Cool?", Bernard offered an idea.

"I can dig it. Thanks, Bernard.", Ricky voiced his appreciation and then disconnected the call.

Now Ricky's mind and eyes could be squarely set on the goal at hand, breaking the fuck out of Canto, he thought. Everyone at the funeral home was on edge and the atmosphere was nervous at best; no one had any idea which version of Ricky would appear on the scene. So as Ricky entered the building there was silence as they waited to gauge his reaction.

"Bettie, get Angelo and Enzo. Tell them to book! I need to see them now!", ordered Ricky.

Everyone within hearing distance realized that he was about planning and business so things appeared to be back on track.

"Yes sir.", replied Bettie then she used the phone to call their meeting room.

Ricky had barely sat down when Angelo and Enzo burst into the office breathing heavily after running the short distance to be at his beck and call. Ricky looked at the pair with a smirk.

"You motherfuckers are out of shape, damn! Sit the fuck down, catch your breath and listen.", instructed Ricky shaking his head at his middle-aged friends.

Angelo was glad to see that Ricky had bounced back and he, himself, was better as well after spending time with his girlfriend. Since he had a clearer head, he set up a watch for Martina as well. Martina was from the streets and always packed a gun, so he had fewer concerns, but concerns nevertheless.

"Ricky, what's your plan?", asked Angelo with Enzo listening intently.

"I had been putting off enacting the plan decided upon in Columbia, but Canto is forcing my hand. I can't delay it any longer. I need you to round up this Maria Santos. Make sure she's not roughed up. We need to deliver her in pristine condition and take photos of her tied up and being dropped off.", Ricky disclosed the plan.

"Why the pictures boss?", Enzo said curiously.

"That's on a need-to-know basis and you don't right now. You dig?", Ricky queried.

"Ok, Ricky. Whatever you say boss.", confirmed Enzo.

"And Canto?", asked Angelo.

"Keep our men on the watch so we continue to know his patterns. Once we have Maria, snatch his ass up and take him to the warehouse.", Ricky provided further instructions.

"For sure. I can't wait to see that punk bitch go down.", Angelo supplied fully vested in the plan of torture for a change.

"Fellas, I'm going to head out for the day. I'm stopping by St. Mary's to see Father Luca.", informed Ricky.

Angelo and Enzo knew exactly what that was about, Ricky was making preparation for the torture and killings he was about to inflict. Angelo laughed at the thought.

"I can't wait to laugh in the face of that arrogant bastard. He didn't know who he was fucking with!", laughed Angelo.

"My man, my man!", laughed Ricky as he jumped to his feet with outstretched arms. He grabbed Angelo and hugged him enthusiastically. "Let's show this dumb fuck!", laughed Ricky. "See you, fellas, later.", Ricky continued to laugh as he exited the building.

This would be the only time; Angelo would appreciate the Reaper making an appearance at the warehouse. He hoped that the Reaper would put on the most vicious performance he'd ever done and he'd have a front-row ticket for the event.

Father Luca was finishing a meeting in the sanctuary when he saw Ricky enter. He was hopeful that Ricky was there to discuss his impending nuptials, but his hopes would fade quickly.

"Father, the confessional please.", Ricky requested.

"Damn. Forgive me, Lord.", whispered Father Luca, "Ok, one moment. Let me retrieve my robe."

"Sure thing, Father.", Ricky said as he pimp-walked to the confessional.

Father Luca entered the small confines after donning his robe.

"My son …", Father Luca began.

"Let's cut the formalities.", Ricky interrupted.

"Ok, so why are you here? Do you have doubts about getting married?", asked the father.

"Hell no!", Ricky denied.

"Language.", reprimanded Father Luca.

"Shit, I just heard you cuss when I asked about the confessional.", Ricky revealed.

"Ok, one time.", sighed Father Luca as he began speaking to God, "Forgive me father, for I have just sinned. It's been more than one time.", then he returned his focus to Ricky, "Spill it before I have another sin to ask forgiveness for.", Father Luca impatiently uttered.

"I'm going to deliver a former sex slave back to her captor so that I can teach a bastard …", Ricky paused as he heard the sigh of Father Luca, "It's' in the bible. I need to teach this bastard a lesson that I'm not the one to be threatened. Then I'm going to kill him; I can't leave a man this evil and ambitious alive. He killed my ex-girlfriend thinking she was my current girl.", Ricky explained his plan.

"Oh, my; do you have Vittoria under watch?", asked Father Luca.

"Most definitely!", Ricky reassured.

"Good man. Protecting family is paramount.", informed the father.

"What are you saying? Are you giving me your blessing?", Ricky asked confused by the words of the father.

He strained his eyes to see through the mesh window and saw no one. He exited the confessional to find the father leaving the sanctuary. Ricky laughed at Father Luca's reaction and took it as support; although, he would carry out his plan regardless of what Father Luca had to say about it.

Isabella had been calling all week asking Lorenzo for help. She had even enlisted Antonella to nag him about it. Lorenzo felt that neither of the women realized just how painful and emotional, he thought it would be to see his brother's things and be reminded of what he had lost. It was the last thing he wanted to spend his Saturday doing. So, he had been dreading agreeing to help his sister-in-law clear out Tommaso's things, but he knew she couldn't depend on help from anyone else. So, he decided to assist as one last act for his big brother. As soon as he arrived, she sent him straight to the basement.

"I have his clothes and the things he stored on the main floor moved out of the house. What I didn't donate, I need you to take down to the alley for the trash pickup. But he has a huge trunk downstairs that I need you to check.", Isabella informed as they walked down the stairs.

She pointed to the massive chest in the corner of the basement; Tommaso had used the space as a man cave of sorts. He had a television and recliner chair in the same area.

"It has a padlock on it and I don't know where he kept the key, but he does have a pair of bolt cutters on his workbench.", Isabella indicated and pointed to the bench on the opposite side of the basement.

Lorenzo dragged the trunk to the center of the room and then retrieved the bolt cutters to clip the lock off. He wondered what his brother would have stored in the trunk. Did he lock away damning evidence on his mob boss for a rainy day? He was quite curious about its contents. He walked over to the workbench to return the clippers when he heard Isabella scream.

Her screams made his heart sink; he fearfully approached her as she dropped pictures to the floor. He looked at the photos on the cement floor and it sicken him to see his brother had pictures of naked girls. Girls that were just that, children, none appeared older than fifteen. Then he looked inside the trunk to see what other sick things were stored when he noticed a video recorder and several nude pictures of Vittoria at various ages.

Lorenzo almost blacked out from shock, rage and disgust; disgust that the man he held in such high esteem was a despicable child molester. The years of Vittoria's unexplainably odd behavior flashed before his eyes as tears began to blind him. Isabella's continued screams and howls were deafening as he staggered up the stairs trying to breathe through his pain. The pain was suffocating and squeezed at his lungs and his heart, twisting both till he thought he would collapse.

He managed to crank the ignition of the vehicle despite shaky hands and drove like a mad man, running red lights just missing his own demise, but he couldn't think clearly. He saw the image of his brother's dead body found on the tracks with his penis severed and shoved in his mouth. There could only be one man responsible for Tommaso's death and Lorenzo would confront that vicious murderer. He drove that road as if he had driven that path a thousand times, yet he had never been there. He pulled up the long driveway just like the mad man that had driven the trek thus far.

The guards were alerted and radioed inside to warn that someone was driving up to the house erratically and to be prepared to shoot. Lorenzo pulled up the circular driveway in front of the mansion and began yelling unintelligibly as he threw the car in park. He stormed the door yelling.

"Ricky! I need to see him. Where is he!", yelled Lorenzo.

Had the men not known him, he would have been shot on sight, but they cautiously escorted him inside. The guards didn't know if something had happened to Vittoria or what and Lorenzo's behavior didn't allow them to voice any questions. Ricky had been alerted and stopped eating breakfast with his parents. He insisted that they remain in the kitchen and he would address the issue alone. As he walked to the foyer, he saw a crazy-eyed Lorenzo pushing passed the guards demanding to see him.

"You killed my brother, didn't you?", demanded Lorenzo.

One of the guards touched the handle of his gun, but Ricky held his hand up to stay his weapon.

"Why would you say that?", Ricky inquired attempting to see what prompted his accusations.

"He had to be killed by the mafia!", screamed Lorenzo as he tried to gather his thoughts, "I was cleaning out his things with his widow and we came across pictures of naked girls … he had pictures of Vittoria! Did she tell you?", screamed Lorenzo.

"Yes.", responded Ricky as he waited for Lorenzo's reaction.

"Thank you.", cried Lorenzo, his cries turned to howls of pain and anguish.

Ricky was not accustomed to showing affection to men, but he realized that it was required at that moment when a father and brother had found out that the man, he looked up to the most had violated what was dearest to him. Ricky approached Lorenzo and Lorenzo fell into Ricky's out-stretched arms. Ricky had never hugged a man that long and he was starting to feel uncomfortable, so to ease his own discomfort he began to speak.

"I did what needed to be done; what you would have wanted to do if you had known. I took that burden out of your hands. I'll fucking kill anyone that ever tries to hurt our Vittoria. Now go home and don't speak of this again.", instructed Ricky.

Lorenzo nodded and left as he was told.

Chapter 14

Vittoria and Martina had bonded at the cabin and the two had started talking a lot; they often talked on the phone a few times a week. Vittoria was relieved to have someone she could speak to about things concerning the life of a mob boss's girlfriend. In most cases, Martina would be privy to the same information as she and that was comforting. They practically would be family soon with Vittoria's fast-approaching nuptials and Angelo's proposal to Martina the previous week.

Vittoria had decided to take a break from going to the meat market first thing in the morning and go later. She planned to take care of some duties for her father but decided to call Martina before heading out. She had lost track of time and had been chatting with her for an hour already when Martina brought up another topic for discussion.

"Are you ready for your bachelorette gathering? We can't call it a party with Eleanor planning it.", asked Martina with a giggle.

"I'm still surprised that she wanted to do that for me. Did she do the same for Bernard's wives?", questioned Vittoria.

"Vanessa told me that she did plan something for her, but not Josephine. From what I was told, Josephine wasn't interested in getting to know her; so, Eleanor never offered anything.", explained Martina.

"Really, I can't imagine Bernard marrying someone who wasn't open-minded about race.", concluded Vittoria.

"Yeah, that's what I thought too, but who knows. Anyway, I'm going shopping in a bit to pick up a new outfit for it. Do you want to come with me?", inquired Martina.

"No thanks. I'm not buying anything new for the gathering. I have enough things that you ladies haven't seen yet that I can wear. Besides, I have an errand to run today.", Vittoria informed.

"Oh, I assumed Ricky had everything covered.", expressed Martina.

"For the wedding, he does. I thought I'd run an errand for my father to give him a break. I know Ricky wouldn't be happy about it, but oh well.", laughed Vittoria.

Neither one felt it was necessary to be on 24-hour surveillance and that it was a waste of time and resources. Vittoria wouldn't have been able to discuss such things with Anna. Anna only cared about sex and money; after a while, that type of talk bored Vittoria.

"I understand how you feel. I'm not going to let a prick like Canto dictate what I do.", Martina shared as she sat on her chaise lounge chair.

"Exactly. Well, I'd better get a move on it. I don't want to be out too long.", announced Vittoria.

"Ok lady. We'll chat later. Be safe.", advised Martina.

"Always. Bye.", added Vittoria.

Vittoria walked downstairs to grab her purse from the coat rack in the living room when she noticed her mother snooping out the window. Antonella had noticed that Ricky had men on the watch, but she didn't ask why and there was a part of her that preferred not knowing.

"Mother, I'm heading out to the warehouse district for Pappa. I won't be gone long.", informed Vittoria.

"Ok, darling. Don't tire yourself out, the wedding planner is scheduled to come after dinner.", suggested Antonella.

"Ok, I won't.", promised Vittoria.

Vittoria exited the house and hopped into her Cougar. Tony, one of the guards, started his vehicle so that he could trail her; he had assumed that she was staying home for the day since she didn't have an early start. As she drove, she considered the rest of her day's activities to complete before heading back home to meet with the wedding planner. She considered swinging by the meat market after running the errand so that she could update her father and see if he needed assistance with anything else. Dating Ricky had changed everything for her; as a woman in her early thirties, she hadn't felt like much of an adult until then. It was more than just finding love that had done it; she had found her voice. Her voice was no longer bound and silenced by the pain inflicted upon her so many years ago. It was an exhilarating feeling and soon, she hoped to experience another joy of womanhood, becoming a mother.

She drove the familiar route not paying much attention to her surroundings; she normally amused herself by seeing if her guard could keep up. But instead, she found herself daydreaming about Ricky and the beautiful life awaiting them. As she approached the intersection, Tony assumed that she was going to stop at the yellow light as she often did as a cautious driver. This time, Vittoria sped through and by the time he realized what she was doing the light was red and the traffic too thick to run it.

He was a nervous wreck and there were so many cars that turned on the street creating barriers to reach her so much so, that he couldn't see where she went. He had never been so afraid in his life; Ricky had made it quite clear that if something happened any guard would pay with their life. Tony accelerated like a drag racer when the light turned green and tailgated anyone in his way.

"Shit, Vittoria! Where are you?", Tony screamed as he looked frantically down side streets.

Unlike Tony, when the light had turned red, Canto's soldier, Mateo, had managed to maneuver around the cars to make a sharp right turn down a side street then drove through a parking lot then back to the main street just passed the intersection. He was able to spot and catch up with Vittoria as she turned down an alley to take a shortcut to the warehouse.

She parked in the parking lot on the Northside of the building which was used for overflow parking. Mateo quickly pulled diagonally near the entrance to the parking lot. He decided to leave his gun in the car; he figured he would have a little fun scaring the beauty before he killed her by taking her somewhere to rape her first. For that reason, when he jumped out to attack Vittoria, he reached for her long hair to bring her close quickly and painfully hoping to throw her into the vehicle. He was clueless that she would cut her hair to the scalp if it meant saving her life.

"Aren't you a sexy mama? I bet Ricky does all sorts of freaky shit with you.", laughed Mateo.

He stuck out his tongue pretending to perform cunnilingus as he attempted to pull her closer to his mouth.

Vittoria whipped out her straight razor blade from her bra and turned her body to face her assailant. He was surprised to see calmness in her eyes instead of the fear from which he had hoped to gain arousal. Vittoria masterfully used her wrist to glide the blade back and forth as it slit his throat with precision. As he loosened his grip on her hair to stop the flow of life from his throat, she raised her leg to kick him in the stomach knocking him to the ground.

Tony panicked when he saw Mateo grab Vittoria as he approached the warehouse, but his panic quickly faded as he watched everything unfold. Mateo was weak from the loss of blood, but he tried to exert enough strength to stand and walk around the car to the driver's seat. He managed to get behind the wheel when he lost consciousness. Just then Tony stopped inches short of the fence and his car jumped the curb in front of the warehouse parking lot. He threw the car in park as it sat perpendicular to Mateo's vehicle.

"Vittoria, are you okay?", asked a stunned Tony.

He peered into Mateo's car to notice him unconscious and bleeding out.

"I'm pissed!", she said as she flung the blood from the blade.

"You better get home. Forget about whatever errand you were doing.", Tony insisted as he contemplated how he would inform Ricky.

"Unfortunately, you are right. Follow me back home.", Vittoria instructed Tony who remained stunned by her actions.

Tony followed Vittoria home as she had calmly instructed; he couldn't wrap his mind around the surprising beauty. She was truly a bad mama-jama, Tony thought and perfect for Ricky. Next was the changing of the guards and he had to report back to Ricky; he prayed that Vittoria wouldn't call him before he had a chance to speak to him.

Vittoria was annoyed that her plans for the day had been ruined; if Tony hadn't witnessed the attack she would have gone inside the warehouse as if nothing had happened. She had returned home and parked out front; she would have to call her father to inform him that he would need to handle the meeting with the warehouse manager after all. So much for helping out, she thought.

She unlocked the door and entered the house, much to the surprise of Antonella who was approaching the living room from the hallway. Antonella was going to speak on Vittoria's early return when she noticed blood on Vittoria's blouse.

"Honey are you okay? What happened? Why do you have blood on your blouse?", questioned Antonella afraid of what she might hear.

"Oh jeez! I didn't notice that at all. My beautiful blouse is ruined!", whined Vittoria not noticing the fear in her mother's eyes.

"Vittoria! Tell me what happened!", demanded Antonella.

Instantly, she realized the gravity of her mother's request and that most people would be scared.

"I'm sorry, Mother. There's no need to worry. It's not my blood. Some goon tried to attack me and I slit his throat, just like Pappa taught me.", Vittoria revealed.

She attempted to scurry past her mother when Antonella reached out and stopped her.

"Are you ready for this type of life?", voiced Antonella who for the first time considered all that comes along with the money and power. "Your father just dabbled in it when we were young, but Ricky's the king of it.", advised Antonella.

"Yes, I've considered it all. I know it's not a Cinderella fairytale; but in reality, I'll be at his side till he or I take our last breath.", Vittoria affirmed then kissed her mother on the cheek before going up to her bedroom.

Tony sat in his car outside the funeral home for what seemed hours as he contemplated what he would say to Ricky and all the things he had done in his life. He began to pray to God to ask for forgiveness for his sins; he figured that could be his last fleeting moments alive. He hoped God would listen without a priest because he didn't have time for that. He also asked for protection during his meeting with Ricky and that Ricky would spare his life. He took several deep breaths as he exited his car to begin his walk inside. The youngbloods outside spoke to him as he passed, but he was zoned out with his mind captive to fear.

He noticed that Ricky's office door was open, but he paused and knocked for permission to enter.

"Come in Tony. What it is?", Ricky greeted Tony as he looked up from his ledger.

"Ricky ... Boss ... Mr. Bianchi.", began Tony nervously.

"What the fuck's got into you?", questioned Ricky.

Tony decided it was no need to prolong the inevitable; so, he cut straight to the chase and updated Ricky.

"Um, Canto's man attacked Vittoria an hour ago.", Tony informed.

Tony's throat became dry with fear and additional words wouldn't come out. He noticed Ricky open his drawer and he knew exactly what Ricky kept there. Ricky's eyes took on an ominous glare that would frighten any man.

"She's fine!", blared Tony as he saw Ricky's hand reach for the gun. "I got caught in traffic and when I arrived at the warehouse, she had already slit the punk's throat with her straight razor. She did it without saying a word or making a sound; she was so calm. The guy managed to shuffle back to the car where he lost consciousness. I'm sure he died there. Please Boss ...", Tony groveled his update.

"Get the fuck out!", yelled Ricky as he sat in shock.

Tony whispered thank you to God as he ran from the office hoping that Ricky would let this pass and not remind him of his failure. Ricky continued to sit at his desk with his fist resting on top as he pictured the punk's attack on Vittoria and how she must have masterfully sliced her assailant's throat. His body began to contort with arousal as he pressed his fist onto the desktop. The need to relieve his throbbing member was too great to ignore; so, he unzipped his pants to masturbate at his desk.

"Fuck!", moaned Ricky not caring who might have heard as he leaned back in his chair completely entranced by Vittoria's bravery.

He looked at the ceiling as his body released its orgasm and pleasure coursed through his limbs. He sighed a pleasureful release and was then ready to address the important issue at hand.

"Angelo, Enzo! Get the fuck in here!", shouted Ricky as he walked to his bathroom to wash his hands and wipe off his member.

Bettie immediately called their private meeting room to ensure that Angelo and Enzo knew they were being summoned. She knew no one wanted to be on the receiving end of Ricky's anger after what she heard Tony report, but she knew it could be even worse if they appeared to ignore his call. Enzo answered the phone.

"Hey, what's up?", asked Enzo.

"Ricky is demanding you and Angelo in his office now. Vittoria was attacked this afternoon!", Bettie warned.

"Shit!", Enzo yelled as he hung up the receiver. "Vittoria was attacked this afternoon!", shouted Enzo to Angelo.

"Oh, shit!", whispered Angelo.

The pair fled the meeting room and ran to Ricky; they tried to prepare their minds for the horror that was about to unfold. However, they were eerily surprised to see their boss sitting calculatingly.

"What updates do you have for me?", asked Ricky sarcastically.

"Updates?", asked Angelo surprised by this line of questioning at that time.

"Yeah, updates motherfucker. I've got one for your ass. Some cunt punk bitch that called himself a man, attacked Vittoria! Thank God, my woman is as tough as she is beautiful. She slit that motherfucker's throat!", hollered Ricky. "Looks like she was right, she didn't need protection; especially not from some weak ass motherfuckers who can't keep up with her if she drives more than 20 miles per hour. Shit!", an exasperated Ricky growled.

"I'll handle Tony or Mario; whichever one was on watch at that time.", reassured Angelo.

"It was Tony's dumbass!", informed Ricky.

"What do you want us to do with him?", inquired Angelo.

"Put him on the most difficult assignments for a while. He'll either get killed or put in jail if he fucks up!", ordered Ricky.

"You got it boss!", informed Enzo.

"It's time to step up my plans. I need that bitch Maria captured ASAP!", Ricky informed.

"Consider it done. Our guys are making their move this evening.", Angelo reassured.

"Good. I want that arrogant fuck Canto captured the moment we have Maria; then fire-bomb his shit. Make it happen. I want this shit wrapped up before my wedding. The only thing I want on my mind then is fucking my wife!", ordered Ricky as he stared at his cousin.

"You got it, Ricky! I promise you.", vowed Angelo.

"Now, get the fuck out!", shouted Ricky then he turned his focus to Vittoria.

He dialed her home assuming that she didn't go anywhere else after what transpired that day, but if she felt stubborn, she might have, thought Ricky.

"Hello.", greeted Vittoria.

"Hey, baby. How are you feeling?", asked a nervous Ricky hoping she wasn't angry at him.

"I'm fine. I'm just meeting with the wedding planner. We'll be done shortly.", informed Vittoria.

"I really need you in my arms tonight. I need to know you are safe. Will you stay the night with me in Grosse Pointe?", fretted Ricky almost desperate enough to beg her.

As quiet as it was kept, she needed him as well; not because she was scared, but because she knew he could relate to killing a man. She had dreamt of doing it many times when she thought about her uncle, but actually slicing a man's throat was surreal.

"Ok, Ricky. I'll come as soon as the meeting ends. I'll pack enough to stay a few days.", conceded Vittoria.

"Out of sight, baby. See you soon.", Ricky said relieved she accepted his invitation.

Ricky had left his office early and spent most of his time pacing around the house waiting for Vittoria to arrive. He informed his men to radio him the moment she pulled up the drive. He was desperate to lay his eyes upon her and to touch her. His body ached for her as if they had never made love before. The moment his men radioed him, he rushed from his office to meet her outside; she had barely exited her car when he swooped her up into his arms to carry her inside.

"Ricky!", giggled Vittoria as she tossed her head back with laughter.

"Grab her bags from the car!", shouted Ricky as he began running.

He jogged up the stairs like a man half his age with the love of his life.

"Ricky, be careful!", giggled Vittoria as she bounced with each running stride.

Bianca and Carlo heard laughter and loud girlish shrills; they were enticed to find out what the playful ruckus was about. They ventured from the kitchen to see what was going on. The two smiled as they saw Ricky running upstairs carrying Vittoria.

"I'm so happy for my precious boy that he finally found his soulmate.", exclaimed Bianca as she leaned on Carlo's shoulder.

"Me too, my love. He truly has found his match. For her to kill that man without hesitation or even a sound …", he said shaking his head in awe.

It reminded him of Ricky's first kill as did the retelling of the scenario for Ricky. Ricky bust through his bedroom door and swiftly laid Vittoria on the bed freeing up his hands to rip off his clothes. He growled with exertion as he desperately stripped. Vittoria was mesmerized by his hunger for her body and the pleasures that awaited them both. She hurriedly removed her sundress and kicked off her shoes, but she didn't move fast enough for Ricky. He took over and ripped her panties from her body then buried his face between her legs as he drank her savory essence mixing his own tears with it as the fluids became one.

Vittoria's cries of joy and pleasure flowed through the halls announcing to all that their love was overpowering, all-consuming and passionate; something that neither of them ever wanted to deny or ever would. Vittoria reached for the hands of her skillful lover to pull his attentions elsewhere; she wanted to feel him deep within her. He climbed on top of her and she took his manhood in her hands to glide it inside her. Ricky fought back his ejaculation; he was like a virgin boy about to come too soon. He wanted to savor each thrust as he masterfully moved his lower back muscles to thrust deep within, first the center of her womb, then the sidewalls until even he wasn't strong enough to hold off the quivers in his body that were demanding control over his frame.

As he quivered, Vittoria's body shook as well as she cried her release. She found pleasure as she always did in his body, in his touch, in his power and fearlessness. She belonged to him and it felt good; fucking good she thought as she heard him say the word. Ricky rolled over bringing her atop his chest so that he could hold her as he kissed her forehead.

"Baby, I think it's best that you move in before the wedding. I know you preferred not to, but it's about to get heated between me and a rival even more than it already has.", he whispered not wanting her to hear the worry in his voice.

"If you really think that's best, I'll do it.", subscribed Vittoria.

"I do. It's the best way to ensure your safety and that also means that you'll have to stop working at the meat market sooner than planned.", Ricky added.

"Ok", nodded Vittoria.

Vittoria kissed his chest to express her agreement and acceptance of his plan. Just then, Ricky's private line rang. He hoped his men had good news; his temper wouldn't tolerate anything less. Ricky reached over Vittoria's body to answer the call.

"What's shaking?", asked Ricky of Angelo.

"Ricky, we got Maria and she's on the plane with Enzo headed to Columbia!", Angelo proudly informed.

"My man, my man. That's good news. Next, that bastard Canto.", instructed Ricky.

"On it!", Angelo reassured.

277

Ricky hung up the phone and sighed as he smelled Vittoria's hair; relief and Vittoria were his comforters that night and vengeance would be his strength tomorrow.

Chapter 15

"So, what's the word from Mateo?", inquired Canto surprised no one had rushed to share the good news.

Miguel entered the room slowly dreading to provide the news to his boss who looked impatient as he puffed on his cigar at his desk.

"Mateo didn't provide an update yesterday and no one had seen him. So, I sent some guys out to look for him.", informed Miguel who hoped the conversation would stop there.

"So, what did you find out? Is Ricky's bitch dead?", demanded Canto.

He sat his cigar down and stared intently at Miguel as he waited for a reply. He noticed Miguel's hesitation; so, he knew Mateo had failed him.

"I want Mateo's fucking head.", ordered Canto.

"Well boss, that's not possible.", advised Miguel.

"Why the fuck not?", shouted Canto.

"Because Ricky's girlfriend slit his throat. Your men found him dead in his car late last night.", Miguel stated hesitantly.

"Mateo was killed by a fucking bitch?", Canto questioned the validity of the incident.

"Yeah, she's tough. Rumor has it she's a dyke. You know dykes are tough.", explained Miguel.

"This shit just got real. Ricky might try to hurt me the same way; so, I need you to pick some guys to go with you to check on my mother. I'm sure he doesn't even know about her, but check

279

just to be sure. She's the only one I care about; he could kill my bitch and I wouldn't blink, but not my mother.", instructed Canto.

"What about you? Do you want more men on duty?", asked Miguel.

"No, he doesn't have the balls to attack me. I'll be fine.", Canto bragged and chuckled.

"Yes, El Jefe.", conveyed Miguel.

Ricky had been on edge all day as he waited on word from Diaz that he had Maria, coupled with him awaiting news from his men that Canto had been captured. Perhaps a glass of brandy would do him good, thought Ricky as he stood to pour the drink.

"Mr. Diaz is on the line.", informed Bettie from the intercom.

"Shit!", Ricky said as he jogged to the phone almost spilling his drink. "Talk to me.", greeted Ricky.

"Hello, my friend. You deliver well on your word!", informed Diaz.

"Of course; just glad to hear that you are pleased.", spouted Ricky.

"Indeed I am. She is just as beautiful as I remembered. You can be assured that I will keep up my end of the bargain and if there is anything else you need, do not hesitate to ask.", vowed Diaz.

"Sounds good. Good day.", beamed Ricky knowing he had reaffirmed their business partnership.

"Adios!", chuckled Diaz.

Next, Ricky was expecting to hear from Enzo that Canto had been captured, but he wasn't going to sit around waiting for the news. Instead, he would take the short drive home to freshen up for his bachelor party. Bernard had suggested hosting a simple get-together at his home, but Ricky had insisted he needed to be close to his operations to receive any updates. So, Bernard reluctantly agreed to host it at the funeral home; they would play cards and drink in the meeting room as they often did.

Bernard and Raymond were prompt as usual and waiting for Angelo and Ricky. Bettie entered the room and noticed that the guys were doing a poor job arranging things. So, she decided she would assist Raymond and Bernard with setting up for the gathering.

"Bettie, thanks for helping us set up. If it were up to us everything would practically stay wherever the deliverymen left it.", admitted Bernard.

"Oh, I'm well aware.", laughed Bettie.

She wanted Ricky and his friends to have a somewhat put-together event in celebration of the once confirmed bachelor. Had Bernard truly had his way, the event would have been announced all over town and he would have thrown a huge event at the Detroit Yacht Club or some other elegant venue. Unfortunately, Ricky was under too much heat at the moment for such a mega affair nor comfortable having it away from his headquarters.

As expected, Angelo arrived before Ricky wearing a blue jean leisure suit with brown leather platforms. Raymond quickly removed a tray from Bettie's hands to play the part of the dependable friend.

"Angelo, you should have been here helping us set up. I should have known you would dodge a little work.", teased Raymond as he winked at Bettie.

"You privileged motherfuckers didn't lift a finger. You had poor Bettie in here sweating while she set things up.", laughed Angelo, "So, where's the bachelor?"

"He's probably getting dressed to the nines.", concluded Bernard.

"You know it. Bernard, you and I are going to look like stiffs next to those Bianchis.", laughed Raymond who at arrival thought he was looking stylish in his navy-blue business suit.

Then the man of the hour walked in as on cue; Ricky entered the meeting room wearing a slim-fit double-breasted black polka dot suit on a white cotton-polyester blend with matching pants. He sported a white dress shirt, a black ascot and a red pocket square. The wide shawl collar accentuated his ascot perfectly. He completed the look with his favorite shoes of late, his patent leather tuxedo shoes. After entering the room, he twirled for his friends to show off his style and flare.

"Niggas always got to show off, thinking they're styling and profiling.", laughed Raymond wishing he had some of Ricky's bravado.

"And we know you know nothing about that!", Ricky teased as he pulled on Raymond's jacket as confirmation.

Canto hadn't heard anything from his men and he was getting restless. He had already drunk a bottle of brandy and had smoked almost a case of cigars. He was getting uneasy that he had not been able to reach his mother; although she had been known to ignore calls when she didn't want to be bothered, he reminded himself. He tossed the bottle of brandy in the trash and began walking back to his chair when he noticed Miguel enter the room.

"Why are you still here? I thought you were going to California to set up protection for my mother.", questioned Canto as he sat down.

"I thought I should stay behind with you to keep watch.", insisted Miguel.

Canto found Miguel's response hilarious; he leaned so far back in his chair with laughter that Miguel thought it would flip.

"Why in the fuck would I be afraid of a pretty boy?", laughed Canto as he fanned at Miguel to stop fretting, "I'm calling it a night. You update me on my mother as soon as my men lay eyes on her.", informed Canto.

"Ok, let me get Jesus to take you home.", said Miguel as he reached for the phone on Canto's desk.

Canto slammed his hand and the receiver down.

"I told you. I'm not afraid of Ricky and his Italian fuck ups. Leave my men here to guard my product. He'd try to steal that before he tried to touch El Jefe. Understood?", growled Canto.

"Yes, El Jefe.", Miguel concurred unwillingly, but who was he to object.

Ricky loved hanging with his fellas, he didn't know how often he would be interested in doing nights like these once he was married. Unlike the rest, he had a hell of a woman that would keep his mind and body preoccupied every night. As they played cards, Ricky discussed his honeymoon plans and his wanting to start a family right away.

"Who knew the great and ruthless Ricky was such a romantic?", declared Bernard as he reached over and squeezed Ricky's shoulder.

"Aye, what can I say fellas. It's just what I do.", proclaimed Ricky.

"I finally rubbed off on you.", bragged Bernard as he sipped his drink.

"You?', laughed Ricky and Raymond in unison.

"For sure. Back in the day.", explained Bernard to his doubters.

"Of the four of us, I'm the only one known to be a great lover!", Ricky alleged.

"Hold the fuck up!", fussed Raymond.

"Being romantic and a great lover are not the same.", Angelo schooled his cousin.

"Exactly, but I'm sure he's neither.", Raymond fussed.

Bernard sat quietly and waited for the Raymond and Ricky show to begin.

"You can't claim to be a good lover if you've only laid the Eleanor Washington-Brown types.", laughed Ricky.

"Oh, shit!", choked Bernard as he attempted to drink his Vodka.

"You were too busy with your head in school books.", Ricky teased as he imitated a young Raymond pushing up pretend glasses, "I have to study my lessons and get out of the ghetto.", Ricky imitated a Poindexter's voice.

"Was she your first?", asked Angelo getting in on the joke.

"Motherfucker, I didn't even wear glasses. And yes, I sure as fuck did get out of the ghetto and know she was not my first. She was just the only one worth bragging about.", Raymond fumed then threw his winning card on the table, "Take that motherfucker!"

The guys laughed almost nonstop; Bernard laughed so much that his face was just as red as his hair. Raymond had to excuse himself to rush off to the restroom.

"This old man's bladder, damn.", said Raymond as he shuffled to the restroom.

"Check your prostate, motherfucker. Check-that-prostate!", laughed Ricky.

Enzo and his crew had been casing out Canto's warehouse and were waiting for the perfect moment to pounce and an arrogant Canto presented the perfect opportunity. Enzo and his crew got a call from a traitor within Canto's own ranks that he was going home alone without a guard. Enzo used his car phone to call his top guy who was already casing out Canto's home to provide the update to ensure Canto's capture. They would either capture him on the road or at his home; either way, his ass would belong to Ricky that night.

Canto drove home without giving much thought to his surroundings at all. Once he thought Enzo's car might have been trailing him, but he noticed that the car slowed down and another car passed it, not knowing the driver was one of Enzo's crew. The closer Canto got to his Southwest Detroit home, the thinner the traffic became and the men took the opportunity to ram Canto's car.

The large Ford vehicles rammed Canto's sporty one causing it to slam into the side of a vacant office building. Ricky's men rushed from their cars with guns in hand, but the dazed Canto wasn't quick enough to draw his weapon. The men managed to grab him from the car and inflicted a couple of blows to the head then covered it with a cloth sack. Enzo and another quickly hogtied Canto and tossed him in Enzo's trunk to deliver him to Ricky at the warehouse.

Enzo and his crew hauled Canto inside the warehouse and tied him to a chair. He nodded at the men to recognize their good work and he walked to a nearby phone in one of the rooms to notify Ricky.

"Get me Ricky!", Enzo instructed Bettie.

"Yes, right away.", informed Bettie then transferred the call to the meeting room.

The ringing phone made every player pause and look at Ricky. Ricky jumped from his seat to rush over and answer the call.

"Speak motherfucker!", ordered Ricky slightly buzzed.

"We got him, Boss! We got that motherfucker Canto!", informed Enzo.

"I'm on my way!", Ricky blared then slammed the receiver, "We got that fuck!"

"Enjoy.", stated Bernard.

"Enjoy?", questioned Raymond as Ricky and Angelo rushed out.

"Yeah, we all know he loves that shit!", laughed Bernard.

"Game over for us and literally for Canto!", announced Raymond.

Ricky ran out of the funeral home and snapped his fingers for his driver. The driver tossed his food in the trash and followed quickly behind Ricky and Angelo.

"Take me to the warehouse. Fly this motherfucker!", ordered Ricky as he slammed the car door.

"Yes, sir!", replied the driver.

The ride to the warehouse seemed long and Ricky's nerves were on edge.

"Watch these fucking lights! I said fly this shit not wreck this shit. I'm trying to go kill a motherfucker not be killed, motherfucker!", sneered Ricky.

"Yes, boss.", the driver acknowledged.

"Ricky, let me get in some blows first.", Angelo requested.

"You got it. I know how much you cared for Giovanna, but the killing stroke will be my own.", Ricky informed.

"Thank you, cousin.", said an emotional Angelo.

The remainder of the ride was eerily silent and the two contemplated the tortures they would inflict upon Canto. The driver opened the door for Ricky who seemed unaware that they had arrived.

"Boss!", called the driver.

Ricky snapped back to reality as he and Angelo exited the car. His arousal started to course throughout his body the closer he neared the torture room. He hadn't decided which devices he would use to torture Canto as he usually had things all planned out in his mind; but not this time. However, he was finding the suspense of it all even more arousing than usual. Ricky entered the room to find Canto tied and gagged with venom and shock in his eyes.

"Who runs this motherfucking town?", laughed Ricky, "You thought you did, but here you are tied up and about to get fucked up."

Ricky smiled a devilish smile as he thought of what else he would reveal to Canto. Ricky looked to Enzo who was approaching with a file folder in hand.

"Ricky, here's what you requested.", Enzo offered.

Ricky nodded to Angelo who quickly put on his brass knuckles. He ran up on Canto and swung two harsh blows to the face and one to the gut. He wanted to make a statement, but he would allow Ricky to do most of the damage.

"You thought you were man enough to bring me down; that you would crush my heart, but she was only kept pussy from my past. Then you found my girl and tried to kill her ...", Ricky whispered as he cracked his knuckles, "When my soldier told me

287

she had been attacked, I thought I was about to nut up, but then he quickly told me she slit your man's fucking throat. That shit turned me the fuck on. I pictured her killing him over and over again and her tossing her long hair and those big tits bouncing as she slit his throat and kicked him. Woo! My cock got so fucking hard … shit it's getting hard now. I ejaculated everywhere.", bragged Ricky as he walked back and forth.

He looked up at the ceiling before continuing.

"You don't know this, but I've already killed for that woman before. Initially, I was just going to cut off your supply, but this act of defiance requires blood.", revealed Ricky as he walked closer to Canto. "I have a question for you? How do you think you were able to get an inside track to secure dope directly from Diaz? Have you thought about that?", queried Ricky of Canto who was frantic and squirming in his chair.

Ricky nodded to Angelo to remove the gag from Canto's mouth.

"Where is my mother? I'll fucking kill you if you harmed her!", screamed Canto.

"Oh, you've got me all fucked up. I don't kill mothers. See, I found out Diaz wanted her; he missed doing all sorts of nasty freaky shit to your mother. He said she loved that freaky shit too. So, he said that if I delivered her to him, he'd stop selling to you in exchange. So, I shook hands on that shit!", laughed Ricky.

Ricky tossed the pictures on the ground so Canto could see his mother tied up and in Diaz's arm upon delivery. Canto began screaming in Spanish and shaking his chair trying to get free.

"Gag him back up. I don't want to hear that crying and shit!", Ricky ordered Angelo and continued, "But I got to thinking you can't just wound a snake, you've got to cut off the head. So here you are.", Ricky said as he stretched out his arms. "I used to have a lot of fun here.", he said as he pointed Canto's attention to

288

his weapons of torture. "But now, I'm an older man; I like to keep it simple with my blade.", he said as he removed it from his pocket to display his moves. "I'll find great pleasure knowing that while you're in hell, you'll be tortured by the fact that your mother is being fucked by Diaz.", sighed Ricky as he smiled wickedly.

Ricky sliced Canto with his straight-blade razor a couple of times. He walked away from Canto and was about to share more of his philosophies when Canto squirmed and somehow loosen his hands and feet. He was able to slip his feet from the rope and stood. Ricky's men were about to shoot him, but Ricky held up his hand to halt their firing. Canto yanked the gag from his mouth and began shouting at Ricky.

"You are nothing but a pretty boy that cowards behind his weapons and his men. Fight me like a man!", Canto's voice boomed.

Canto wanted to go out with a fight if that was his fate. Ricky tossed his blade behind him out of reach of either of them. Ricky crossed his arms at his wrists as his fingers seemed to transform into claws as his knuckles cracked. His face became crazed and his eyes menacing as if being possessed by something unworldly. His men recognized the beast that he was becoming; they had seen the Reaper much too often. Canto lunged toward him and Ricky swung with the force of all his might hitting Canto's jaw sending two teeth flying. Canto's body twisted and he hit the ground face down; his body was immobile near unconsciousness. Ricky pounced atop Canto like a wild beast as he pounded Canto's face into the cement floor. With each forceful contact, Ricky grunted and growled as the beast who had taken over, desperate for its appetite to be quenched leaving Canto's face a bloody pound of flesh and his cries barely audible. Ricky stood and pressed his right foot on Canto's back.

"Give me your gun!", Ricky ordered as he extended his hand to Angelo.

Angelo gladly handed over his weapon to his cousin. Ricky nodded as he accepted it and placed a single bullet in Canto's head.

"Y'all motherfuckers need to get better at tying motherfuckers up!", Ricky scolded his embarrassed crew.

Epilogue

Ricky had secured his family seat of power in Detroit for years to come providing him enough time to develop his legitimate affairs; then when the time was right, he planned to hand the reigns over to Angelo. Until then, the Bianchi family and Bernard were overjoyed to see the day when their beloved Ricky would declare to the world the happiness he had found. Finally, that day of celebration was at hand. Similar to Carlo and Bianca, Lorenzo and Antonella were the happiest and proudest they'd ever been. Lorenzo prepared to walk Vittoria down the aisle if he were able to see; he wiped his eyes countless times, but every time he looked at her tears began to flow all over again. Vittoria was finally happy, finally free to live a life of happiness with a man who truly cherished her above all else.

Ricky stood next to his best man, best friend and brother, Bernard; he glanced at Bernard with the brightest smile anyone who knew him had ever seen. Bernard gave him a playful nudge and teased him.

"Don't get cold feet on us. We don't want you to be a runaway groom.", laughed Bernard knowing full well that Ricky smiled with joy, not nervousness.

"No, that was almost you at your wedding to Vanessa.", Ricky playfully jabbed back, "Besides, Vittoria still owes me a dance. And you see me, I look too good to be running away like a frightened punk.", he bragged then reeled his best friend in for an emotional hug.

Ricky was in true Ricky fashion, dressed to the nines; no one other than Vittoria could compete with his good looks. He wore a three-piece silver and black floral tuxedo with a black shawl collar, black pocket square and a black ascot that sealed his suave appearance. Black patent leather tuxedo shoes rounded out the look.

The pair fought back tears as they hugged, but it was unlikely that anyone noticed as all eyes were more likely to be fixed on Old St. Mary Catholic church's glory. It was made even more beautiful by the fresh flowers that adorned its sanctuary; white roses and green fern used as streamers lined the aisle at the end of the pews along the center aisle. Bernard and Ricky stood with Father Luca along with Martina under a beautiful bridal arch of white roses representing the loyalty of their love and vibrant tree fern; the green represented their rebirth and growth as a couple.

The bridal march began to play and everyone stood turning their attention to the entrance waiting to be awed by the future Mrs. Ricardo Jilani Bianchi. The massive doors opened to reveal the breath-taking Italian jewel of the ball; Vittoria stood proudly arm-in-arm with her father. She wore a cuffed long-sleeved V-neck wrap dress in soft cream with a huge sash bow at the waist. A huge jeweled button decorated each cuffed wrist. The gown was long and flowed to her ankles; it moved with each stride as if being blown by the wind. Vittoria made sure her bustier paired well with her V-neck to please Ricky; however, everyone's eyes strained as they jumped from one beautiful feature to another. She wore silver and cream strapped heels with a Cinderella plastic vamp with a white silk rose atop and a jeweled buckle.

The curvy Vittoria walked elegantly toward her groom; his eyes were alive with desire, love and hope for their future. Ricky wanted to shout hurry up woman if it meant getting her one step closer to having her in his bed. He was completely mesmerized by the sway of her hips, the bounce of her breasts and her hair. Her thick long mane was curled and then put in an up-swept style with some free-falling curls. The stylist placed white roses, tree fern and pearl hairpins in her hair; Vittoria looked like an angel.

Lorenzo proudly presented his daughter to Ricky and stepped aside as she prepared to become Mrs. Ricardo Jilani Bianchi. A day no one could have imagined would happen on that fateful day she attended the fundraiser so many months ago. His daughter had come a long way indeed.

Ricky reached for her hand and he brought it to his heart so she could feel his heartbeat. Vittoria had never felt it flutter so fast; it was beating almost as fast as her own.

"It's yours forever.", Ricky whispered and then kissed her hand.

The couple turned to the priest as Ricky held Vittoria close as if afraid that the day and that moment weren't real. Victoria needed his touch as well to ensure it wasn't all a dream, as she stood in front of the altar ready to vow her life and love to the most incredible man that had ever breathed the breath of life. She was ready to take that step into their new life surrounded by love, children and the comforts of life; but most importantly, she would live out her days in the arms of the man she loved.

www.ingramcontent.com/pod-product-compliance
Lightning Source LLC
Chambersburg PA
CBHW070603260626
47161CB00002B/698